
★

All he could think to say was "I *know* what I saw. It wasn't you."

Cochrane nodded. "That's right."

"Then...?"

"I didn't kill Chris Berry. I didn't kill the boy at the brewery. I *did* kill three boys ten years ago."

There was no ambiguity in that. It was either a lie or a statement of fact, and Daniel didn't think Cochrane was lying. Fear knotted up his stomach.

Cochrane moved closer. He lowered himself into the straw at Daniel's side. "I want to tell you about it. Then we'll decide what happens next. At least—" he flickered a graveyard grin "—I will."

★

"Bannister skillfully moves her characters through an intriguing tale of tragedy and death in a small town, exploring their thoughts and motives."

—*Publishers Weekly*

Jo Bannister

TRUE WITNESS

WORLDWIDE®

TORONTO • NEW YORK • LONDON
AMSTERDAM • PARIS • SYDNEY • HAMBURG
STOCKHOLM • ATHENS • TOKYO • MILAN
MADRID • WARSAW • BUDAPEST • AUCKLAND

TRUE WITNESS

A Worldwide Mystery/December 2005

First published by St. Martin's Press LLC.

ISBN 0-373-26550-6

Printed in U.S.A.

TRUE
WITNESS

ONE

DANIEL HOOD looked at the sleeping child and his heart swelled. The brown hair tumbled on the smooth brow, the long lashes dipped on the rounded cheek, the stubby thumb caught between pursed lips in a defiant last stand against the end of infancy. He thought she was the most perfect thing he'd ever seen.

At five years old she was poised on the cusp of life, all its possibilities opening before her, the magical nowhere she sprang from still close enough behind to clothe her in its wonder. Six years ago she hadn't existed in any shape or form; even the idea of her had not been formulated. Then a chance encounter between two disparate organisms began the sequence of events that led to this child, this Paddy Farrell, this marvellous child lying asleep in his bed at two o'clock on a May morning.

Seeing her like this, the knowledge that she wasn't his—that she didn't belong here and wouldn't be staying—was an ache in him. Daniel liked living alone. It was pleasant and undemanding; he had no one to satisfy but himself, he had never felt the need of another person to make him whole. But if you wanted one of these you needed another person, and now, watching Paddy Farrell sleep in his bed on the night of her fifth birthday, he understood the urge to pair off. It wasn't about sex or companionship; the first was available to anyone with the right number of heads, the second to anyone with a few good friends. But having a family required commitment. At two o'clock this spring morning, Daniel felt the temptation.

He was a sentimental man: he knew if he went on watching the sleeping child his eyes would fill. But he couldn't bring himself to wake her, to trade that fey creature woven of light and potential for the real flesh-and-blood child, grouchy with not enough sleep, complaining of the cold, demanding food, demanding attention, demanding amusement. Maybe he'd be glad enough to hand her back to her mother after breakfast.

He thought he'd get the telescope ready before he woke her. Saturn was coming into a comfortable position for viewing. Jupiter would be easier in half an hour. He'd woken in plenty of time although he didn't own an alarm-clock. After fifteen years of watching the night sky his Circadian rhythms were attuned to the music of the spheres.

Still barefoot and with his clothes pulled over his pyjamas—not from laziness, it was the best way to stay warm outdoors in the coldest part of the night—he padded across the living-room, his sleeping-bag crumpled on the sofa, lifted the telescope from the safety of its corner and carried it out to the little balcony. The iron bit like ice and he hurried back inside for his shoes.

The sound of him moving about had penetrated Paddy's sleep. A mumbled plaint just recognisable as his name reached him from the bedroom. "Daniel?"

"I'm here. I'm just setting up the telescope."

"Is it there?"

"They're all there. I promised you a clear night."

"Is it raining?" This was her birthday treat, she'd been looking forward to it for weeks—now she was looking for excuses to stay cocooned in the warm bed.

"No. But it is cold—you'll need all your warm clothes on. Tracksuit, coat, boots. Do you need a hand?"

"No thank you," she said primly. On the first day of her sixth year she was already conscious of the proprieties.

Outside, Daniel carried the heavy telescope carefully down the iron steps to the shingle shore. His flat over a netting-shed a few metres above high water suited him in every way except this one. He needed to extend the balcony to give him a full field of view, but it would take money he didn't have and didn't expect to have soon. If what he wanted to observe was north or east he had to carry the telescope to the other side of the building.

Oh yes: and the stool, without which Paddy wouldn't be able to reach the eyepiece. He went back for it and found her waiting. At least, he supposed it was Paddy: it might have been an Eskimo with a poor sense of direction. "Your mum didn't want you getting cold," he guessed.

Paddy nodded. With so many layers on she couldn't bend her arms, she looked like a teddy-bear.

"First rule of astronomy," said Daniel. "You catch your death of cold, you don't get to name a comet."

"Can I see a comet?" asked Paddy, pressing her mittened hand into his.

"Er—no," said Daniel. "Sorry. But I can show you the moons of Jupiter, and the rings of Saturn, and some binary stars, and a stellar nursery, and we might see some meteors. Shooting-stars."

"You can wish on those," said Paddy knowledgeably.

"I know."

"What will you wish for?"

"More meteors," said Daniel. "What will you?"

"To stay at your house again."

Daniel planted her on the stool. He glanced through the finder, made a tiny adjustment and indicated the eyepiece. "Look through there. Don't touch the telescope or it'll slip out of alignment. What can you see?"

The child looked, and blinked, and jerked back and looked up directly at the night sky. "A big white…" She tailed off, puzzled that it had gone. "Where is it?"

Daniel pointed at the bright dot that was Jupiter, a spot of brilliance among a hundred others. "There. That's what it really looks like from here. The telescope makes it look bigger."

She looked again. "Wow!"

"Can you see four dots lined up with it, two on each side?

Those are Jupiter's moons—like our moon. Actually there are
fourteen, but these four are the biggest."

"They're tiny!"

"They're a long way away. And Jupiter is much bigger than
Earth. It's the biggest planet in the Solar System."

Daniel wasn't sure how much of this she was taking in. He
was a teacher by profession, but not of children of this age.
He talked to her more or less as he'd talk to an adult with no
knowledge of the subject: she'd make it plain when she'd had
enough.

"Show me something else."

He quartered the sky with the little finderscope until the
curious oval that was Saturn appeared. "Saturn's the one with
the rings. Can you see—like ears on either side?"

"Cool!" said Paddy Farrell, peering. "Can I call Mummy
and tell her?"

Daniel doubted Brodie would appreciate being woken at
two-fifteen a.m. with the news that Saturn had rings. "Maybe after breakfast."

He was never afterwards sure if he heard voices first, or
the sound of running feet hollow on the rotten boards of Dimmock's pier.

Either would have been sufficiently unusual at this time of
night to attract attention. The pier was supposed to be closed,
although no one stopped the children who played on it or the
anglers who fished from its end. Occasionally on summer
nights lovers availed themselves of the privacy offered by its
ruined concert-hall, two hundred metres out over the English
Channel. Occasionally in the hour after closing time young
men who were too drunk to go home would clump around out
there, trading beery dares that ended in a splash.

But it was a Monday morning in May, too late in the night
and too early in the year for any of the usual suspects. Still
with his hand on Paddy's shoulder Daniel turned towards the
pier, brow gathering under the fringe of yellow hair, grey
eyes troubled behind the thick glasses. The moon was low,

bathing the shore in a flat half-light. He could see two figures on the pier, one behind the other, occulting the westering stars as they ran. At this time of night Dimmock couldn't manage a background of traffic noise, so the thunder of feet on boards and the angry voices carried easily across a hundred metres of shingle shore.

Daniel couldn't make out the words but the tone was unmistakable. Quietly he lifted Paddy down from her stool and took her up to the flat. "Stay inside," he said softly. "I'll be back in a minute."

He wasn't sure what he was witnessing. It might be a police matter, it might not. He wanted to check, and he didn't want the child with him just in case. He walked towards the pier.

The shouting stopped, the feet were still. The figures had vanished in the shadows where the concert-hall canted drunkenly at the end of the pier. Perhaps the drama was over, the differences resolved, the protagonists making up over the dregs of a six-pack where once Madam Astarte had told fortunes and a Laughing Policeman had performed for small denominations of a forgotten currency.

Daniel vented a pent breath and turned for home, glad fate had let him off the hook. He'd no idea what he'd have done if he'd stumbled on real violence. He wasn't built for knocking sense into people. A God with a funny sense of humour had given him Robin Hood's urge to ride to the rescue, and Maid Marion's muscles.

A man screamed.

Daniel froze. The blood in his veins turned to ice and the hair on the back of his neck stood up.

The sound of another human being in that much distress would, and should, have pulled anyone up short. But Daniel Hood knew about pain and terror. The last man he heard screaming like that was himself.

Someone else, mindful of what can happen when decent citizens tackle vicious thugs, might have hurried on up the iron steps, locked the door and told himself it was none of his business and he'd call the police if it was still going on in half an hour. But Daniel knew how long half an hour can feel. No one had been close enough to help when he needed it. But he *was* close enough to help whoever was up there, and he couldn't turn his back on him. It wasn't sensible, it wasn't logical— he could have had the police on the scene in just a few minutes. But he couldn't abandon someone in pain for even a few minutes. He headed for the pier at a slithering, skittering run.

All he had in his pockets were a star-chart and a torch to read it by. It wasn't even a normal torch but a red one: the night-blindness induced by white light takes minutes to clear. So the only weapon he had was his own presence. As he reached the weed-bearded struts of the crumbling pier he raised his voice—and hoped he sounded strong and deter-mined rather than, as he rather suspected, small and afraid. "What's going on up there?"

Perhaps they were too involved in their own drama to hear him. Certainly no one answered. There was the shuffle of movement and when Daniel stood back he could see them, against the end rail, five metres above the incoming tide. He heard grunts of exertion, a panic-stricken sob, and one of them cried out, "Get away from me. Get *away* from me!"

They were wrestling for some kind of implement. Daniel couldn't make out who was the aggressor and who the vic-tim. Finally one of the two figures broke away with the thing in his hand, raised it above his head and swung it mightily to-wards the man cowering against the rail.

Daniel gasped. There was a thick choked wail, then silence.

Then the man still on his feet bent and lifted the other against the rail, and bending again lifted his legs and tipped him over. The injured man fell silhouetted by stars and disap-peared with a splash where the sea gnawed at the timber piles.

Shocked to the core, Daniel yelled something—he had no idea what—and the man above him, already running back to-wards the promenade, startled and froze. He seemed to real-ise for the first time that he'd been observed. He looked down at the same moment as Daniel shone the red torch up. Then he jerked back and hurried on up the pier. The beat of feet diminished, and then there was nothing but Daniel and the sea.

And the man who went into the sea, plainly injured but perhaps not dead. Panting with shock, trying to think, Daniel turned his torch towards the breakers. He could see nothing beyond the foam. But he could see most of the timberwork. Only a little past slack tide, much of the pier was still high and dry—a man might wade almost as far as the splash before he was out of his depth.

Having thought that, the rest was inevitable. Daniel wasn't a strong swimmer but he didn't need to be. All he had to do was stay on his feet and grope in the darkness and the foam for an injured man who might still be saved. He threw off his parka, kicked off his shoes and waded into the surf.

The sea was both colder and rougher than expected. He plunged on, drawn by the hope of a miracle that might be had now but not in five minutes' time. He regretted not calling the police when he had the chance. But it was no longer an option: if he turned back now there would be only a corpse to recover.

By the time the water was round his hips it was hard keeping his feet. The thick piles broke the tide into eddies and undertows. Still well short of his goal the sea swept Daniel hard against the timbers and took the legs from under him.

He swallowed brine but somehow found his feet and broke the surface, coughing and gagging and flinging the water out of his hair. He found the corroded iron of a crossbrace and clung to it.

Water broke around him like an avalanche. Chilled to the bone, unable to feel his fingers knotted round the ironwork, he clung to the pier and knew he would risk his own life if he ventured one step further into the Channel.

He sucked in the salt-laden air and raised a voice cracking with despair. "Where are you? Tell me where you are. I can help you. Please…"

Hard as he listened, no answering cry sounded above the

tumult of the waves. The water surged around his chest, the cold of it like razor-blades. It was dark under the pier, he could see nothing but the chiaroscuro breakers, only knew where the shore lay from their direction and the shingle sound. His glasses had gone when the sea swept over him. It hardly mattered. He could have seen nothing from here, and he had neither the strength nor the courage to go further.

The tide was coming in. He had to give way before it. He reached behind him, fumbling with dead hands for the next brace. Tears of disappointment and exhaustion mingled with the rest of the ocean.

Something touched his hip. It could have been anything—a clump of weed, a baulk of drift-wood, a Great White Shark for all Daniel knew. But he so wanted it to be the man who'd been thrown from the pier that he released his grip on the cross-bracing and reached into the water, groping as far as his arms would stretch.

He found it; and it wasn't wood, and it wasn't weed, and it didn't feel like sharkskin so much as denim. He fastened his hands in what he recognised as the belt of someone's jeans and pulled, and a man's body surfaced and bumped flaccidly against his own.

In his own mind he had already accepted defeat. He'd thought the only prize left was his own safety. Now, against all odds, he'd stumbled on what he came for and suddenly time was of the essence again. This man had been in the water for minutes: if he hadn't managed to breathe in that time he was already dying.

All Daniel knew about life-saving he'd picked up from a ten minute lecture at Dimmock swimming pool when he'd been covering for a missing sports mistress. He knew there were two ways to save lives, and both worked. One was the proper way—ABC equals airway, breathing and circulation, clear the mouth of obstructions then five compressions of the chest followed by one breath into the lungs.

And the other was the bodger's way, which recognised that

if someone was dying in front of you it was impossible to make things worse, just forcing some air down their throat might keep them alive long enough for someone more knowledgeable to reach them. That he could do here and now, clinging to the pier with one hand and the drowning man with the other.

Actually, he had to let go of the pier because he needed both hands to hold the man's head above the water. All Daniel could see of his face was a white blob, but he found the mouth and fastening his own over it exhaled as deeply as his recent exertions would permit.

Heavy in the surging tide, the man's body rolled and dragged at his grasp. Daniel struggled to keep the face out of the water. But the hiss of air and the movement of his chest as the man breathed out kept him trying. He ventilated again, then with the man's chin in the crook of his elbow set off for the shore, his left hand guiding him along the corroded ironwork.

Twice more he lost his footing. The first time he was able to hang onto the bracing until he found it again; the second time he tumbled his length in the breaking surf, lost his companion and for terrible seconds thought the man was going to die for his weakness.

When he found him Daniel hauled his face above the foam, breathed for him once more, then set off determinedly for the beach whose proximity he could hear like an orchestra of tiny flat bells. Again the feet went from under him; this time he sprawled in shallows and a few metres of dogged hauling brought him and his burden clear of the waves.

The tide was coming, but it wasn't coming that fast. Daniel let the man slump on the shingle and dropped beside him, lungs heaving, a cocktail of shock and cold and reaction shaking every muscle.

But there wasn't time to rest. Out of the waves' reach was not the same as safe. Daniel forced his weary body to move again, rolled the man onto his back and pumped and breathed and pumped and pumped and breathed because he didn't know what else to do. The chest expanded when he pushed air into it, contracted when he rocked back on his heels; he thought that meant the man was alive. He couldn't leave him to find help. Between breaths he tried to raise the alarm, but he knew that his gasping cries could never carry up the beach, across the deserted promenade and as far as the nearest house where a light sleeper might be roused. He knew he was on his own. He knew this man would live only if Daniel Hood, unaided, could force him to.

He pumped with the heel of his hand on the man's chest, he breathed for both of them, he yelled for help. No one came. The tide marched closer. Daniel dragged him by the arm until their legs were out of the sea again. Then he pumped some more and breathed some more. He knew time was passing, had no idea how much. The man at the swimming pool had said you keep going until you can't keep going any longer, and that point was coming but it wasn't here yet. Daniel stopped shouting—he needed all his breath. He pumped and breathed, and the sea snapped again at his heels.

Suddenly there was someone else on the shore. Daniel heard the distinctive chime of hurried footsteps in the shingle, and his own name in a woman's voice. A familiar voice, mingling anger and concern as if he'd gone out of his way to frighten her. "Daniel! Answer me, damn it!"

"Over here." He didn't think she'd heard him, tried again. "Brodie. I'm over here."

The frailty of his voice alarmed Brodie Farrell, but it was enough to take her in the right direction. She quartered the shore with the big torch from her car and found him, on his knees at the water's edge, crouched over what could only be the figure of another human being. "Dear God! What—?"

There was no time to explain. "Can you take over?" It took him two breaths to get it out. "Can't—any more—"

She had the little Eskimo with her. Before she did anything else Brodie took her back a few metres up the beach and sat her down. "Now, you stay there. You understand? You don't move an inch." Paddy nodded solemnly.

Hurrying back, Brodie dropped to her knees on the other side of the inert form, ran her torch over it. He was barefoot, dressed in jeans and a black T-shirt. When the beam reached the head Brodie blinked and straightened up. Her voice was quiet. "Daniel. Stop now."

He spared her two seconds for a stare, then lunged again at the man between them. "No! He's breathing! Help me."

Brodie shook her head, the dark hair clouding round her face. "He's dead, Daniel. I think he's been dead for a while."

"How can you *say* that?" Then he saw what the light of her torch had shown Brodie: that the left side of the skull had been pulped by a mighty blow. The tall man; the implement they fought over; the raised arm and the wail in the dark. It had been over then? He'd done it all for nothing?—risked his life for a dead man?

"No," he choked, applying himself once more to the task. But he had nothing left to work with.

Brodie regarded her friend with compassion. He'd given everything he had, drained himself to the dregs. Now he needed her help, not to continue with the futile exercise but to stop.

She rose and put her arms around him, stilling him. "Daniel. It's time to stop now. Let him go. Give him peace."

He hadn't the strength to struggle. She felt his body go slack in the compass of her arms and he sat back on his heels, head bowed, softly panting. Then he began to cry.

TWO

THERE WAS A WHISPER of shingle and then the Eskimo was there with them, wrapping thick short arms as far round the sobbing man as they would reach. The little voice was muffled by clothing. "Don't cry, Daniel." And hopefully: "Kiss it better?"

A hug was what he needed most in the world. He returned it with gratitude. "Love you, Paddy Farrell."

"Love you, Daniel."

Brodie pulled herself together with an effort. "All right. Daniel, take Paddy inside and put her back to bed. I'll call the police and I'll stay here till they arrive."

Releasing the child, Daniel shook his sodden hair in protest. "I should stay. The police will want to talk to me."

"I'll tell them where you are. Daniel, if you stay outside any longer you'll freeze solid. Go inside and get changed. I'll be up in a few minutes."

Brodie used her mobile to call the police, waited with the body until they arrived. She hurried back to the flat.

He'd done as she said, got Paddy out of her Eskimo outfit and tucked her into bed, before grinding to a halt. She found him in the kitchen, still in his wet clothes, sitting in the corner in a pool of salt water.

She said nothing. She went into the bathroom and ran the hot tap. Then she went back for Daniel.

"I can't. The police…"

"Will get more sense out of you if you haven't collapsed with hypothermia." As she spoke she stripped the wet clothes from him as if he were a child. "Now, get in there and don't get out until you're warm."

She went to boil the kettle and put three mugs on a tray. They wouldn't be alone long, and she had a fair idea who would be joining them.

Through the bathroom door Daniel said indistinctly, "I don't understand. What are you doing here?"

"Paddy called me," said Brodie. "I came over to knock some sense into you for leaving a five-year-old alone at night. When I found you, of course, I realised why."

"I'm sorry. I didn't seem to have any choice."

"I see that." She couldn't quite bring herself to say he'd done the right thing. But if he hadn't achieved what he'd hoped, at least no harm had been done.

"Smart kid," he mumbled. Brodie heard the water slosh as he lay back. He said nothing more, and when she opened the door to check that he hadn't drowned he was asleep.

SHE HEARD Jack Deacon before she saw him. Other men's feet made the iron steps ring too, it was impossible to climb them in silence, but Detective Inspector Deacon had a unique ability to project substance, doggedness and the utter refusal to suffer fools at all through the soles of his shoes. Brodie opened the door as he made a fist to knock. He was not surprised to see her but nor did he look particularly pleased. "Where is he?"

"In the bath. I'll tell him you're here." She offered to take his coat but Deacon kept it on. It settled round him like a bat's wings as he sat. Brodie poured his tea, which he regarded with mistrust, then went to rouse Daniel.

"Make yourself decent, it's Inspector Deacon."

Fifteen minutes in a hot tub had restored some colour to his fair skin. He emerged from the bathroom wrapped in an oversized green dressing-gown, his fair hair roughly towelled. "Inspector."

"Daniel," responded the policeman guardedly. When he was irritated with him he called him Danny; when he was really angry he called him Mr Hood. "Tell me what happened."

Daniel took a mug and settled on the sofa. He began with

when he took the telescope outside, ended with Brodie's arrival. He omitted nothing, ventured no speculation. His voice was steady; but both these people knew him too well to think he was over it.

Deacon was watching him hawkishly. "You saw the whole thing? The boy running, the man chasing him. You saw them fight for the wheel-brace, you saw the man swing it, and you saw him tip the body into the sea. Daniel—you actually saw this murder taking place. Is that right?"

Daniel's breath caught in his throat. "Boy?"

"Not much more," said Deacon. "Eighteen maybe. What—didn't you realise?"

Daniel shook his head. "I never saw his face. It was dark, I lost my glasses… He was just a kid?"

Brodie was watching Deacon. There was something going on in his expression that she couldn't put a label on. He was listening to Daniel—yes, that was it—as if he already knew what he had to say.

But Daniel hadn't noticed. He was still trying to explain what happened, not even to Deacon so much as to himself. "I tried to stop it. It happened too quickly. I couldn't get to them—they were on top of the pier, there's no way up from the beach…" He heard himself making excuses and fell silent.

"Just as well," grunted Deacon, "or we'd have had two bodies on our hands. He's a powerful man, you couldn't have stopped him. But you can stop him doing it again. You saw his face?"

Daniel shrugged narrow shoulders inside green towelling. "Yes. But not clearly. He was above me, the only light was a little red torch I use to read star-charts, and it was only a split-second before he turned away and ran."

"Would you know him if you saw him again?"

"Maybe."

"Would you know him from a photograph?"

Brodie fixed him with her gaze. "You know who it was, don't you?"

Deacon hesitated, then nodded. "I have an idea. I may not be right. We'll have to see."

Brodie's eyes saucered in disbelief. Jack Deacon *never* considered that he might be wrong. If he was being this careful it was because of the consequences of failure.

Daniel said softly, "He's done it before."

Deacon nodded again. "Yes, he has."

"Done what, exactly?"

Detective Inspector Deacon folded his hands across his midriff and eyed him thoughtfully. He was a big man with a big man's gestures. Soon he'd be a fat man too, but not yet. For now the bulk cladding his strong bones was mostly muscle.

He answered obliquely. "Daniel, if we get this man you are our best chance to put him away. You saw his face, you saw what he did. If I tell you anything that could contaminate your evidence, he could go free. And sooner or later he'll do it again. I won't risk that."

Daniel understood. "You want me to look at some photographs?"

"Yes. Come down to the station at eight o'clock, we'll do it then."

Brodie saw him to the top of the steps. He reached behind her to pull the door closed. "I still don't understand what your daughter was doing here."

She smiled. "It's her birthday. Daniel promised her the stars."

"She stayed here? Alone?"

Brodie wasn't sure what he was getting at. "Inspector, Daniel's my friend. I'd trust him with my life *and* Paddy's."

"He left her alone with a murderer running loose."

"He thought he could save the boy's life. You're saying he was wrong to try?"

Deacon shrugged. "No. But I would if she was my five-year-old."

She regarded him speculatively in the light filtering through the curtained windows. "You're never going to give him a chance, are you? Once, for what he believed were good reasons, he refused to do what you wanted him to, and you're going to hold a grudge for the rest of your life. Nothing he does from now on will ever win your respect. He could have died tonight, trying to save that boy. If he can give you the murderer he will. But none of that matters to you. As far as you're concerned, he let you down once and you'll never forgive him. Have you any idea how sad that makes you, Inspector Deacon?"

The detective bristled. Part of him agreed with her. But most of him had spent twenty years sorting the sheep from the goats, those who obeyed the law from those who didn't, and he wasn't going to start forgiving trespasses now. He liked and admired her; there had been a time when he liked Daniel. But when Deacon had demanded his unconditional support, Daniel hadn't given it. Deacon would never forget that.

"I'm just doing my job, Mrs Farrell," he said heavily. "It really doesn't matter what you think of me, or what I think of Daniel. There's a boy dead on that beach and I want to find the man responsible. Let's concentrate on that and keep our personal opinions to ourselves, shall we?"

BRODIE AND DANIEL sat for an hour, occasionally talking, mostly coming to terms with what had happened. At length Brodie went into the bedroom, squeezed into the narrow bed without waking Paddy, and sank into a troubled sleep.

Daniel remained alone in the dark, hunched miserably on the sofa, too tired to sleep, unable to rest for the churning of his mind. He thought about what he might have done differently. How he might have shouted before he did, or called the police when he had the chance, or—in his own head he had absurd expectations of himself—somehow clambered up the cross-bracing onto the pier in time to snatch the weapon before it did murder. Inspector Deacon said it was a wheel-brace. It could have been: Daniel only saw it for a moment and didn't recognise it. But then, he didn't own a car.

A man had chased a terrified youth out onto the pier, and

when he'd caught him he'd smashed his skull with a wheel-brace; and Daniel had watched. He despised himself for not finding an alternative. He sat in the dark thinking the boy had two bits of rotton luck that night. He met his murderer; and the only person close enough to help was too stupid to. And maybe too scared to.

DI DEACON WASN'T wasting time on punishing himself, not when punishing the killer would be so much more satisfying. With DS Voss beside him he drove due north up the Guild-ford road.

Behind Dimmock the South Downs spread in a patchwork quilt of hillside pasture and little woods dotted by tiny ham-lets, often just a farm and its attendant cottages. It took a de-tailed map to show anything but contour-lines.

A detailed map was exactly what Jack Deacon had in his head. He needed no other. He hadn't been here for years, but not once did he think he might lose his way. The little lanes edged with grass banks and overhung with trees might all seem identical, but Deacon could have come straight here on a moonless night, in a howling blizzard, in a total eclipse of the sun. Pigeons navigate by atuning themselves to the Earth's magnetosphere. Deacon homed in on criminals in much the same way.

He didn't drive into the farmyard. He didn't want to an-nounce himself until he'd had a look around. He stopped the car in the lane and turned off the lights, and he and Voss got out. Deacon waved to the occupants of the second car to stay put. There were four of them, and he'd need them all if he found grounds for an immediate arrest. If not he'd leave one car and two officers on surveillance when he returned to Dim-mock. But he'd be back as soon as he'd been through the fam-ily album with Daniel Hood.

Hood. Of *course* Hood, who else? Who else would be wandering about the beach at two in the morning? Yes, the man lived close by; and yes, he was often out in the middle of the night. Half of Dimmock knew about the eccentric young teacher who lived over a netting-shed on the beach and came out at night to watch the stars. Who didn't go out much apart from that. Who used to teach maths at Dimmock Comprehensive until someone tore him up for reasons that were never satisfactorily explained. Not to Deacon they weren't. Hood knew. Deacon *knew* he knew, he'd as good as said so. He'd refused to say more in order to protect an innocent party. Brodie Farrell was right: Deacon would never forgive that. It wasn't Hood's place to judge innocence and guilt.

Deacon had told him something. In his office, when he'd given Hood a last chance to help the police with their inquiries and Hood hadn't taken it. He'd said, one day Hood would need his help and he wouldn't get it. And now...well, now he needed Hood's help again. And he was pretty sure he *would* get it. And that didn't make him feel better about anything.

Except that, if Hood looked at the photographs and picked the right one, and because of that Deacon was able to charge a man who should have been behind bars for ten years, maybe he'd revise his opinion of Daniel. Neither forgive nor forget, but make his peace.

Deacon was getting too far ahead of himself. First he had to establish if Cochrane was here. Then he had to establish that, an hour and a half ago, he hadn't been.

There were no lights on, in the farmhouse or the outbuildings, and front and back doors were both locked. A green Land Rover was parked under the kitchen window. Deacon felt the bonnet and the exhaust but both were cold. Of course, it was nearly four in the morning; there had been plenty of time for it to cool down.

Somewhere in the clutter of sheds a dog began to bark. A light went on and someone shouted a curse. Deacon sniffed. It was time to announce himself anyway. He hammered his fist on the back door. "Mr Cochrane, it's the police. Will you come down and open up, please?"

Jack Deacon would have recognised Neil Cochrane across

a busy street anywhere in the world. The converse was probably also true. It had been years since they last talked, but Deacon had never gone more than a week without thinking of the sheep-farmer living alone in his fastness in the secret heart of the Downs. He believed Neil Cochrane was a serial killer, and that he'd almost managed to prove it.

Ten years ago Deacon was a keen new Detective Inspector who thought he would make Chief Inspector, Superintendent, Chief Superintendent. He was a big man then, as tall if not quite as broad, making up for his limited experience with a wealth of confidence. Now he knew more, and he knew better. He knew that every murder isn't solved, that every murderer isn't found, and that every murderer who *is* found doesn't go to prison. Ten years ago his failure to make Neil Cochrane pay for the murder of three teenage boys had stuck in his throat till he almost choked.

The man who opened the back door in corduroys and his pyjama shirt was also ten years older. He hadn't got broader, he'd grown gaunt, but the framework was the same—the long bones, the powerful muscles knotted over them, the strong square jaw and the oddly light eyes at bay under the heavy, beetling brow. He looked at Deacon as if he'd been expecting him. "What now, Inspector? Somebody tripped over a kerb, have they? Wandered in front of a bus? So you thought you'd find out what I know about it."

"Can I come inside?"

"Have you got a warrant?"

"Do I need one?"

"No. You could do with a new watch, though." He turned inside, leaving the door open. Deacon took that as an invitation and followed him into the kitchen, Voss at his heels.

Cochrane neither took a seat nor offered one to his visitors. "What d'you want, then?"

"Have you been out tonight, Mr Cochrane?" Deacon's tone was uncommunicative, his face expressionless.

"Been out to check the sheep. That what you mean?"

"No. Have you been into Dimmock?"

"Yesterday evening. Needed some drench from the vet."

"What time did you get home?"

Cochrane shrugged. "Dunno. Middle of the evening."

"Seven? Eight?"

"Maybe."

"Your vet works late," commented Voss.

"The money I pay him, he'd better work any time I want him to." He glared at the younger man, then switched his gaze to Deacon. "All right. What's happened?"

But Deacon wasn't ready to talk about that. "Who is your vet?"

"John Cummings," growled the farmer.

"And if I ask Mr Cummings, what time will he say you called with him?"

There was a pause. Then: "About seven. I went to the pub afterwards."

"Which one?"

"The one in Rye Lane." *The Rose*—the only pub in Dimmock that never tried to get a theme, attract a younger clientele, or even sweep the floor on a regular basis.

"When did you leave?"

"About eight. What's this about, Mr Deacon?"

The policeman fell back on the old mantra that served as both shield and weapon. "Routine inquiries, Mr Cochrane."

"Routine inquiries?" Cochrane's accent was thicker than the standard south coast argot, with a bit of a Devon burr in it. "In my kitchen, at four o'clock in the morning? That's not routine, Mr Deacon, that's personal. And if you're accusing me of something, maybe I'd better call my lawyer."

Deacon shrugged. "Your prerogative, Mr Cochrane. But it's an expensive way to get rid of me when just answering a few questions would have the same result."

"I answered your questions." The lantern jaw came up. "You're still here."

Deacon nodded. "So you were in Dimmock earlier but

you came home about eight and you haven't been out since except to check the sheep. That about the size of it?"

The tall man nodded.

"So if somebody says he saw you on the pier at two o'clock this morning he's mistaken."

Neil Cochrane's expression turned wary. "Not necessarily."

Deacon's heart thumped. Surely to God the man wasn't going to confess? After ten years of taking everything Dimmock CID, first led by DCI George Ennis, later by Deacon himself, could throw at him? "No?"

"No," said the farmer. "He might be mistaken. Then again he could be a damn liar."

Deacon swallowed his anger, nodded slowly. "All right, Mr Cochrane, that'll do for now. I'll drop by again if there's anything more." He headed for the door. "Oh—one thing. Could I have a look in your Land Rover?"

Cochrane didn't even blink. "You got that warrant in the last five minutes?"

"No."

"Then no."

DANIEL WAS EXPECTED. When he announced himself at the front desk of Dimmock Police Station at five to eight, the Duty Sergeant ushered him immediately into the warren of corridors and stairwells and delivered him to Detective Inspector Deacon's office on the second floor.

Deacon waved him to a chair. Daniel looked round uneasily. The last time he was in this room he was thrown out almost bodily, and Detective Inspector Deacon was not a man to gloss over past differences. He was a man to wrap them carefully in tissue-paper, store them in a dark cupboard and bring them out in mint condition time after time.

Of course, he wanted something. But Daniel wanted it too. He wanted to identify the man he'd watched beat the life out of a teenage boy. He wasn't here as a favour to Deacon: he was seeking justice.

DS Voss was in the room too. They traded a non committal nod. Daniel knew what the sergeant's presence meant. Deacon wanted a witness. He didn't want any doubt over whether Daniel recognised the murderer in the volume of photographs on his desk. He didn't trust him. Daniel felt the colour prick his cheeks. "Do you know yet who he was?"

"Oh yeah," said Deacon. "I've got a pretty good idea."

"The boy," said Daniel in a low voice.

Deacon's lips formed an O that he had marginally too much tact to voice. "His name was Chris Berry. He was eighteen, working with his dad as a house-painter. In his spare time he was a runner. Won cups for it. Nice kid. And someone beat his head in with a wheel-brace. You want to look at some faces and tell me who?"

There were hundreds in the bound volume CID called the family album. But Deacon didn't expect him to look at them all: he passed the book to Daniel already open. Daniel looked.

When he'd inspected every face on the page he turned it over. Deacon and Voss exchanged a fast, worried, uncomprehending glance.

"Hang on a minute," objected Deacon, turning the page back. "There are twenty faces there. I want you to look carefully at all of them."

"I have," Daniel said, surprised.

Deacon scowled. *"And?"*

"None of them is the man I saw."

Deacon stared at him in disbelief. Then he turned the book round and had another look himself. Could he possibly have opened it at the wrong page?

But no. The photograph of Neil Cochrane, second from the left in the bottom row, gazed up at him. For an instant Deacon could have sworn it winked.

THREE

"LOOK AGAIN," Jack Deacon said through clenched teeth.

"I *have* looked," said Daniel indignantly. Then he caught the real anger in the inspector's manner. "It wasn't who you thought."

Deacon's eye could have set off fireworks. "Damn sure it was who I thought. I *know* who did this—I just need the only witness to identify him. If that isn't asking too much."

Daniel looked again, mostly to appease the policemen. Then he sat back. "I'm sorry. None of these is the man I saw on the pier."

Charlie Voss said, "Are you *sure?*" He sounded perplexed but not suspicious: a younger man than Deacon, he didn't share his general mistrust of everyone under thirty.

"Pretty sure," said Daniel. The regret in his tone was genuine. He'd have given them what they wanted if he could.

Deacon breathed heavily. If he hadn't been a senior detective in his own office, in the presence of his own sergeant, his next move would have been to grab Daniel by the lapels and slam him against the wall. As that wasn't an option he had to think.

"All right," he said gruffly. "That photograph's ten years old. People change in ten years—well, their appearance does. The man you saw: describe him again."

Daniel was anxious to co-operate. He didn't like annoying Inspector Deacon. He didn't like annoying anyone, but particularly not people with the build and temperament of a bull buffalo in the rutting season. "I got the impression he was tall. Not just taller than me: when they were together he was taller than—than—"

"Chris Berry was six foot," said Deacon baldly. He would be the last man in England to go metric. "To be noticeably taller he'd have to be six-two or above."

"Not heavily built. Not thin, but he was a tall man rather than a big man. Aged maybe fifty, fifty-five—though he didn't seem it when he was running. Chris wasn't leaving him behind."

"Fit, then. And strong. Someone with a physical, outdoor sort of life maybe?" He ignored Voss's warning look. "What was he wearing?"

"I couldn't see."

"Hair?"

Daniel shook his head. "I don't know."

"Eyes?"

"Red."

Deacon blinked. "What?"

Daniel lifted one shoulder in an apologetic shrug. "It was a red torch. Everything looked red—his face, his eyes, the surf. Everything light looked red, everything dark looked black."

"So light eyes rather than dark ones. Blue or grey." Deacon folded his arms on the desk, regarded his witness over the top of them. "You're describing my suspect as clearly as could be expected in the circumstances. I know it isn't easy to pick someone out from a photograph, particularly an old photograph, particularly when you've only seen him for a couple of seconds. What about an identity parade?"

"I'll do anything you think might help," said Daniel. "But Inspector, if your suspect is one of the men on this page you're not going to get a result. I'm sorry."

Jack Deacon's temper was a permanently lit fuse. Smouldering quietly in the dark, it never needed more than gentle fanning to make it explode to life. He came to his feet, slamming one leg-of-mutton fist hard enough on the desk to make the family album jump. Daniel jumped too.

"Damn it, Danny," he yelled, "you're doing it again! Why are you protecting this one? The last one only hurt you, maybe you were entitled to a say in what happened to him, but this one? This one kills boys. Four in ten years. If I don't stop him—if you don't help me—there'll be more. Now, do you want to give a little more thought to your evidence?"

Daniel had been shouted at by experts, by people who made Jack Deacon sound like a Sunday school teacher in a pet. It had achieved nothing then, and would achieve nothing now, for the same reason: he had no more information to give. Whatever Deacon thought, his task could not be advanced by bullying his witness.

He looked up, daring the big man's scowl. "Inspector Deacon, what is it you want me to do? If you wanted me to lie you could have pointed out your suspect. Since you didn't do that I assume you want the truth. Well, inconvenient as it may be, that's it. If your prime suspect is one of the men on that page, I'm not going to be any help to you. I don't believe I've seen any of them before."

Deacon opened his mouth for a fresh tirade but Sergeant Voss got in first: partly to protect Daniel but mainly to protect his boss. "Are you absolutely sure of that? Or are you just saying none of them looks familiar?"

Honesty was a virtue which Daniel Hood plugged away at until it became a vice. If he'd stuck to his guns, probably they'd have shown him the door and his involvement would have ended there.

"Of course I'm not absolutely a hundred percent sure! How could I be—it was dark, it was over in a few seconds, I got a glimpse of a man's face several metres above me by the light of a torch designed for another purpose. If you're asking me to ID one of the photographs you've shown me, I can't. If you're asking if there's a possibility that I'm mistaken then yes, of course there is. I'm doing the best I can but I can't give you a guarantee. I'd put money on what I'm telling you. I wouldn't stake my life."

"But you're happy to risk other people's, aren't you?" snarled Deacon. "The fact is, Danny, you're safe enough.

You're—what?—twenty-six? You're too old for him. Even
Chris there, at eighteen, was getting past his sell-by date. The
others were sixteen and fifteen.

"He rapes them, Danny. He snatches them, ties them up,
beats them with his fists, rapes them, then finishes the job with
a wheel-brace. He's done it four times. He's going to do it
again. Even though you caught him in the act, he's still going
to get the chance to do it again. Chris Berry died for nothing."

DANIEL DIDN'T GO home, he went to Brodie's office in Shack
Lane. He got there before she did. He wasn't wearing a watch
but knew it must be nearly nine. He leaned against the wall
and waited.

After six months the business was beginning to look part
of the scenery. The slate shingle with her name on it was
weathering nicely and the easel in the window displayed an
impressive collection of discreetly edited testimonials. Behind
the easel was a burgundy velvet curtain. Nobody coming here
wanted to do their business in full view of passers-by.

She'd called it *Looking for Something?* Combining the
wistful with the faintly pugnacious, the name struck Daniel
as an accurate reflection of the proprietor. He'd never heard
of a finding agency before, but apparently it wasn't that unusual in London and Brodie was a Londoner. She lived in
Dimmock because she'd married a local man. She still lived
in Dimmock now they were divorced because she had contacts here and, unfashionable as it was, she thought it was a
good place to raise a child.

Daniel thought so too. It offered fresh air, sea views and a
hinterland of open countryside. Dimmock might have seen
better days, the Georgian squares and Victorian terraces a little cobwebbed now, but basically it was a decent middle-
class town with decent middle-class values and safe streets.
Muggers with any ambition sought out more prosperous
towns. Actually, anyone with any ambition tended to leave
Dimmock, so even the traffic remained manageable.

Daniel didn't have asthma, didn't have enough money to be worth mugging and didn't have a car. He also didn't have any children to consider. But though there was nothing holding him here now, he didn't see himself leaving either. He'd acquired some modest contacts of his own, and also some obligations.

He'd come to Dimmock to teach. Returning to school seemed impossible at the moment—the doctors called it Post Traumatic Stress Disorder; what it really meant was his nerve was shot—but if the time came that he could cope with crowds again, Dimmock Comprehensive was as good a school as any.

In the meantime he was taking pupils for tutoring. Daniel Hood was that rare specimen, a teacher who could make maths interesting, and what had begun as a favour to a couple of struggling thirteen-year-olds who panicked when he had to leave his job was now providing him with an income. And also the satisfaction of making a difference to a group of children who, if he turned them away, might never learn to navigate the numerical world. He had no ties anywhere else, nothing pulling him away. If tutoring was all he could do, he could do it as well here as anywhere.

On top of which Brodie and her daughter, and even her odd Polish neighbour, were the closest friends he had. Closer than what remained of his family. They were reason enough to stay in Dimmock. Also he rather liked his flat.

There wasn't much parking-space in Shack Lane: Brodie used an empty lot behind the seafront shops. She came round the corner on foot and waved when she saw him. "Have you been waiting long?"

"A minute," said Daniel. "How's Paddy?"

"She seems fine," said Brodie. "I left her having breakfast with Marta and she was chattering away about staying at your place and going out in the middle of the night and seeing the moons of Jupiter. I don't think she's altogether aware she got to see a dead body too."

"It may hit her later."

"If it does she's in good hands. Paddy's OK, don't worry about her. Tell me how it went with Deacon."

He told her. Brodie felt her heart sinking. "Why does God hate us so?" she asked plaintively.

Daniel chuckled. "He doesn't hate you, he hates me; possibly because I don't believe in him. I don't mind God hating me, I just wish Inspector Deacon didn't."

"He doesn't hate you. He just doesn't understand you."

That made Daniel laugh out loud. "When men complain their wives don't understand them, usually it means they understand them too well." The amusement drained from his face, leaving it pale. "I can't get over what it is we're talking about. Somebody died last night. I watched one human being end the life of another. Chris Berry isn't going home to his mum any more. His dad's going to need a new assistant with the painting business. Someone put an end to his future, and I watched it happen and did nothing to stop it."

Brodie gripped his arm. "There was nothing more you could have done. If he could have been saved, you'd have saved him. With the possible exception of Jack Deacon, who's as stubborn as you are—and that, by the by, is the reason you rub one another the wrong way—I don't know anyone else who would." The echo of what he'd said caught up with her. "Chris Berry? That's who it was?"

"Do you know him?"

"I know who he is. Was. A fell-runner. There's a race they do round here—the Three Downs, it's about eight miles across rough country. Chris Berry's won it twice in the last three years. The first time he was sixteen, the youngest winner ever."

Daniel was staring at her. "How on earth do you know?"

"I met his mother at the Civic Ball at Christmas, it was her sole topic of conversation. Nice woman, bit of a one-track mind." Remembering, she gave a vinegar smile. Mrs Berry hadn't been the only one she'd bumped into: her ex-husband had been there with his new wife.

Time had not yet erased the hurt. Though she knew—as

the wife and sometime clerk of a solicitor, how could she not?—that half of all marriages end in divorce, she had felt hugely betrayed. In a way it was easier that John had wanted to marry the other woman, it saved Brodie having to try to forgive the unforgivable. The divorce wasn't messy because both of them wanted it. Brodie walked away with her daughter and enough capital to buy her flat and start her business.

Daniel gave a low whistle. "He didn't believe in making life easy for himself, did he?"

Brodie was still thinking about the Civic Ball. "Who?"

"Whoever killed Chris Berry. He was an eighteen-year-old endurance runner at the peak of his physical strength. He should have been able to take that wheel-brace off whoever was chasing him and wrap it round his neck. Why would anyone wanting to abduct a boy pick one who was famous for his ability to run for miles, who trained relentlessly, who'd know exactly where to shove a wheel-brace so it was no longer a threat to him?"

They were staring at one another across Brodie's desk. It was a small office: there wasn't room for both of them on one side. The more they considered, the more valid the question seemed. Criminals don't *want* to be caught. Why would anyone select a target so obviously capable of defending himself?

"What did Deacon think?"

Daniel shrugged. "Deacon thinks I'm wrong about who I saw on the pier. He thinks he knows who killed Chris Berry; apparently he's done it before. He was ready to make an arrest. But his prime suspect isn't the man I saw, and he isn't interested in looking for anyone else."

"Whatever else he is," said Brodie, "Jack Deacon's a pro. When he's finished shouting, he'll think about what you told him. If only as insurance, he'll look into it."

Daniel was chewing the inside of his cheek. "This Mrs Berry. Do you know where she lives?"

Immediately Brodie's expression turned wary. "Why?"

"I'd like to go and see her. To—I don't know—apologise."

His gaze came up and she saw the pain in his eyes. "I was her son's best chance and I failed him. I'd like to tell her I'm sorry. That I'd have helped if I could."

Brodie shook her head. "I don't know, Daniel, I'm not sure it's the right time. Deacon will have told her what happened, so she knows there was someone there who cared enough to try and save Chris. The fact remains that she lost him, and I don't know if she could cope with meeting you just now. Give her a little time. Later she'll be glad of the chance to thank you, but right now it's just asking too much."

He thought she was right. He nodded slowly and flicked her a fragile smile. "I don't know what to do for the best."

"Daniel, you've already done it. There's nothing more you can do. It's up to other people now."

FOUR

As soon as he had his search warrant Detective Inspector Deacon returned to Manor Farm. Now he regretted his earlier visit: it hadn't advanced his inquiries, only served to warn Cochrane that he was under suspicion. Any evidence that Chris Berry had been here would be harder to find now. The constables left on surveillance had seen Cochrane rise at six and tend to his beasts. They could not say if he had also been busy with a bucket of soapy water and a scrubbing brush.

It takes a lot of people a lot of hours to search a building thoroughly. Deacon had brought a lot of people, and they had nothing more important to do with their time, but he still wasn't confident of success. They did all this ten years ago and found nothing; and Cochrane wasn't worried enough.

The Land Rover was probably their best chance of finding some forensics. Cochrane hadn't been near it: whatever was in or on it at four o'clock this morning would be there still. As soon as Cochrane had seen the warrant the Inspector waved up a low-loader to take it away. He wasn't going to do this on his hands and knees with a torch. It was going to the police garage for a thorough workout.

"How long's that going to take, then?" asked Cochrane dourly. He'd pulled on a waxed jacket so old it was impossible to judge its original colour, wellingtons with as much tread on them as tractor tyres, and a tweed cap. He was a farmer, had no wish to be mistaken for a gentleman. When he had trouble with vermin he solved it with a double-barrelled shotgun, not a horse and a bunch of dogs.

"A couple of days," said Deacon. "Look on the bright side.

When you get it back—if you get it back—it'll be spotless. Think of it as a free valet."

"In the meantime, how'm I supposed to feed my sheep?"

Deacon's gaze travelled round the farmyard, lit on a wheel-barrow propped against a wall. "Plan B."

Leaving Manor Farm, he headed back into Dimmock with Frick Down on his left and Menner and Chain Downs stretching away to his right. The Three Downs. Dimmock hadn't many claims to fame, but the fell race was one. Runners all over Britain knew of it, counted its plain silver cup as one of their glittering prizes. For three years this had been Chris Berry's kingdom; till he met a rampant old goat and made the mistake of running the one way his speed could do him no good.

When Deacon got back to the police station Sergeant Voss was waiting. "Mrs Berry's here."

"Has she done the formal identification?"

"We're just back from the hospital. Her husband was there too but he couldn't hack it. I had Jill Meadows take him home."

"Is she all right?"

Charlie Voss looked askance at his boss. "Well, she didn't faint and she didn't get hysterical, if that's what you mean. Now she wants to see you."

Deacon had wanted to talk to her again too. He'd broken the news to the family himself at six o'clock this morning, but he hadn't stayed long. It was too soon to tell them anything that made it easier, and his time could be better spent than on meaningless condolences. When he'd caught their son's killer he'd sit down with them and talk.

Except that Mrs Berry wanted to talk now. Deacon threw his coat at the rack and missed; Voss picked it up. It was a ritual they performed a couple of times a day. "Where is she?"

"In your office. I didn't want to put her in an interview room. Meadows is with her."

Mrs Berry didn't look like an athlete's mother. She was rather small and dumpy, and wore a grey cloth coat over a purple sweater and grey tweed skirt. She'd only known for four hours, but already she was observing the proprieties.

She also remembered his name, which was an achievement in the circumstances. Perhaps that ability to focus through the pain was what Chris inherited from her. She'd just been to view the body of her murdered child. Someone who'd seen less of grief than Jack Deacon might have found her dry eyes and steely self-control unnatural if not unnerving. But Deacon knew that people cope with disaster in a wide variety of ways, and any which leave them sane are valid. Mrs Berry was getting involved. She couldn't help her son but she could follow the hunt for his killer. "I wondered if there'd been any developments, Inspector Deacon."

He wasn't sure what to tell her. She desperately needed some good news but he wouldn't raise her hopes only to dash them. If he'd been able to get more sense out of Daniel Hood... But he hadn't.

"We're following a line of inquiry, Mrs Berry," he said, dropping into his chair. "I've interviewed a man, and we're searching a house and a vehicle. I can't tell you yet that we have your son's killer. But I'm doing everything I can in the hope of making an early arrest."

"When you came to the house," she said, "you told us what had happened. I'm sorry but I didn't take it all in. Did you say there was a witness?"

Deacon nodded. "A man who lives near the pier. He happened to be outside and heard shouting."

"He saw...?" She couldn't quite bring herself to say it.

"He saw something." The policeman shrugged awkwardly. "It was the middle of the night. But yes, he saw the struggle. Then Chris went into the water and the other man ran. The witness got a glimpse of his face. I'm hoping it'll be enough."

"And then—did I get this right?—he pulled Chris out of the sea?"

Deacon nodded. "He thought he might still be alive. He found him and started artificial respiration. But it was too late."

"He could have died. Trying to save my son."

"Yes," nodded Deacon. He looked surprised. "Yes, he could."

"Would you thank him for me?"

"Yes, Mrs Berry, I will." It had taken the mother of the murdered youth to think of it. Deacon didn't remember saying a single appreciative word to Daniel Hood when he stood, shocked and exhausted, in front of him. For a moment he regretted that. But he knew the feeling would pass before he saw Daniel again.

While he had her there Deacon took the opportunity to ask a few questions of his own. "You told me Chris went out training yesterday evening. Do you know where he'd have gone or who he'd have been with?"

"He'd have been with Nathan. They did all their training together. They did *everything* together." She smiled wanly. "We used to say they'd have to marry Siamese twins."

"Nathan?"

"Nathan Sparkes." She gave him an address in the Woodgreen estate. "They're—were—best friends since they started school. The year Chris didn't win the Three Downs, Nathan did."

"So they were running yesterday evening."

"They might have gone running," said Mrs Berry, "they might have gone to the gym. They might have decided to skip a night and go to the pub. They weren't just athletes, Inspector, they were young men. They enjoyed their lives. It's the one consolation in all of this, you know? Chris may not have had a very long life but it was a full one. He'd done as much, achieved as much, as men twice his age."

"It ought to make it better," Deacon agreed softly. "Somehow it makes it worse. I'm going to get this man, Mrs Berry. Count on it."

He saw her out. When he got back to his office there was a message waiting. "A Mr Ennis to see you. He says he knows you."

Deacon's eyes widened. "George Ennis? Of course. Send him up."

If the girl on the desk had been doing this job for longer she'd have known who George Ennis was too. Ten years ago he was Detective Chief Inspector Ennis, leading the hunt for the man who murdered three Dimmock youths over the course of thirteen months. Deacon knew that his failure to make anyone amenable—more specifically, to bring charges when the whole of CID knew who committed the crimes—influenced his decision to take an early retirement a couple of years later. He hadn't been much older than Deacon was now.

He headed for the stairs to meet Ennis on the way up. There was also a lift, and most men in their fifties would have taken it, but Ennis had always been a fitness fanatic. He'd got salad put on the canteen menu at a time when self-respecting policemen ate steak and chips. When he retired he opened some kind of a health club. Deacon hadn't seen him for years, but he still knew better than to wait for the lift.

They met at the top of the stairs and shook hands, Deacon uncharacteristically warm in his welcome. Of course, this was the man who'd taught him nearly everything he knew. "Good of you to come round, George. I was going to call you, let you know he's back in business." It wasn't true but it might have been.

But he'd misunderstood the reason for Ennis's visit. He wasn't for the moment concerned with Neil Cochrane. "Jack, they're saying it was Chris Berry. Is that right?"

"Yes," said Deacon.

"There's no mistake? You're quite sure?"

"I'm afraid so." He steered Ennis into his office as if it hadn't been *his* office until eight years ago. "Did you know him, then?"

"Of course I know him!" George Ennis was an inch taller than Deacon and a lot of inches narrower, and if anything he looked younger than the day he retired. But he also looked desperately troubled, his angular face creased with anxiety, his eyes stunned. "Knew him. I trained him, Jack. From when he was a scrawny little kid about thirteen years old. His mum sent him to me to keep him off the street, and the first time I saw him run I knew I had a champion. And now he's dead." He dropped into the chair recently vacated by Mrs Berry. "You're sure? You are sure?"

"George, the boy's mother ID'd the body. There's no doubt." The pieces were snapping together with a click. "She said something about him going to the gym. Your place?"

Ennis nodded. Now the last hope was gone he slumped in his chair and sighed. "Yes. One of my star pupils, and as nice a kid as you could hope to meet. It's an absolute tragedy." He shook his head, still struggling to believe. "Can you tell me what happened?"

Deacon told him everything he knew. He stopped short of telling him everything he suspected; but Ennis had no need to be cautious any more.

"You know who did this, don't you?"

Deacon bit his lip. "I have a good idea. But George—that's not your business any more."

"I know." Ennis straightened, pulling himself together by sheer force of will. "And I know it's in safe hands. But—oh dear God, Jack, if I'd got him ten years ago Chris would be alive now!"

"Damn it, George," growled Deacon, "you can't think like that. It isn't fair on either of us. We did our best. We found the man responsible. It wasn't our fault that the evidence didn't satisfy the Crown Prosecution Service."

He let out a long, slow breath and leaned back in his chair. "And actually, that isn't fair either. We couldn't give them enough. If there'd only been some DNA. But whatever else Cochrane is, he's not stupid. He was never overtaken by an irresistible urge. He planned carefully, meticulously. Well, maybe this time will be different. This time he didn't have things all his own way."

Ennis was looking at him, the question he was reluctant to voice stinging in his eyes. "Did he…rape…Chris too?"

Deacon shrugged, not unkindly. "I don't know. The post

mortem's going on about now. Maybe not—he still had his clothes, maybe he got away before Cochrane could over-power him."

"In that case there won't be any forensic."

That was Deacon's fear too. "George, we simply don't know yet. He may have been in the Land Rover; he may even have been in the house. If he was there'll be some evidence somewhere; and however little it is, we'll find it."

But he was talking to someone who knew the pitfalls as well as he did. "We're going to lose him again, aren't we, Jack?" whispered Ennis. Behind rubbed lids his eyes were bitter. "We couldn't get him ten years ago, and we're not going to get him now. He's too clever for us."

Deacon stumbled to his feet as if someone had kicked the chair from under him. "Don't give me that! *Nobody* is that clever. Nobody is fireproof. Ten years ago we were unlucky. We did our damnedest, but we were unlucky. We scared him, though. We put him off trying again for ten years. How many boys have grown up safely in that time because of how close we got to him?

"This time it's going to be different. We know exactly when the crime occurred, we got to the pier while the scene was still fresh, we had Cochrane and his house and Land Rover under surveillance within a couple of hours. We were never in that position before. Forensic techniques have improved in ten years. And this time we have a witness."

Ennis was staring at him, a coal in the grief-muddied blue of his eyes. "Somebody saw?"

"The whole thing. I have the time, the place and a damned good description. I'll get him, George. I promise you."

THEY MET ON THE shore. Both wanted it though neither intended it. Daniel thought Brodie was right when she said it was too soon to express his regrets to Chris Berry's mother; and Frances Berry didn't even know Daniel's name. She went to the pier because something deep in her was saying that she knew how and where her son came into the world, she ought to see where he left it; and alone because she didn't believe anyone would understand.

Charlie Voss had arranged for a police-car to take her home. But she'd had it drop her here, said she'd make her own way. WPC Meadows wasn't happy and she didn't think DS Voss would be either. But the woman was calm, apparently in control of herself, and giving someone a lift somewhere they don't want to go is kidnapping. Jill Meadows told her to call the station again if she needed them, gave her the number of a taxi firm, and left her on the promenade.

Daniel was on his way home. He sat in Brodie's office, sipping her coffee, until she got busy, then he left. It was a five minute walk from Shack Lane to the netting-sheds, but half way he was suddenly so tired he could go no further. He dropped onto a bench and stared out to sea, and didn't notice his eyelids growing heavy.

He may have dozed for a few minutes or an hour. He woke cold and stiff with a small woman in a grey coat watching him. He started, thinking he'd done something stupid; and then he knew who she was. It was the quality of her gaze that told him: plummetingly sad, and yearning, as if she wanted something from him. He stood up, unsure what to do with his hands. "Mrs Berry?"

She nodded. "You're him, aren't you? The man who tried to save my son."

Daniel nodded, a shade reluctantly. "I'm Daniel Hood."

"I asked Mr Deacon to thank you for me—for Chris's family. I'm glad to have the chance to do it myself." The words were coming out just a little faster than they should have done, but Daniel marvelled that she could hold an intelligent conversation at all.

"I'm so sorry it wasn't enough," he said, his voice low. "For a while I thought I'd got to him in time. But—"

When his voice faltered her gaze turned compassionate. Eight hours after the event, and those few minutes of exhausted slumber on a promenade bench were clearly all the sleep he'd had. He looked drained and grey, and despite her own misery—perhaps, in a way, because of it—her heart went out to him. "I'd like to talk to you, if that's all right. Is there somewhere we could go? I'll buy you a coffee."

For an instant he saw himself through her eyes—frail, pathetic even, running on empty, too weak to make it home—and winced. This woman had raised a big, strapping, athletic son with endless strength and energy. Even at his best Daniel was not an impressive physical specimen. Today the contrast between the man who died and the one who lived was painfully acute.

He gestured awkwardly. "My flat's just here. Come inside, I'll put the kettle on."

While he assembled the cups she stood in the kitchen door, still with her coat on, and began talking to him as if to herself. Anyone would have served: a friend, a stranger, the cat. Daniel let her talk, only responded when a response seemed necessary.

"I can't go home," she said. It wasn't a plea for sympathy, merely a statement of fact. "If I go home the reality that Chris isn't there, that Chris is never *going* to be there, will be unavoidable. As long as I keep moving—going to the hospital, going to the police station, coming here—I can keep it at arm's length. I'm doing something useful; I'm helping. If I go home, and sit down, and stop, it's going to break over me like one of the waves out there."

It wasn't the happiest analogy. The picture it conjured made her mouth tremble. She ploughed on determinedly. "I'm treating my husband very badly. Chris doesn't need me any more but Bill does. He needs to put his arms around me and feel mine round him. He needs us to hold one another and cry.

"I'm not ready for that. If I start I won't be able to stop. I need to do everything that needs doing first. Like coming here, talking to you. I don't know why it feels more important than going home and grieving with my husband, I only know it does. There'll be time for that. This needs doing now."

Daniel carried the tray into the living-room. Mrs Berry took a seat, hugging her coat around her. The flat wasn't cold, she was in shock.

She bit her lip. "Now I'm here I don't know what to say to you. Thank you, obviously, but…"

Daniel thought for a moment. "It happened very quickly. He was on his feet and running, then he was in the sea. I think it was all over at that point. I don't think there could have been much pain." He wouldn't lie to her, lies would demean what she was going through, but he knew as he said it he was being less than honest. The boy was running for his life. He knew he'd taken a wrong turn, that the pier was a dead end, and that the man behind him would kill him if he caught him. No pain? Chris Berry had been hunted to his death, must have spent the closing minutes of his life in an agony of terror.

But even Daniel, who had a zealot's reverence for the truth, saw no need to bludgeon a stricken woman with it. If he couldn't make things any better for her, he could at least try not to make them worse.

She looked at him with haunted eyes but a tiny tremulous smile. "You're very kind. If there's a grain of comfort in this, Mr Hood, it's that my son didn't die alone with his killer; that there was someone nearby who cared enough to try and help him, and he just may have known that."

Daniel didn't know what to say. He'd let Brodie persuade him it was too soon for this meeting in part because he was afraid how Mrs Berry would react. He was overwhelmed that in her desolation she could find the strength to be gracious to him. He sipped his coffee in silence.

Frances Berry belonged to a generation that believed in self-reliance, in picking yourself up and dusting yourself off. She was fighting to stay positive. She sat up straight and pushed her shoulders back. "Inspector Deacon is hopeful of making an early arrest." She sounded more like a press release than a bereaved parent.

"Yes?" murmured Daniel, not looking at her.

"He said you saw him. The man who…" For a moment the blackness bent over her, the chaos loomed and her composure faltered. She sucked in a sharp breath, fingernails digging into her palms. "The murderer."

"Yes," Daniel said again. "Um—"

It would be days before she knew if she was warm or cold, hungry or full, tired or rested. But in this one matter her awareness was crystalline. She heard the hesitation in his voice and knew it was significant. "What?"

His only choice was between hurting her now and hurting her later. He thought it would be cruel to give her false hope. "Inspector Deacon had a suspect. Maybe he's right but…"

"But?"

"I don't think his suspect is the man I saw."

The room went perceptibly cooler and stiller. The mutter of the shore receded, the rumble of traffic on the promenade sank to a whisper. Daniel felt the woman's eyes fixed in his face like talons.

"You're not going to identify him?" She was holding her voice level by an effort of will.

"I am," protested Daniel. "When I see him again."

"But surely," said Frances Berry, struggling to understand, "Inspector Deacon *knows* who did this. He's already interviewed him, he's searching his house. He told me he expected to make an arrest."

Daniel nodded. "I know he does. I think he may be mistaken."

"May be?" echoed Mrs Berry. *"May be?"*

He knew his delicate conscience was like a knife twisting in her side. He tried to explain. "Mrs Berry, it won't help to go after the wrong man. I'm sure Inspector Deacon has good reason for his suspicions. But you don't want to see somebody who might have killed Chris, who could have done it, behind bars. You want the man who actually did it. I saw that man. I'm sure Inspector Deacon will find him. It just may take a little time."

She was staring at him like a hawk at its prey. All the empathy between them had dissipated. A note of revelation in her voice, she stated: "You're afraid."

"Afraid?"

"You saw a man commit murder. You think he saw you too. You're afraid of what he'll do to silence you. You think if you refuse to identify him he'll realise you're no threat and leave you alone. My God! You're going to let a killer go free because you're afraid he'll do to you what he did to my Chris."

Daniel shook his head unhappily. "I swear to you, if I thought the police had the right man—"

She wasn't interested in his excuses. "I thought you were a brave man, Mr Hood," she said imperiously. She stood up. "I see I misjudged you."

She didn't slam the door behind her. She closed it precisely, with a crisp click that ricocheted through Daniel's brain, and bloomed on his cheek, like a slap.

FIVE

DANIEL HOOD NEVER WAS a social animal. For one thing, he had better things to do with the dark hours than sit in smoky clubs listening to music he didn't like and unable to hear people he did. He had always been self-contained. He liked people and on the whole people liked him, but he had never craved companionship.

So it was bizarre suddenly to be the centre of attention. Hardly had he recovered from Mrs Berry's parting shot than there came another knock at the door and it was Tom Sessions from *The Dimmock Sentinel*. Daniel groaned but let him in anyway. He owed Sessions a favour.

The reporter looked him up and down and said with characteristic candour, "You look like shit."

Daniel chuckled and waved him to a chair. "Do you want some tea?"

"I'd sooner have some information."

"Take the tea," advised Daniel, "so you won't have wasted your journey."

The kettle was still hot. Sessions took the mug, but he also got out his tape-recorder. "I take it there is at least some truth in the rumour."

"What rumour?"

"That you've taken to changing into tights and a cape in telephone kiosks."

Daniel laughed out loud. He found Sessions' attitude oddly bracing. There was no malice in the man, he was just a natural cynic. "You heard about last night."

"I heard *something* about last night. I thought I must have got it wrong. Did I?"

"I don't know how much I can tell you," said Daniel. "Deacon's talking about arresting someone."

"Really? I bet that put a smile on his face."

"Well…not the last time I saw him."

Sandy brows knit over Tom Sessions' keen eyes. "Daniel—what is it you're not telling me?"

So Daniel told him.

The reporter whistled at the ceiling. "Oh, you *must* be popular with Dimmock CID!"

"I don't understand," complained Daniel. "Surely he wants to arrest the right man? Why's he trying to tell *me* who the murderer is when I'm the one who saw him?"

"Because of the history," said Sessions. "Do you know the background to all this?"

"I know something happened ten years ago. I didn't live round here then."

"Well, I did," said the reporter, "and it was a bad time. I thought you'd be interested so I brought you a paper. Well, a photocopy, of an article I wrote when things were at their scariest." He put a manilla envelope on the table.

"Give me the highlights."

There were three victims. The first was sixteen, so when he failed to return home one night there was much winking and elbowing and references to hormonal overload. Even three days later, when it was clear that something had happened, the police were still thinking in terms of a young man off to see the world, or just possibly an unreported accident. Then a body was discovered at the end of the pier, naked, battered, ravaged and finished off with a volley of blows to the head with an iron bar. The sense of shock reverberated around Dimmock like TNT.

"George Ennis was DCI in Dimmock then, Jack Deacon was his deputy. They used all the manpower and all the science available to them, but none of it gave them a suspect," said Sessions.

"Four months passed, and if the chances of solving the crime seemed to have passed too, so did the danger. We all thought it was something you might see once in a career, if you were unlucky, and whether it was inspired by rage or passion or drugs, whoever was responsible had gone back where he came from. Either it was the result of a brainstorm in someone who'd then returned to his ordinary life reading meters or serving groceries or whatever, or—and this was a favourite—it wasn't a local man at all, it was someone who'd been passing through when the madness struck."

That comfort vanished when a second body turned up at the pier. In those days there was still a summer season, but from the end of October until Easter there were no concerts in the concert hall and no fortune teller in the booth. The pier was just a wooden cul-de-sac sticking far enough into the Channel that something left there could go unnoticed for days.

"That, presumably, was why he took them there," said Sessions. "It was handy, and out of season it was deserted; and George Ennis reckoned the killer got a kind of thrill out of performing under the very noses of Dimmock's notoriously respectable citizens. Dumping the boys up on the Downs wouldn't have been nearly as much fun."

Daniel shuddered. He'd seen what this man's fun meant a lot closer than Sessions had. "Were they killed here?"

Sessions shook his head. "Apparently not. Ennis thought they'd been killed where they were kept, and the bodies brought here late at night when no one was about."

"Kept? For how long?"

"Jamie Wilton—the first boy—probably died the night he disappeared, though the body wasn't found till a couple of days later. The second boy, Peter Krauss, was missing for four days and probably alive for three of them. He wasn't on the pier all that time, but the police never found out where he was instead. He vanished while buying chips for a family supper. In the middle of town, in the middle of the evening, no one saw a thing. And no one saw when his body was returned four days later."

"In the same state?" asked Daniel softly.

Sessions nodded. "Ennis had the pier watched from then

on. Nothing. For five months, and then a lorry driver tipping at the foot of Chain Down saw an arm sticking out of a pile of rubbish. No one had heard or seen anything amiss, and the site was covered with tyre-tracks anyway so that was no help. The pathologist reckoned the body'd been there a couple of weeks."

"Another boy?"

"Gavin Halliwell, also sixteen, also raped and battered to death. He'd been missing for eight days and no one had even told the police. The family thought he really had gone to London to seek his fortune. Apparently he'd talked about it, he'd had a bust-up with his father, they thought he'd better get on with it. Only he never got as far as London. He was tied up somewhere long enough for the abrasions on his ankle to fester, and the killer had hacked his leg down to the bone before finishing him off. This time he left the murder weapon behind. A wheel-brace was found with the body."

"A wheel-brace," murmured Daniel. "Is that what I saw?"

Sessions shrugged. "I don't know. Is it?"

Daniel bit his lip. "What's a wheel-brace?"

Despite the gravity of what they were discussing, the reporter couldn't help but grin. Daniel Hood was clearly a very intelligent man, just not all the time. "An iron bar with a kink in it. You use it to change a wheel. On a car."

Daniel nodded slowly. "That's what I saw."

By now the town was panic-stricken, the police under massive pressure to make an arrest. "To give them their due," said Sessions, "they didn't just go through the motions, pick up the usual suspects and wait for the heat to die down. They didn't want just anyone in the cells, they wanted the right guy."

But there were no leads. No witnesses, no physical evidence, no forensics. He'd brutalised three teenage boys, held two of them captive for days, without leaving anything that could be traced back to him. Which meant he was not a man tormented by urges he couldn't control. He could control them well enough to take his pleasures only after he'd protected himself. He was going to be hard to find and harder to convict.

"Nine months into the investigation, with three teenage boys in the morgue and not a single viable lead, the police were reduced to seeking suggestions. They did an appeal on television. Of course they were inundated with suggestions. Many were well-meaning but checked out as groundless. Some were people settling scores. But there were also a handful of names that couldn't readily be dismissed.

"One of them was Neil Cochrane. Four different people advised the police to interview him. He was a farmer, a single man in his forties running sheep up on Menner Down. No family, no friends, no social life at all that anyone knew of. He used to drink in *The Rose* on a Friday night, and that was all anybody knew of him.

"But there was something about him that made people uneasy. I know: I felt it too. I saw him in *The Rose* a time or two, and he was always on his own. I don't mean he came in alone—people left a space round him. I never saw him make trouble, but he gave off the sense that this was someone you didn't want to know any better. If the place was full, people who didn't play darts went to play darts rather than sit with him."

Daniel shrugged uncomfortably. "People who live alone—sometimes we get a bit—eccentric…?"

Sessions nodded. "It could have been that. But Neil Cochrane wasn't the only single man living in Dimmock ten years ago. But he was the one that people kept suggesting the police should visit.

"When they did, they started to think they were finally onto something. The first of the boys had done some work on Cochrane's farm a few weeks before his death—which didn't prove anything except that the two knew each other. Of course, a lot of boys help on a lot of farms at harvest time: it didn't have to be significant. The police searched the farmhouse and Cochrane's Land Rover and found nothing. They had him in for questioning and got nothing out of him.

"But I know for a fact that George Ennis thought he'd found his killer, and so did Deacon. They questioned him for every minute that the law allowed, and maybe a few more. But they never found a scrap of physical evidence connecting Cochrane to the boys, and they never managed to break his story."

"He had an alibi?"

Sessions shook his head. "He said he was at home, alone except for his sheep, on all three occasions. He didn't remember the boy who'd worked for him, or any of the boys who'd helped him. Boys were boys, he said, they charged too much for doing too little, but a couple of times a year he needed help on the farm. His only interest in boys was how many beets they could lift."

"Could it have been the truth?"

"Of course it could. If you spend your evenings in pubs there's a good chance someone will remember seeing you: if you spend them lambing ewes there isn't. Just because you can't prove you weren't abducting teenage boys doesn't mean you were."

"Then why were the police so sure?"

Sessions shrugged. "You'd need to ask Jack Deacon. Maybe because Cochrane fitted the profile. They had a mental picture of the man who did this, and it looked like Neil Cochrane. Maybe they were wrong. Maybe he was never more than a dour outsider who made people uncomfortable. But when I heard who was under investigation, I can't say I was surprised."

Daniel nodded slowly. He knew about being an outsider. There was hardly a community, a concept or a belief to which he subscribed.

He wandered to the window and looked across at the pier. In the twelve months he'd lived here it had never been dressed with fairy lights, the concert hall at the end packed with trippers. Until today it was just a pile of rotting timbers a hundred metres up the shore and the vague concern that an equinoctial gale could one day send a bit of it through his basement. Now it had acquired a presence, almost a personality, like a sea-monster resting its bones along the beach. Waiting. Speculating on what his next move might be.

"It's not my move to make," he said softly.

"Sorry?" Tom Sessions looked puzzled.

"Thinking aloud," Daniel said apologetically. "Mr Deacon doesn't really confide in me. Ever, but especially not now. I'm not his favourite person."

"You're his witness."

"Yes. I'm *not* the German Shepherd on his parcel-shelf: I won't nod whenever he nudges me."

Sessions was good at his job partly because he was good at hearing what hadn't been said. "He's leaning on you? To make Cochrane?"

"That's not entirely fair," said Daniel, who cared about being entirely fair. "He thinks Cochrane did it, and he thinks I saw him do it. He thinks I'm being over-cautious."

"And are you?"

"No. It's not that I'm only eighty percent sure it was him. I really don't think it *was*. Unless he's changed a lot since the photograph was taken."

Sessions put down his mug and stood up. "Daniel, don't tell anyone else what you've told me. It doesn't matter if Deacon's pissed off with you, but there are other people in this town who won't be restrained by the Police & Criminal Evidence Act. You don't want them thinking you could have put a monster behind bars if you'd wanted to."

Daniel turned to him in astonishment. "I did want to! I still want to. But none of the faces I was shown were the man I saw on the pier."

"I know," said Sessions. "Daniel, I believe you. But I know you, and this town's full of people who don't. They'll want to blame someone for this, and if they can't have the killer nailed to a gate they may settle for someone else. Humour me: keep your head down."

FINALLY, JUST BEFORE ONE, Daniel answered a knock at the door and it was three young men he'd never seen before, shoulders hunched, fists thrust deep in the pockets of their jeans, standing at the top of the iron stairs not looking at him. His heart fluttered. They were younger than him but every one of them was bigger. "Hello."

They looked at the steps, at the sea, at the pier, at one another—still everywhere except him. One said gruffly, "Are you him?"

Daniel considered. "Could you be more specific?"

It was saying things like that which made people wary of him. They thought it meant he was cleverer than them, which was often the case, and would use it against them, which wasn't. Daniel was an intellectual, but he wasn't an intellectual snob. He was well-read, but people who thought he came from a privileged background were mistaken. He was born in a terraced house in Nottingham. It wasn't a class thing, the way he spoke, the way he thought. It was a Daniel thing.

Another of the youths said, "Can we come in?" and stepped towards him.

Daniel Hood wasn't built for heroics. On average, he had to start looking up at students by the time they were fifteen. Some small men have hearts like lions, but Daniel knew he was vulnerable in a confrontation.

What he had instead was a kind of moral courage. He refused to be ruled by fear. He hated how it made him feel enough to straighten to his full five-foot-seven, hold his head up and look his problems in the face. Which meant that occasionally he got a black eye but most of the time he earned a puzzled respect.

He took a step out onto the iron stairway, closing the door behind him. "No. Now, who are you and what are you doing here?"

"We're from the gym," said one of the youths, finally looking at the man they'd come to see. "We're friends of Chris Berry's."

"I see. Then, I'm sorry about what happened."

"You saw it?"

"Some of it."

"You saw *him?*" Venom dripped dangerously from the word.

"For a second."

"Enough to recognise him?"

"I'd never seen him before."

"Enough to ID him?"

"Perhaps. If I see him again."

It was clear where this was going. But they were young men, athletes rather than philosophers, and they didn't know how to get there. "Look," one of them said. "The police know who did this. All you have to do is tell them that's who you saw."

Daniel drew a steadying breath. "They may think they know. But if they actually knew, they'd have arrested him years ago. They wouldn't have waited for another death on the off-chance that there'd be a witness. If they knew, if they could prove it, he'd have been behind bars for half your lifetime."

They had no answer. But they wouldn't be shooed away by someone they'd come here to bully. "Look," said the young man again. "It's easy. All you have to do is co-operate with the police. Ask to see a photograph and tell them that's him. It's the least you can do. For Chris and everyone else."

Daniel chewed on his lip. He looked at the young men with their stubborn expressions and their hard muscles and thought this was probably a black eye occasion.

He said quietly, "I know how angry you must be. You've lost your friend, and it shouldn't have happened. I'm sorry I couldn't prevent it. But pretending to have seen something, or someone, I didn't won't bring him back. If you're wrong it'll compound the tragedy with a terrible miscarriage of justice. And if you're right it'll get the case kicked out of court and set a killer free. Be patient. Inspector Deacon wants this man as much as you do. He won't rest till he has him."

One at a time he'd have persuaded them. They were angry, they were upset, but they weren't vicious. Each alone would eventually have seen the sense in what Daniel was saying. But they weren't alone. They'd come here together because they were resolved to make a difference, and as a rallying call Patience doesn't cut the mustard.

Perhaps if he'd cowered from them they'd have dusted their hands, sauntered away and told one another they'd shown him, and never come back when they learned that actually they'd changed nothing. Grief and rage made them feel they had to do something, and listening to a lecture wasn't what they had in mind.

"Are you going to stop that bastard or not?"

"You mean, am I going to say I saw someone I didn't," said Daniel. "No, I'm not."

He didn't even see the fist that floored him. His head snapped suddenly back, lights exploded behind his eyes, then the iron steps came up to meet him and a couple of the boots he'd fallen among were aiming kicks.

A voice cut through the scuffle like a crystal dagger. "The last one of you down those steps is going to suffer the indignity of being thrown over the rail by a woman."

Though Daniel couldn't see her for legs, he knew who it was. The three young men from the gym didn't, either who she was or what she was capable of. Because she wasn't wearing a star-spangled leotard they were fairly sure that they could overpower her. But then they'd have had their mums to deal with. The average British male is about forty before he stops worrying how he's going to explain things to his mother.

The boots moved, shuffling a bit at first, then in an orderly procession down the steps. There was a bit of muttering but none of them was brave enough to cheek the tall woman with the cloud of dark hair and the angry eyes. Perhaps they thought she *was* Wonderwoman and just hadn't had time to change. Feet crunched on the shingle; a voice shouted back, "Think about it"; then they were gone.

Daniel uncurled from his protective ball, found his glasses and gave Brodie a wry smile. "Good timing."

"Are you all right? Who *were* they?"

"I'm fine," he said, standing up; and though reaction showed as a tremor in his hands it wasn't enough for her to call him a liar. "Friends of Chris Berry's, from the gym."

"That's a reason to beat the crap out of you?"

Daniel led the way inside. "They think I'm protecting his killer."

Brodie's eyes flew wide in amazement. "Why would they think that?"

"His mother was here earlier. She thought the same."

"But *why?*"

He shrugged. "Because they think Deacon's suspect must have done this, so I must have seen him, so if I won't identify him it's aiding and abetting."

Brodie dropped onto the sofa and tossed her handbag irritably into a corner. "Daniel, how do you *get* yourself in these situations? Ten hours ago you were the hero of the moment; now you're the villain of the piece. How does that *happen?*"

He had no answer. He knew he hadn't done anything wrong. He didn't even think he'd done anything stupid. "Beats me." He smiled again. "To coin a phrase."

"You'd better call Inspector Deacon."

It was Daniel's turn to look startled. "Why?"

Brodie shut her eyes for a moment while the urge to slap him went away. "Because three guys big enough to use you as a football tried to! Because next time I might not turn up to bum some lunch off you and they might succeed."

He shook his head. "They won't come back. They made their point. I think they scared themselves nearly as much as they scared me. They might be big but they're only kids. They were upset. About now they'll be feeling pretty foolish. They won't bother me again."

"Maybe they won't," agreed Brodie. "But if the feeling's going around that this is somehow your fault, someone else may. And a sock in the eye may be the least of it."

"So what do you want me to do?" asked Daniel, with more levity than was wise. "Enter a witness protection programme? Change my name and move to Brighton?"

"Maybe," retorted Brodie, her voice and her temper rising. "Maybe that's exactly what you should do. Tell you what: you

can ask Jack Deacon when you tell him what just happened."
She lifted the telephone and thrust it at him.

Daniel looked at it and then at her. Then he went into the
kitchen for some ice.

Brodie swore at his departing back. She dialled the number herself, but put down the phone before anyone answered.
"All right," she growled, "we'll leave Deacon out of it, for
now. That doesn't mean they get away with this."

Daniel returned holding a packet of frozen peas to his face.
"Let it go, Brodie. It wasn't important. Let the dust settle.
When Deacon stops worrying about the man who didn't do
this and starts looking for the one who did, nobody'll be interested in me any more."

Exasperated, she left him nursing his eye and went to make
them some lunch. Everything she could think of required peas.

SIX

BRODIE LEFT the netting-sheds at five to two to walk back to her office. But as she went to turn into Shack Lane a sign further up Fisher Hill caught her eye. *The Attic Gym.* She stood and stared at it for perhaps half a minute, then with a determined sniff set off up the slope.

There was, of course, more than one gymnasium in Dimmock. Off-hand, she knew of one attached to the golf club and one attached to the squash club. Neither seemed the natural habitat of young fell-runners. Perhaps *The Attic Gym* wasn't either, in which case she'd have wasted a few minutes and a brisk walk; but perhaps it was.

It wasn't above the narrow shop outside which the sign swung, it was beneath it. So it was a reference not to the location but to the Greek ethos: a sophisticated play on words not likely to earn many kudos in Dimmock, Brodie thought as she descended the area steps. Dimmock's idea of sophistication was cake doilies and a plastic heron by the goldfish pond.

She wasn't sure if the gym was open. No lights showed, but when she tried the door it swung wide with the cheery tinkle of silver bells.

Inside were running machines, cycling machines, weight-lifting benches and a boxing ring: very much the sort of place young men would feel at home. But no one was working out right now. Probably the lunchtime shift had already cleaned up and returned to their offices while the leisured afternoon class had yet to arrive.

But someone was here or the door would be locked. Brodie raised her voice in peremptory summons.

A man appeared from the locker-rooms. "I'm sorry, miss, we're not open today. I only came in to get something—I should have locked the door. We've had a bit of a tragedy."

"Chris Berry," Brodie said stiffly. "I know."

George Ennis raised an eyebrow. But of course it must be common knowledge by now. "Was it one of the ladies' classes you were interested in? If you could come back tomorrow…"

"Thanks," she said brusquely, "but I get all the exercise I need in the course of a day's work. Do you want to know what I was doing this lunchtime, for instance?"

Ennis wasn't sure he should hazard a guess. But she waited so he did. "Aerobics?"

"In a manner of speaking," she nodded. "Specifically, I was stopping three young thugs from beating the living daylights out of a friend of mine. Since they seem to be pupils of yours, I'm here to warn you that if I see hide or hair of them again I'll have them down at the police station, and then I'll have you."

People who had known Brodie Farrell as a girl, and then as a young wife, were always startled to meet her again since the divorce. They remembered her as a quiet, modest person, almost demure, not someone to go round threatening six-foot athletes. But demure was of limited value to a woman who, at the age of thirty, suddenly found herself without a husband, a home or the means to make a living but with a three-year-old child to raise. She learned what her strengths were and how to use them, and because it was urgent she learned quickly.

She found she was much tougher than she'd ever guessed. From rock-bottom at the time of the divorce, her confidence had grown in step with the growing success of her business until now she had no reservations about sharing the great secret with all and sundry. The secret was: Women aren't soft. They're strong.

Ennis frowned, plainly bewildered. "I'm sorry—what are we talking about?" So she told him what had happened.

George Ennis heard her out but the anger behind his eyes

was mounting. Not at her—he'd been threatened before, lots of times, by people who intended him much worse—but at the direction events had taken. "Those damned idiots!" he exploded when she'd finished. "I can develop their muscles, I can increase the capacity of their hearts and lungs, I can get them to the peak of physical fitness. But I can't knock any damn sense into them. Your friend: is he all right?"

Mollified slightly, Brodie nodded. "He's holding a pack of frozen peas to his eye, but otherwise he's fine."

"Thank God for that at least," said Ennis. "Mrs Farrell, you have my absolute assurance there will be no repetition of this. I can guess who your visitors were: I'll have them down here within the hour and they won't leave until they've written an apology. If Mr Hood will accept that I'll be very grateful. But if he wants to involve the police I'd understand."

Brodie had marched in here ready for battle. His immediate surrender left her room to be generous. "There's no need for that. When it happened I was angry enough to call the police but Daniel wasn't. I think he feels that nobody's at their best today. Chris's friends have every right to be upset. If some of them were distraught enough to strike out at the first person they could find, well, it was a heat-of-the-moment thing and there's no great harm done. If you'll make sure it doesn't happen again we can draw a line under it."

"Thanks," said Ennis. "You're right, we've all been turned inside out by this. They're good lads, they're not thugs, in the normal way of things they don't go round threatening people. I dare say they're feeling pretty ashamed of themselves already—by the time I've seen them they'll be feeling a great deal worse. I'll point out that they could have found themselves in court for their stupidity. And also that your friend risked his life trying to save Chris."

He saw her to the door. The business between them disposed of, Brodie unbent enough to say what she should probably have said at the start. "I am terribly sorry about what happened to Chris. Murder is always a monstrous thing, but it's worse when it's someone with his whole life ahead of him. I didn't know him, but it's obvious he's going to leave a big gap in a lot of lives."

Ennis nodded. His brow dipped, and Brodie knew that if she stood here much longer he'd start to cry.

"Thank you for your help." She left him alone to his grief, her heels beating a sharp tattoo on the area steps.

JACK DEACON WAS starting to get information back, and none of it was helpful.

Preliminary findings on the post mortem indicated that Chris Berry had not been sexually assaulted, but there did appear to have been a struggle. It had left him with fist-sized marks, that would have developed into bruises if he'd lived long enough, on his jaw, ribcage and arms. None of them were serious injuries. He succeeded in defending himself until his assailant stopped trying to punch him into submission and beat his head in with a wheel-brace. No, Deacon corrected himself pedantically, with a smooth hard implement with a rounded profile approximately three centimetres in diameter. Death must have been instantaneous—no salt water reached the lungs.

Hood didn't see the fight but he did see the murder. So there was a struggle somewhere else, possibly where the killer and his victim met, and Chris Berry repelled his assailant long enough to take to his heels. The older man then armed himself with his weapon of choice and gave chase. It was impossible to judge how far they had run, but finally Chris made the mistake of turning into a dead-end. The man pursued him to the end of the pier and killed him there.

The whole thing might have lasted no more than a few minutes from beginning to end. Deacon was glad, even if it made his job harder. If Chris's death was frightful, at least it was quick. He hadn't suffered days of terror, pain and degradation first.

The forensic examination of Neil Cochrane's Land Rover was not coming up with the desired results. There was evidence of the farmer in there, and his sheep, but not so far of Chris Berry. But if Cochrane had cleaned the vehicle out thoroughly enough to remove traces of an unwilling passenger it should have been a lot cleaner than it was.

"So he used something else for transport," mused Deacon. "He doesn't own another vehicle. So he borrowed one, or stole one, or…" His train of thought screeched to a halt as the guard leaned out the back waving a red flag. "A trailer. He's a farmer, he's bound to have something for moving livestock. Maybe the boys were never in the jeep. And the inside of a trailer could be power-hosed as soon as he got it home."

For five minutes Deacon sat bolt upright at his desk, wondering why he hadn't thought of that ten years ago, trying to convince himself it wouldn't have mattered if he had. The trailer would have been as clean then as it would be by now. But at least it explained how Cochrane could transport youths who desperately didn't want to be there without leaving any physical evidence.

After five minutes Deacon got up, yelled for Charlie Voss and headed for his car.

THOUGH SHE THOUGHT it unlikely, Brodie didn't want Daniel making a liar of her. She called from her office to tell him about her meeting with George Ennis and what had been agreed.

Clearly Daniel hadn't given any thought to calling the police. Preoccupied with something else, his voice was low. "What did he say?"

She'd already told him what Ennis had said. She repeated it. "He apologised. He said it wouldn't happen again."

"About me," said Daniel distinctly. "Does he blame me too?"

"Damn it, Daniel," exclaimed Brodie, "are you still fretting about that? Will you get it into your head that it wasn't your fault? Not that Chris Berry died, and not that his killer is still at large. You did everything humanly possible. Lying would not make things better."

"Not everyone would agree. Not Mrs Berry, not Chris's friends, and not Inspector Deacon."

"Mrs Berry is a special case. It's only a few hours since she lost her son: she may look to be coping but in fact she has no idea what she's doing or saying right now. It would be cruel to hold her responsible for anything she does in the next few days.

"And his friends are not only shocked and grieving, they're also scared. What happened to him could happen to them. They're desperate to see the bastard caught. Desperate enough to think they could speed things up by giving you a hard time. But then, they are only young. Young men aren't noted for making good decisions under pressure.

"And you're wrong about Jack Deacon. He doesn't want you to lie. He was taken aback, that's all—he thought he knew who was responsible. By now he'll be looking for alternative suspects. Don't read too much into his manner: you know he has all the social grace of an alligator. That doesn't make him a bad man, or a bad detective. He'll sort this out. He doesn't need to like either of us in order to do it."

"Just as well." But Daniel sounded a little reassured. "I'm sorry, I'm behaving like an idiot."

"You're behaving like someone who hasn't had much sleep," said Brodie. "Why don't you get your head down for a couple of hours?"

"Maybe I should," said Daniel. He didn't fool her for a moment. It was the sort of thing he said when he wanted to avoid an argument without actually fibbing.

OF COURSE THERE was a trailer at Manor Farm. An aluminium beast-box designed to confine a ton of seriously displeased dairy bull would be more than adequate to imprison a man.

And it wasn't pristine from the power-hose. Nevertheless, the policemen didn't expect it to yield much evidence. Cochrane had half a dozen sheep penned in it.

Hope springs eternal. Deacon had the sheep driven off and

the trailer towed to the police garage. If just one of those boys had understood what was happening he might have left his mark scratched into the aluminium with a belt-buckle in a spot where only a trained searcher would find it.

Deacon knew it was a long shot. He was prepared to try anything that might stop Neil Cochrane before another young man went missing.

SEVEN

"YOU DON'T SUPPOSE," ventured DS Voss, in the tone of someone about to gamble with his life, "that Hood could be right? That it wasn't Cochrane he saw?"

In his own way, Jack Deacon was as honest a man as Daniel. He didn't make a fetish of it. He was happy for people to think of him as Jack-the-lad, a hard man, a believer in ends over means. But when the time came to give each thing its name he was as straight as a die. He didn't bear false witness, even against those he knew deserved it; he didn't use his fists unless someone else started it; he didn't massage the statistics by coaxing men who were going down anyway to have unsolved crimes taken into consideration. Brodie was right: he was a good policeman. By most definitions he was a good man. He just didn't like word getting around.

He glared at Voss with an exasperation that the sergeant, who had been working for him for about a month now, was beginning to recognise as displacement activity for doubt. "You still haven't read the CID handbook, have you? Inspectors do the thinking; sergeants do the running after people and getting thumped."

Voss grinned. People had commiserated when he'd drawn the short straw, but actually he rather liked working for the man known throughout Dimmock Police Station as The Grizzly. It was never boring. "I read the first chapter. You know—*Constables Make The Tea?*"

Deacon found himself grinning too. Charlie Voss was younger and more cheerful than his last sergeant. He'd thought that was a drawback. He was beginning to wonder if he'd been wrong. But that was the only thing he thought he might have been wrong about.

"Daniel Hood is an arrogant little sod. He thinks too much, and he thinks that being clever makes his opinion more important than other people's. He doesn't lie—I've told you about that, haven't I?—not because he thinks it's wicked but because he thinks it's beneath him. I never see the man without wanting to give him a slap.

"In spite of which, or perhaps because of it, I know he's trying to describe accurately what happened at the pier. He isn't being difficult deliberately: he genuinely didn't recognise Cochrane as the man he saw.

"But you know as well as I do, Charlie Voss, that eye-witness testimony is about the weakest evidence you can have. Honest reliable people with no axe to grind make mistakes all the time. Both ways: they ID people who couldn't have dunnit and miss people who did. It's not easy to remember a stranger's face, glimpsed briefly in the midst of chaos, and recognise it from a still photograph taken under duress. It's like passport photos only worse. The wonder is that anyone *ever* spots a villain that way."

"I know," said Voss. "I just wonder if we should consider the possibility that he's right."

"Well, of course there's a *possibility*," said Deacon nastily. "There's a *possibility* that the Liberal Democrats will form the next government, that Elvis Presley was abducted by aliens and that if you opened my bottom drawer you'd find back issues of *Men in Tights: the Official Organ of the Transvestite Community*. Anything's possible. But in the real world, things make sense. This looks like Neil Cochrane's work because it is."

Voss hadn't been in Dimmock ten years ago. Ten years ago he'd still been at school. "It's that good a match?"

"Pretty much," said Deacon. "The victim was a couple of years older than the others but that's the only difference. The scene of crime was a place Cochrane used before; the murder weapon was the same he used before; and he smashed that boy's skull in exactly the same way he did the other three."

"The other three were raped."

Deacon shrugged. "Chris Berry was a bad choice. Cochrane couldn't overpower him as easily. He got away, and Cochrane had to give chase because otherwise Chris would have come to us. He needed to silence him. At two o'clock in the morning he didn't expect to be seen."

"But the fact remains that he was—at least the killer was—but Hood doesn't think it was Cochrane he saw."

Deacon's thick eyebrows canted. "So it's a coincidence? Somebody else had taken to preying on Dimmock's teenage boys, taking them to the pier and beating their heads in with a wheel-brace? Somebody of about Cochrane's age, size and build?"

"But not with Cochrane's face," murmured Voss. "According to Hood."

"Daniel Hood is a stubborn man who can't deal with the possibility that he might be wrong," growled Deacon, and never even saw the irony of what he was saying.

BRODIE'D HAD A funny sort of a day. It started ridiculously early with a corpse on a beach; it got quite bracing at lunchtime when she thought she was going to put those sixth-form self-defence lessons to a purpose for which they were never intended; and at quarter to five in the afternoon a woman she'd met twice wrote her a cheque for eight thousand pounds.

As word began to spread of the service she offered people came to her with an ever wider range of problems. She would find, or try to, anything for anyone who could meet three conditions. They needed a lawful reason for wanting what they sought—early on someone had asked her for three Uzis and a Kalashnikov. It had to be a thing, not a person—the one time she'd agreed to find someone rather than something events had run horribly out of control. And they had to be able to afford her help. Where the item had a significant monetary value she took a commission of twenty percent. Where the value was more sentimental she put a price on her time. Either way, eight thousand pounds was the most profitable job she'd done so far.

Of course, Selena Trimble had stood to win or lose a sum which even today might be counted a fortune. Her claim to it hung on whether it was her mother's posterior immortalised in a painting entitled "Bathsheba In Flagrante" by the sought-after Hastings artist Cedric Wymes. His will included a sizable bequest to "his Bathsheba" or, should she predecease him, her children: if the posterior was indeed that of Mrs Trimble, the money was Selena's. However, artists use many models, all of them have posteriors, and one may look very much like another.

Of course Ms Trimble had photographs of her mother, but they showed only her face and the painting showed everything else. Selena soon realised that a comparative analysis of 1950s models' backsides would quickly run through even forty thousand pounds. Failing to find a solicitor who would take the case on a no win, no fee basis she decided that Brodie Farrell working for twenty percent was her best bet.

Brodie didn't rate the odds much higher than the solicitors had. But she didn't have partners to explain herself to, and the problem amused her enough to take a gamble. If she failed she'd settle for the start-up fee and a good laugh.

In fact she soon realised that the mission was achievable. She visited every gallery and art dealer on the south coast, and used the internet to call up as much information as she could not only on Wymes but on other artists working on the south coast in the same period. She ended up with a stack of images comprising the definitive study of the female nether regions in post-war Britain.

And since many artists were more diligent about recording who was modelling for them than Cedric Wymes, she was soon able to compile a dossier on Mrs Trimble's person as viewed from every angle. Happily, even behinds have distin-

guishing features, and Mrs Trimble's had a trio of small moles
formation-flying across it. Two other artists had noticed the
same peculiarity that Cedric Wymes reproduced on Bathsheba, with Mrs Trimble on record as the model on each occasion. The bottom line was that the executors were satisfied and
Selena Trimble got her bequest.

Brodie felt about *Looking for Something?* much as Charlie Voss did about working with Jack Deacon. No two days
were the same. She locked up at five o'clock with a smile on
her lips.

But it had been a long day by any standards. By the time
she reached the car-park she was yawning, looking forward
to a quiet evening at home with her daughter. Almost the last
thing she wanted to see was Daniel Hood waiting by her car
with that shy, stubborn expression she knew so well half-hid-
den by his straw-coloured fringe and a manilla envelope under his arm.

She sighed. He was her friend, and he'd had a harder day
than she had. If he wanted to talk they'd talk. "Come up for
tea," she suggested.

He had the grace to look faintly embarrassed. "I didn't
mean to invite myself for another meal. I just wanted to pick
your brains."

Brodie opened the car. "My brain's five pounds of wet spa-
ghetti right now. You want to pick it, try again when it's eaten."

Driving across town she said, "How long were you waiting for me?"

"Oh, maybe"—sometimes lying would be so easy!—
"twenty minutes."

She took her eyes off the road long enough to stare at him.
"Why didn't you come to the office?"

"Because that's where you work. I make enough demands
on your time without invading your working day as well."

One of the most irritating things about Daniel Hood was
how hard it was to stay angry with him. Unless you were Jack
Deacon, of course.

Brodie felt her heart lift. They were two people with nothing in common who'd met in circumstances which should have been impossible for them to transcend. But somehow they'd forged a real friendship, and this was what Brodie got out of it: Daniel made her feel good. She'd read somewhere that owning a dog made people feel so much better about themselves that it was reflected in their state of health. Well, knowing Daniel did the same for her.

He caught her grin and frowned. "What?"

Brodie had no compunction about lying when it suited her. "Just thinking about Selena Trimble's mother's bottom," she said airily. Then of course she had to explain.

Paddy had already had her tea with Marta Szarabeijka, the Polish music-teacher upstairs. She curled up in front of the television, leaving Brodie and Daniel to talk over reheated casserole.

"So what's in the envelope?" asked Brodie.

It was lying on the kitchen table beside then. Daniel looked at it but didn't pick it up. "An article Tom Sessions wrote for *The Sentinel* ten years ago. About the killings. About the victims."

"Ah," said Brodie softly.

Daniel was still looking at the envelope rather than her. "It doesn't make pleasant reading. And I can see why Mr Deacon assumed that whoever committed those murders also killed Chris Berry."

"A lot of similarities?"

"An awful lot. But…"

"Daniel?"

Finally he looked at her. "Differences, too. Will you read it? I may be kidding myself and I'd like an unbiased opinion. But I think there are enough discrepancies to back up what I told Deacon: that the man I saw wasn't who he expected."

Brodie bit her lip. She knew what he was doing. "Daniel, you don't have anything to justify. It's not your job to make sense of what you saw, it's Deacon's. And if he can't, well, he couldn't ten years ago either. Maybe *because* he was wrong about his suspect. Maybe what you saw will finally set him on the right track. But for heaven's sake don't get any deeper involved. You've done your bit."

Daniel knew she was right. If half of Dimmock had seen what he'd seen, and everyone else agreed that Deacon was right about the killer, he wouldn't have been persuaded. He would rather make an honest mistake than tell a fortuitous lie. But he'd much rather be right than wrong.

"Will you read the article?" he asked. "Tell me what you think? It won't change anything, but I'll sleep easier tonight if…" He let the sentence peter out.

Brodie finished it for him. "If you don't think you're standing between justice and a killer."

IT HAD BEEN A huge news story spread over thirteen months, from early 1991 into 1992. Tom Sessions was a junior reporter when he wrote this resumé, but already he knew how to handle difficult, important material without hitting the parallel verges of sensationalism and triviality. He'd worked a wealth of detail into the text without losing the narrative thread. It was the sort of work that won awards for young reporters and set them on the road to the nationals, where for the most part everything they had learned, all the skills that had earned them advancement, had to be set aside.

Which was why Tom Sessions, and a lot of other good reporters, continued to work on smaller papers for smaller wages when they could walk into prestigious jobs if they didn't mind leaving their principles at the door.

By the time he was writing this, all three deaths had occurred and most of the facts that would emerge were already known. This wasn't a breaking news story, it was a recapitulation. It told Brodie everything she'd have known if she'd come to Dimmock twelve months before she did, including something about the victims. There were also photographs. Jamie Wilton on a canoeing holiday in France; Peter Krauss with his afghan hound; Gavin Halliwell on a speedway bike.

Finally Brodie put down the photocopy and leaned back. "I'm with you. It doesn't look to me as if the man who killed Chris Berry also killed these boys."

Daniel's relief was almost palpable. He shut his eyes for a second and sighed, "Thank God." Then, remembering he was an atheist, cast her a wry grin. "Why not?"

Brodie thought for a moment, marshalling her arguments. "Because the man who chose those three as victims wouldn't look twice at Chris Berry."

"Because he was older?"

"Not even that. He was a whole different sort of guy. He was big, strong and athletic. Physically he was a grown man. These other three were boys."

She pushed the report across the table, indicating the photographs. "Look at them. Those are not rough, tough, boisterous youths. Some sixteen-year-olds are physically adults and some aren't. These weren't. They were small for their age, looked younger than they were. If you were a pervert looking for boys to brutalise, these would attract you. Chris Berry and his muscle-bound mates wouldn't."

"Then how do you explain the similarities?" Now he'd got what he'd wanted, someone to say he was probably right, Daniel couldn't keep from playing Devil's Advocate. "The details of Chris's murder could have come straight from that ten-year-old newspaper. It *can't* be a coincidence. *I* don't believe that, let alone Jack Deacon."

"I don't believe it either," said Brodie. She regarded him across the table. "What's the best place to hide a tree?"

Everyone knew the answer to that. "A forest."

"So what's the best place to hide a murder?"

She saw understanding dawn in his face, the initial relief turning to horror as he realised what that meant. "You mean— the man who killed Chris Berry worked out how to pass the crime off as someone else's work, and only carried it out when he knew what clues to leave?"

Brodie nodded sombrely. "Not exactly a spur-of-the-moment thing, was it? Not a crime of any sort of passion."

"We have to tell Inspector Deacon!"

Brodie's shapely eyebrows soared. "Tell him what? That he's wrong?—you've already told him. That if he'd abandon his preconceptions and think about the facts he'd come to the same conclusion we have?—go right ahead, but I'll wait for you outside. He'll get there in his own good time."

"But time is important! There's a killer out there—"

"But not necessarily a serial killer. If that's how he wanted it to look, it's because Chris Berry's murder was something quite different. He killed Chris because he wanted him dead— not just anyone, him. He took this much trouble to disguise the fact precisely because there won't be another victim."

"You make him sound pretty smart," said Daniel in a low voice.

"I think he is pretty smart," said Brodie. "I think *he* thinks he's pretty smart. Smart enough to try messing with Deacon's head. He'd worked out, before he went after Chris, that the best way to shift suspicion from himself was to put it on someone else. He knew Deacon's spent the last ten years wanting another crack at whoever killed those boys and designed Chris's death to look as if it had started all over again."

Her voice warmed to the theory. "The pier, the wheel-brace, the nature of the injuries—it's camouflage. Chris Berry wasn't killed by a paedophile. He was killed by someone who knew him, who had a reason to want him dead, and who was afraid that a good detective with an open mind would work it out. His best defence was to plant the idea that this time Deacon could solve all four murders. If you hadn't seen him on the pier, he'd have succeeded."

Daniel was watching her open-mouthed. There were times when Brodie Farrell seemed only and exactly what she appeared to be: an intelligent, slightly harassed young woman juggling her home and business commitments. But sometimes the veil parted, giving a glimpse of iron intellect and steely will. He blinked. "And you still don't think we should tell Deacon what we know?"

Brodie shook her head impatiently. "Daniel, we don't *know* anything. It's a theory. It sounds good. It may well be the truth, at least as far as it goes. But it's pure speculation, and when Deacon's got over the shock of being wrong he can do his own speculating. If we march into his office and tell him what to think he'll reject the idea on principle. We could set the investigation back a week. Much better to let him get there under his own steam."

"If he does."

"He will. Any time now, if he hasn't already, he'll do what you just did: get out photographs of the boys from ten years ago and compare them to one of Chris Berry. He'll see how unlikely it is that they all died for the same reason. The rest will follow."

Daniel was feeling better. His refusal to tow the CID line wasn't inviting further tragedies. On the contrary, it should lead the police to Berry's murderer when they could still have been sniffing round someone who'd never even met him.

He wasn't mad, he wasn't stupid, he wasn't undermining the investigation by putting all his trust in an image imprinted on his brain in less than a second, and there weren't going to be any more deaths. He had, as well as a real fondness, a huge respect for Brodie Farrell. He trusted her judgement. That she believed in him was a weight off his shoulders.

Taking the pots to the sink, she put her head into the sitting-room to make sure Paddy hadn't found a way of accessing the Playboy Channel. When she came back Daniel was finally asleep, his head cradled on his arms on her kitchen table.

IF THERE WAS ever any evidence in Neil Cochrane's trailer his sheep had obliterated it. And the more Deacon thought about it, the less sure he was that Chris Berry had ever been in it.

Cochrane hadn't got as far with Berry as he had with the other boys. Something alerted the young man to his danger and he ran for his life. He must have expected to get away. But speed was never going to be the deciding factor on a pier two hundred metres long. When they came together it was strength that mattered, and the fact that one of them was armed with an iron bar.

It was quarter to eleven before the policemen knocked off for the night. They'd been working for twenty hours solid. Deacon gave his sergeant a ride home.

Voss had been disobeying orders and thinking again. "You don't suppose this could be a copy-cat killing? Someone who's read the '92 reports and thought it would be a clever way to disguise his own identity?"

Deacon shook his head wearily: "I think he's even cleverer than that. I think that's what he wants us to think."

He was in bed by eleven, asleep by five past. When the alarm-clock rang he fumbled for it, swearing, sure it was still the middle of the night.

The worst thing was, he was right. It was the police station. "Sorry to wake you, sir. But we've found another one."

EIGHT

HIS NAME WAS KEVIN SYKES, he was seventeen years old, and he didn't look like he'd had a square meal since hitting puberty. His clothes were worn and dirty. Under them the emaciated body was dirty too, and there were lice in the tangled hair. There was also blood, a lot of it, and fragments of bone, and a quantity of whitish matter ejected from the massive wound to the side of the head.

"Was this one raped?" asked Deacon, stifling a yawn. He wasn't bored but he was still very tired. It was half past one: he'd had just two hours of sleep in the last twenty-four.

"Not sure," said Dr Roy, the Forensic Medical Examiner. He crouched over the filthy, wasted body in his bright white suit and moved the rags of clothes aside. "There's some blood, but there's also some old damage. This may be how he made his living. I'll be able to tell you more after I've taken him home." He meant, to the mortuary where he could carry out a full examination. But it wasn't really a joke. He looked on his work as a kindness to the dead.

"I don't suppose I need ask what killed him," said Deacon grimly. "How long's he been dead?"

"Not long. His temperature's still dropping. Maybe an hour or so?"

"Has he been moved?" He might not have been. On paper this was a brown-field site, formerly used for industrial purposes and now awaiting redevelopment. In fact it was a derelict brewery, not so much demolished as allowed to fall down, and redevelopment presupposed someone with a desire to live or work here. This was the grimy underside of

Dimmock, neither solid town nor leafy suburb: no one had a use for it and almost no one came. The occasional car turned in at the gates, rocked on its springs for ten minutes and then left. A couple of times a year Dimmock's small homeless community, evicted from the old Roxy Cinema, gathered here for two or three days until it was safe to return. Apart from that, no one. Even the local drunks staggered home by a more scenic route.

"No reason to think so. No unexplained lividity, and the ejector"—he meant the blood and brain tissue splashed on the ground— "is consistent with him having died here."

"And the murder weapon?"

Dr Roy regarded him quizzically. "Murder is a legal concept, not a medical one. He died because something caused a massive comminuted fracture of the skull. Since there's nothing handy for him to have jumped off I don't see how it could have been self-inflicted. But murder is something you have to prove."

Deacon breathed heavily at him. "Then, could the damage have been inflicted with a wheel-brace?"

Dr Roy shrugged white shoulders and pursed dark lips. "I'm not sure. There's so much damage it's hard to say. I mean, yes, conceivably it was caused by a hail of blows with a blunt instrument. But there are other things it could have been too."

"Such as?"

"I've seen damage like this in road accidents."

So had Deacon, but not in isolation. He looked down the length of the skimpy body. "There's no damage to the legs." The bumper invariably caught the legs first. If the victim was thrown up into the air, the damage to the head was secondary, incurred when he landed.

Roy nodded. "I know. That was just an example."

Jack Deacon had worked with a lot of pathologists in his time, the good, the bad and the inspired. The one thing they all had in common was this reluctance to commit themselves.

Roy would still be hedging his bets if he'd actually witnessed the murder of Kevin Sykes.

He changed tack. "How do we know his name? Has he been identified?"

The FME shook his head. "The kid's still wearing his old school shirt. It's got a name-tape inside. And he's scratched his initials on his boots."

Somehow, that struck Deacon harder than the murder itself: the fact that, within the last couple of years, someone thought enough about this boy to sew his name inside his clothes. What had gone wrong? Why had he ended up, ragged and filthy and selling his body for what it would make?

There was an answer. More often than not it was the right one. "Drugs?"

"Oh yeah," said Hari Roy. He stretched out a thin arm: the veins were visible as dark tracks of infection. "To be honest, murdering this one was a wasted effort. I doubt he'd have lasted the month."

It didn't make it better. The anger rose in Deacon's throat like bile. It may not have been much of a life but it was the only one Kevin Sykes had and it shouldn't have ended like this. If Cochrane thought that destroying a guttersnipe was the safe option, that less effort would go into solving the murder, he was going to find out that he was wrong.

Right now. Deacon whistled to Sergeant Voss like calling a dog and got back in his car. There was nothing more he could do here. Roy would learn whatever the body had to tell, Sergeant Mills was the scenes of crime expert, forensics would analyse anything that would bear analysis. More than ever, modern scientific methods left detectives free to focus on the people involved.

"Where are we going?" asked Charlie Voss.

"Guess," snarled Deacon, heading for the hills.

BRODIE HAD THE radio on as she made Paddy's breakfast. Details of the night's events were still sketchy, but the reporter connected the death of Kevin Sykes with that of Chris Berry and so did Brodie. She left the toast half-spread and picked up the phone.

It was only eight o'clock, she hoped she'd be getting Daniel out of bed. If he'd been asleep she could break the news herself. She wasn't sure why that was better than hearing it on the radio, only knew that it was. But his phone rang and rang and no one answered, and she knew then that he already knew.

As soon as Paddy had eaten, before she had time to wonder if she'd like another slice, Brodie took her up to Marta. "Would you walk her to school? I have to go and see Daniel. There's been another…" She indicated with her eyebrows the nature of the omitted word. Marta signalled her understanding.

Paddy had a perfect instinct for when she was being kept out of the loop. "Another what?"

"Another hike in the price of fish," said Brodie.

Paddy didn't know what that meant but she knew when she was being flanneled. She squinted at her mother as she brushed past into Marta's flat, but for a moment Brodie thought she'd got away with it.

Then the little girl turned and announced firmly, "I was at Daniel's house yesterday. I saw a dead person."

Brodie's heart stumbled.

Marta put a bony hand on top of the moppet's head and steered her inside. "Well, don't boast about it," she said briskly, "there aren't enough to go round."

Brodie drove straight to the netting-sheds. But Daniel didn't answer her anxious rapping any more than he'd answered the phone, and finally she accepted that he wasn't there. She phoned the police station and asked for Detective Inspector Deacon.

"I'm afraid he's busy," said the woman on the switchboard. "Can someone else help?"

"Probably not. I'll try again later." A thought occurred to her. "You don't happen to know if Daniel Hood's on the premises?"

"Are you a relative of Mr Hood's?" asked the woman warily.

"Just a friend," said Brodie. "And you've already answered my question."

DANIEL SAT IN AN interview room in the bowels of Dimmock Police Station, not being interviewed. Occasionally DS Voss looked in, apparently to check he was still there; once someone brought him a cup of tea. No one asked him anything or told him anything. He hadn't seen Inspector Deacon since he arrived.

The next time Voss stuck his head round the door Daniel was ready for him. "Wait a minute. Tell me what's going on. I don't even know what I'm doing here."

Of all the tools in a policeman's armoury, a look of slightly miffed surprise is one of the most versatile. In five years with CID Charlie Voss could hardly recall an inquiry where he hadn't pressed it into service. He did it now. "I'm sorry? I thought you came here to help with our inquiries?"

"I did," nodded Daniel. "Two hours ago. Nobody's been near me since." Voss looked pointedly at the paper cup. Daniel felt himself bridle. "Except for the tea-lady. That isn't why I came."

"You wanted to help."

"*Yes,*" said Daniel. "I heard about… On the radio this morning."

Voss nodded. "Have you remembered something you didn't tell us? Have you thought better of something you did tell us?"

"I told you everything I saw and heard! I'm not going to tell you anything more or anything different."

"I see," said Voss evenly. "So you came to do—what, exactly?"

Daniel shut his eyes. Put like that, he wasn't sure. "*I* don't know. Maybe we should do that identity parade. Maybe Inspector Deacon's right and I'm wrong. Maybe if I see his suspect in person I *will* recognise him. Damn it, there has to be *something* I can do."

But Voss knew what Daniel didn't, that identity parades are a double-edged sword. While a successful one will help towards a conviction, an unsuccessful one is a powerful weapon for the defence. The most diligent jury will be wary of convicting a felon unrecognised by the witnesses.

"He's up to his eyes right now," he said apologetically. "I'll have a word with him. If he's not going to be free this morning there's no point you waiting."

Daniel was beginning to think so too. When Voss returned five minutes later he was glad to be dismissed.

"The inspector appreciates you coming here," said Voss tactfully. "He'll call you when he has a spare minute. Let me show you out."

They didn't go the way Daniel had been brought in. Voss took him down the back stairs and out by the back door. "It's quicker. The front office is like Piccadilly Circus."

In the long corridor they moved aside to let three men pass. The first was Jack Deacon. Daniel thought he'd changed his mind, but Deacon only grunted an acknowledgement and turned into a room on his right. The others followed: a tall man in work clothes and another policeman. Daniel didn't know either of them.

As soon as he was rid of his charge Charlie Voss hurried back down the corridor. Deacon was waiting outside the shut door. "Well?"

"Not a flicker," said Voss. "From either of them."

Deacon's scowl was like a gathering storm. "I don't understand. It *had* to be Cochrane he saw."

"There are only three possibilities," said Voss. "Hood is lying. Or it was Cochrane but the light was too bad. Or it wasn't Cochrane."

Finally Deacon seemed to give some consideration to the last option. "An accomplice? It's not the sort of crime you'd expect two people to be involved in, but it does happen. But

Cochrane's a loner in every other respect: why would he involve another party when what's at stake is the rest of his life?
He never needed a partner before."

"As far as we know," amended Voss. "He's older now. And
Berry was older, and stronger."

"So why pick an athlete?" There were too many questions
he couldn't answer. The chain was broken: the thing should
be making more sense than this if what he thought had happened had indeed happened. "Damn it, Charlie Voss," he
swore thickly, "you don't suppose the little sod was right all
along?"

"HE WAS RIGHT ALL ALONG," said Daniel dully. "He said there'd
be more killing if I didn't help him, and he was right. I only
saw the man for a second. I thought I'd know him again, but
I was wrong. My mistake cost a teenage boy his life."

Brodie watched him with compassion. If there'd been anything to say that would have made him feel better she'd have said
it, true or not. There wasn't. "I'm so sorry," she said quietly.

"I should have—" said Daniel miserably, and stopped.

Brodie had kept trying his number until finally it rang
twice and was cut off. She shut up the office and came straight
here, and kept knocking on his door until he opened it.

She took his hand. "But that's it, isn't it? There was nothing you should have done differently. Maybe Deacon *was*
right. That's no reason to say you saw something you didn't.
You had to stick to what you believed, there'd be no value in
your evidence otherwise. Anyone could lie for him. Only you
could tell him the truth."

His pale tormented eyes raked her face. "But I was wrong.
Don't you understand? I was wrong, and now someone else
is dead. Deacon could have stopped it. I could have said I
wasn't sure, that maybe his suspect was the man I saw. I
didn't have to lie, just say I didn't know."

"You made an honest mistake," murmured Brodie.

"Don't," gritted Daniel, his fair head bowed. "Just—don't

tell me that the man who never made a mistake never made anything."

"I wasn't going to."

He looked up again, ashamed. "Deacon wouldn't see me. He knows what I've done."

In the same way that he pushed his honesty until it got up people's noses, he tended to do the whole sackcloth-and-ashes number over things he could not have prevented. Brodie knew he was hurting. Other men when they were hurt hit out; Daniel turned the violence inward. She supposed it was nobler to absorb the pain than to spread it around, but it was no less destructive and hardly more attractive.

"For pity's sake, Daniel," she growled softly, "get a grip. The boy's dead because someone beat his head in with a wheel-brace. That's where the responsibility begins and ends. It's not your fault you didn't recognise the man. You haven't done anything wrong.

"Except this wallowing in guilt. That's wrong. It's stupid and unproductive, and it's self-indulgent. You seem to think this is about you. It's not. It's about a serial killer and his victims. You're just a bit-part player: you've said your lines, now leave the stage to those who can carry the action forward."

He flushed as if she'd slapped him. Brodie heard the breath catch in his throat. After what felt a long time he nodded. "You're right. I'm sorry. I know I'm being stupid."

Remorse tweaked at her heart-strings. She had to stop herself from taking it all back. "You're still in shock, Daniel. Since this began you've had a lot to deal with, physically and emotionally. Your blood's full of chemicals your brain can't process. Be gentle on yourself for a couple of days."

"In a couple of days someone else could be dead," he murmured miserably.

Patience no longer came as naturally to Brodie as it once had. "You're right," she agreed tersely. "Keep this up and it could be you."

NINE

"YOU HAVE TO RELEASE HIM," said Chief Superintendent Fuller.

"If I release him," said Inspector Deacon, tight-lipped, "he'll kill someone else."

"You have no grounds to hold him," said Fuller, as if explaining the basics of police procedure to a new recruit. "No forensics, no witnesses, no suspicious behaviour, no incautious remarks to barmaids. You not only haven't got any evidence that isn't circumstantial, you haven't even got any that is."

"I have a witness," insisted Deacon desperately. His last hope was that Fuller hadn't read further than the top sheet of the file.

But Dimmock's senior police officer had been in this business even longer than Deacon. He knew that being lied to by members of the public was the least of his problems. Being told half-truths by members of his own force was much more likely to get him into trouble with the Chief Constable. "A witness who states categorically that Neil Cochrane is not the man he saw!"

There was nowhere left to hide. Deacon had given the Police & Criminal Evidence Act a run for its money but it had caught up with him in the end. He sighed and took the chair he'd been offered minutes before. "Yes. I know. I'll send him home. I'll give him his Land Rover and his trailer back, and I'll apologise, and I'll send him home."

Chief Superintendent Fuller was not an unkind man. And despite suspicions in the CID offices upstairs, he preferred to see criminals in prison rather than wandering the streets cooling their fingers in the breeze. "I can't spare the manpower for a full surveillance. I also couldn't justify it: not when the witness has effectively ruled him out. But the area car could do drive-bys. That ought to discourage him from any extra-mural activity; especially if the drive-bys aren't too discreet."

"Constable Huxley?" suggested Deacon.

Fuller gave an unctuous smile. "Seems the right man for the job."

It was better than nothing and Deacon nodded agreement. In a perfect world he'd have had twenty-four hour surveillance on Cochrane, and he wouldn't have put Constable Huxley, who was six-foot-three with red hair and a voice like a fog-horn, in charge of it. The game plan would not have been to scare the suspect into staying at home but to catch him stalking another boy.

But a perfect world would have no need of detectives. If Deacon couldn't be sure of catching Cochrane in the act he had to make sure there would be no more acts. Constable Hux-ley and the area car would make no contribution to solving these murders, but they would buy some time in which Dea-con might solve them.

Solid police work can achieve a lot in a few days. But per-haps not, Deacon thought glumly, on a case which it has fail-ed to advance significantly in ten years.

SOME CRIMES HAPPEN mostly in the day, some happen only at night. Some happen in the hour after the pubs close.

Daniel was sleeping. He'd been listening for the phone all day, waiting for Deacon to call. He hadn't dared go out for fear of missing him. He cancelled a couple of maths pupils who were coming after school because he wasn't sure he'd be here.

Even when the day waned he told himself that a murder squad can't work office hours, the detective would call when he was free to, day or night. At nine-thirty he made tea and toast, the first food he'd contemplated all day. He took it in-to the living-room and put his feet up on the sofa, and fell asleep with his supper reproaching him from the coffee table.

The thunder of fists on his door jerked him awake. A surge of pure, primitive fear galvanised him in the second before he knew where he was and what was going on. He knew, at an emotional level, that terrible things had happened, and for that second he didn't know what they were. He didn't know what the fists meant. He fumbled for his glasses, knocking over the cold tea, and stared at the door in a terror that only began to dissipate as his senses caught up. This wasn't a fearful place, it was his home; the terrible things hadn't happened to him, not this time; and though he wouldn't have been astonished to find an angry mob on his steps in the middle of the night they'd hardly have addressed him this politely as they tried to beat down his door.

"Mr Hood? Mr Hood! Open up. I've got to talk to you."

It was a young man's voice. The last time young men came here he was in trouble, but though there was urgency in the voice he couldn't detect a threat. After a moment's hesitancy he padded to the window by the door and pulled the curtain aside.

The wash of light spilling out caught the face of another tall young man standing on his steps, about the same age as the others, identically dressed in denim and leather, but alone. Still Daniel hesitated. But the idea of fear, of yielding to it and making himself its slave, worried him more than a reality which could be faced and dealt with. He didn't know that the youth outside was his enemy; but if he was, Daniel wasn't about to talk to him through a locked door. He took a deep breath and opened it.

No hiding hordes leapt from the shadows, nor did his visitor grab him by the throat. He just said. "You're Daniel Hood?"

Daniel nodded. "Who are you?"

"Nathan Sparkes. George Ennis sent me. You have to get away from here."

"What? Who's George Ennis?" Then he remembered. "Why—?"

The boy shook off Daniel's questions like a dog shaking water from its coat. His voice rattled like gunfire. "There's no time. There's going to be trouble. Not the guys from the gym—someone's been stirring it down at *The Rose*. Blaming you for… And now they're on their way. I've got wheels, I'll take you somewhere safe."

Daniel stared at him more in astonishment than alarm. "I'm not leaving my flat to a mob! I'll call the police."

"George is calling them, they'll be here in five minutes. But *The Rose* is closer: *they* can be here in three. If they find you they'll break your legs."

It could have been a ploy—if he went with this boy he didn't know he could find himself up a dark alley where half a dozen more were waiting. But Nathan Sparkes certainly seemed anxious. He kept looking over his shoulder to the promenade. That he saw nothing didn't reassure him for long. "Please! You have to come. Hurry!"

Thinking too long would leave no time for action. Daniel snatched a decision out of mid air, grabbed his parka, kicked his feet into his shoes and turned off the light. Then he thought better of that, switched it on again and drew the curtains back. If they could see there was no one hiding in the dark they might not stay. He locked the door and followed Nathan's retreating back, entirely failing to keep up with him over the shifting shingle.

By the side of the road was a black van with the words *The Attic Gym* picked out in gold paint. Nathan was already behind the wheel. Daniel scrambled up beside him, panting. "You're another of these fell-runners, aren't you?"

The boy nodded, too distracted to reply. He revved the engine and wrenched the vehicle off the kerb. There was still no sign of a mob.

"Then you must have known Chris Berry."

Nathan didn't glance at him. His voice was thick. "He was my best friend."

"I'm sorry," said Daniel quietly.

The young man kept his eyes on the road. "It wasn't your fault. I know you tried to save him." The street-lights found tears on his cheeks.

He made a couple of quick turns off the promenade, checking the road behind them in the mirror. Daniel thought he wasn't used to driving something as big as this van: every time they passed a parked car he watched the wings.

When they were back in the centre of town and there were no signs of pursuit Nathan glanced at his passenger and said, "Where do you want to go?"

Daniel came up with the same answer he always did. Sometimes it embarrassed him how much he relied on Brodie Farrell. He felt sure he was a considerable nuisance to her at times. He hoped he gave her something in return, but was aware that if the friendship ended he would be the one left alone. He sighed and directed Nathan to the big house in Chiffney Road.

It was late: the doorbell got her out of bed. He could hear the annoyance in her voice. "Whoever you are, you'd better have a good excuse."

He swallowed. "It's Daniel. I'm on the run. Can I come in?"

Immediately she threw the door open. "What do you *mean* you're on the run?" Then she saw the young man standing behind him, and remembered she was wearing only an oversized T-shirt with the words "Investigators do it in the dark" emblazoned across the front, and waved them in with a gesture that was more despair than embarrassment. There was a dressing-gown in her bedroom: she came back a moment later with it wrapped around her. "What's happened now?"

Daniel introduced his companion and repeated what Nathan had told him.

Brodie was reaching for the phone before he finished. "And George Ennis was calling the police?"

The youth nodded. "He thought it would save time if I went on ahead."

She approved of that. "Good thinking." But she phoned the station anyway. When the police confirmed they'd been called to a disturbance at the netting-sheds she merely told them that Daniel was safe with her. She turned back to her visitors. "Who's wanting to beat the crap out of you this time?"

Daniel winced. "Some men in a pub got talking about the killings and decided it was all my fault. That's about the size of it, isn't it?"

Nathan nodded. "When George realised where it was heading he told me to collect Mr Hood in the van. He was calling the police, but he reckoned I could get there quicker than they could."

The veteran of numerous phone-calls to police stations, all processed with the same meticulous attention to detail and conspicuous lack of urgency, Brodie agreed. But it wasn't the obvious thing to do. "Does he know something about the police?"

"He used to be a detective," said Nathan.

Which explained a lot. Looking back, Brodie thought she should have guessed. The tall, strong frame; the ability to deal with an angry stranger without losing his own temper; his reluctance to have to explain himself to Jack Deacon. Even the fact that he was running a gym when most men of his age would be at the peak of their careers. Policemen have the option of early retirement. George Ennis had taken it and directed his energies into *The Attic Gym*.

"Sit down," Brodie said wearily, "I'll make some coffee." It was a reflex reaction she shared with women the world over: in a crisis you look for someone to feed.

But Nathan shook his head. "I'd better go. George'll need his van back."

"All right." She showed him out. "Listen: thanks. We owe you one."

Returning to the flat Brodie said, "Stay here tonight. I'll make up the spare bed."

"It's probably all over by now," said Daniel. "I'll ask the police if it's safe to show my face."

"Just because this lot have been sent packing doesn't mean someone else won't get the same idea," objected Brodie.

Daniel hesitated. "We don't know if anything actually happened. They may have got half way to the shore, sobered up and gone home. Beer talks big."

Outside the gravel crunched again. They exchanged a tense

glance. When the bell rang Brodie reached for the intercom but Daniel got there first. He tried to make his voice deeper. "Who is it?"

"Detective Inspector Deacon." It was, too. No one could have copied that heavy, faintly disparaging tone.

Daniel opened the door. "Is everything under control? Can I go home now?"

The policeman gave that some thought. "Yes, in a manner of speaking, and not really."

Brodie joined them. Deacon gave her dressing-gown a surprised glance and then avoided looking at her. "What do you mean?" she frowned. "Either you've dealt with the situation or you haven't."

"We have," said Deacon, gazing at the ceiling. "The Fire Brigade haven't. I'm sorry to inform you, Mr Hood, that the bastards burnt your house down."

THEY WENT TO HAVE a look. Brodie didn't want Paddy to see this so she woke the long-suffering Marta to stay with her downstairs.

Daniel was quiet. Brodie wasn't sure what he was thinking. What *she* was thinking was that if it hadn't been Paddy's birthday he would probably have slept through the events on the pier and none of this would have happened. No one would blame him for anything, no one would be threatening him, and his house would still be standing.

The Fire Brigade were rolling up their hoses. The tarred timber shack had burnt alarmingly quickly, only the iron stairway and a few charred uprights remaining. Everything else was smoking, steaming ash. There was no one to rescue, no nearby buildings to safeguard and nothing to defend from looters. The destruction was total. But for George Ennis's intervention, probably Daniel would have died in the inferno.

"Terrible business," said Jack Deacon without much sincerity. He plainly thought Daniel had brought this on himself.

"Did you catch them?" asked Brodie through her teeth.

"We made some arrests. Not sure yet if we got generals

or grunts. Doesn't matter: if we got grunts they'll give us the generals."

"How organised was it?" Daniel's voice was thin with shock.

"Well, it wasn't the Berlin airlift. On the other hand, people don't go to a pub armed with their best darts *and* five litres of petrol. The beer inspired some tough talking, then they started egging one another on. They were just drunk enough to worry more about losing face by backing down than losing their liberty by carrying on."

"They could have *killed* him!" exclaimed Brodie.

"When they sobered up they'd have been sorry about that." Daniel knuckled his eyes. "But—*why?*"

"You know why."

"No, I don't. This isn't because when I pulled Chris Berry out of the sea he was already dead. It isn't because of the murder of another boy none of them cared about when he was alive. It's because you haven't made an arrest. Why aren't they burning your house down?"

The policeman was never sure if Daniel's logic was very simple or very sophisticated, but it caught him off balance every time. "They know I'm doing my best. They don't think you are."

Daniel's voice soared till it cracked. "If I could do what you asked, if I could do what they want, don't they think I would?"

Deacon sighed. When he had the men who did this in the interview room, one at a time, sober and with no one to reinforce their prejudices, he'd make them feel like shit, not only for behaving as they had but for thinking as they did. But in fact he understood it. He too believed that Neil Cochrane killed Chris Berry and Kevin Sykes. He was also aware that Cochrane and Daniel Hood looked dangerously like natural allies.

They were both loners. They lived alone—Cochrane in his rambling farmhouse out on the Downs, Hood on the shore. Neither had any family that anyone knew of, neither could boast many friends. Cochrane showed his face in *The Rose* once a week, mostly to prove he wasn't afraid to. Daniel's social needs seemed to be satisfied by a platonic friendship with a sharp-tongued divorcee five years his senior.

They were outsiders, Cochrane with his sheep and Hood with his stars, and in the smoky tap-rooms of Dimmock it seemed more than a coincidence that the one would be having a confession beaten out of him at the police station but for the protection offered by the other.

Deacon didn't believe that Daniel was shielding a man he knew to be a murderer. But he saw how it could look that way to people who didn't know him. He couldn't condone their actions but he understood their frustration. And fear. Ten years ago they lived through a nightmare. Now it was back and they were afraid. They were sorry about Chris Berry, they were even a little sorry about Kevin Sykes, but they were afraid for their own sons. No one's thought processes are impeccable when their children are in danger.

But he wasn't going to explain any of this to a man standing in the ashes of his home. It didn't alter anything. Whatever the reason for it, what happened here was, briefly, mob rule and Detective Inspector Deacon wasn't going to be their apologist. Understanding where it came from was part of his job. If he sympathised, just a little, that was no one's business but his own.

"I think," he said carefully, "that they're frightened people looking for someone to blame, and you're here where they can see you and the guy who's actually responsible isn't. I think it would be sensible, when you're looking for somewhere to stay, to look outside Dimmock."

"He's staying with me," Brodie said flatly.

Deacon opened his mouth to argue. But Daniel rendered the argument redundant. "No, I'm not."

Brodie frowned. "Have the spare room. I've put you up before."

He was pale but adamant. "Brodie, I'm not setting foot in your flat until this is finished. What happened here could happen again, wherever I go. You think I'm going to bring it to you and Paddy?"

She knew he was right. "You have nowhere else to go."

"That's what hotels are for: people who have nowhere else to stay." He turned to Deacon. "Can you get me in somewhere tonight? I've no money. I'll go to the bank tomorrow, get something organised."

Deacon thought. "Hastings. I know someone in Hastings who'll take you in."

But Daniel shook his head. "I'm not running away."

The policeman's brow darkened. "Daniel, now is not the time. Those men from *The Rose,* they didn't mean to kill you but they could have done. If you stay in Dimmock, someone else in a flush of alcohol and righteous indignation might finish the job. I'm not suggesting you live your life under a false name and a false nose. I'm asking you to avoid provoking any more trouble for the next few days."

It was only sensible. Brodie willed him to agree, but she knew he wouldn't.

He shook his head again, doggedly, the yellow hair spun by the breeze. "If someone's determined to see me dead they'll find me in Hastings, Halifax or Honduras. Everyone else can get used to the idea that I haven't done anything wrong and I'm not running away. If I go now I'll never come back. It'll go down in Dimmock mythology that I fled because I was guilty of something. I like this town, I want to stay here. I don't want everyone I meet for the next ten years to wonder where they've heard my name before, and then remember and hurry away.

"Besides, I have things to do, things to sort out. I don't have a car, and you can't do everything by phone. I need to find somewhere to live. I need to go shopping, and before that I need to get some money. So I need to convince the bank that it's mine, and I don't know how to set about it when everything that proves who I am has just gone up in smoke!"

"Don't worry about that," said Deacon grudgingly, "we'll sort you out. I won't see you on the streets."

"*You* won't see me at all!" exclaimed Daniel, turning on the policeman because he didn't know how else to vent the emotion building in his breast. "I wasted the whole day waiting to hear from you. God knows why but I'm still trying to help with your inquiries. I told your sergeant, he said you'd call me."

"I've been busy," growled Deacon.

"Busy getting nowhere!" snapped Daniel. "Use me, for pity's sake! I may not be the witness you hoped for but I'm the only one you've got. Put your suspect in a line-up, let me see him. Maybe I was wrong: maybe it was him. But I can't tell from photographs. Let me see his face."

"You already have," muttered Deacon.

For a moment the silence was so complete they could hear not only the waves creaming on the shore but the hiss and spit of the few hot-spots left in the debris.

Brodie looked at Daniel but his face was blank. She said, "When?"

The policeman looked at Daniel. "This morning, at the nick. When Voss was showing you out and we met in the corridor. Neil Cochrane was the man with me. You didn't recognise him."

"No," breathed Daniel.

Deacon couldn't quite leave it at that. "You want to give it a bit more thought? Now you know?"

Brodie had been a solicitor's clerk: every instinct was outraged at what he was doing. She spat: "You can't—!"

He turned on her fiercely. "Shut up! There are lives at stake here. And his is one of them, and yours isn't, so stay out of it."

She was so astonished she fell silent.

Daniel didn't know what to say. His breath was unsteady, his eyes devastated. Finally he managed, "You didn't *trust* me?"

"It's not a question of trust," said Deacon dismissively. "If you'd recognised him without help I could have used it as evidence. I can't do that now; but you can still tell me if I'm looking at the right man. If I am, I'll find the evidence."

For long seconds Daniel's expression didn't alter. Then he

blinked and moistened his lips, and Brodie saw him trying to remember. To strip away what had come afterwards and get back to what he had seen, what he knew.

But it was too hard. Too much had happened; too many stones had been thrown, disturbing the surface of the pond which was the mind's mirror. He shook his head and his voice was defeated. "I don't know. I don't think so, but I'm not sure any more."

Deacon breathed heavily at him. His jaw clenched and unclenched, and Brodie thought that if there'd been a dog handy he'd have kicked it. But he didn't kick Daniel, or even look as if he might. Under the granite veneer she glimpsed compassion.

And it was the moment for it. If he was only going to do one kindness this year, no one needed it more than Daniel. He was diminishing visibly before them, the moral courage that was his only defence slipping away. He could face his enemies: what he couldn't handle was the uncertainty. He no longer knew where he stood, who he stood beside or where he was going. Turning helplessly in the ruins of his home he looked like a lost child. "I don't know what to do," he whispered.

Deacon sighed. There were only the three of them here: there was no reason this should get back to Voss, who he hoped still thought of him as a bastard. He set strong hands on Daniel's shoulders and stopped him, and steered him away from the smouldering wreckage towards his own car. "Come home with me for now. We'll sort something out tomorrow."

TEN

PERHAPS AS A RESPITE from his own troubles, Daniel spent the short drive wondering what kind of place was home to a man like Jack Deacon. Did he live alone, or was there an extensive family and a noisy chaotic kitchen where children tripped over pets and vice versa? Was he into industrial chic or overstuffed Victorian comfort? Or was his house just a box for living in until he could go to work?

Whatever he'd decided, *chez* Deacon would have taken him by surprise. It surprised people who knew the policeman much better than Daniel did. Detective Inspector Deacon lived in the single-story square stone structure between The Lanes and the foot of the Firestone Cliffs which was once Dimmock's gaol.

Earlier owners had removed some of the grimmer trappings but Deacon had restored as many as he could. There were grills in front of the windows and the wood-plank front door was studded with nails. "Nice," murmured Daniel, sidling round a wrought-iron hall stand that might have served as a gibbet.

A snarling hiss behind made him startle and Daniel found himself being eyeballed by the biggest, meanest cat he'd ever seen, its mottled coat a cloak of darkness, its ears flat against its wedge-shaped head, its fangs like scimitars. He thought they might actually be dripping saliva but wasn't prepared to get close enough to check. "Nice moggy," he ventured.

"His name's Dempsey." Deacon showed every sign of pride. "Don't try to stroke him."

Nothing was further from Daniel's mind.

Deacon opened a door on the far side of the kitchen. "The spare cell's through here."

The tiny room was rather pleasant. The iron bedstead bolted to the floor was clearly original, as were the bars at the window, but the stone walls were whitewashed and there were a few pieces of simple furniture. Deacon turned on a radiator under the window and after a minute the heat began to come through.

"Get some sleep," he advised, "we'll talk in the morning. If I'm not back by then, make yourself some breakfast."

Daniel blinked. "Where are you going?" It was after one o'clock.

"Back to work. I've got some arsonists to interview, remember? And I've still got two murders to solve."

It seemed odd being left alone here by a man he hardly knew. "Is there anyone else in the house?"

"Just Dempsey."

He was on his way out of the door. Daniel said, "This is good of you."

Deacon grunted as if he'd been accused of something.

THERE'S NOTHING LIKE a killer at large to stop people fretting about trivia. Last week Brodie was rushed off her feet looking for first edition books, rare china, settings for a TV period drama, a suitable retirement home for a superannuated greyhound and, of course, authenticated representations of Mrs Trimble's bottom. This week the work had thinned to a trickle. Fortunately *Looking For Something?* produced enough cashflow these days that the odd quiet week was more bonus than disaster. Anyway, Brodie would have put her work on hold while she tried to help her friend.

Not since the earlier days of their acquaintance had she seen him so unsure of himself. As when Paddy came to her in tears, she ached to make things right for him, to wipe the hurt from his eyes and see the secret smile stray across his face.

His smile did things for her. He had a very ordinary face,

amiable but quite unremarkable; but his smile played on her heart-strings. It said that the world, with all its failings, was still a wonderful place. It made an optimist of her, and she liked knowing it was there for the having whenever she needed cheering up. Her life was richer for knowing Daniel Hood and she hated seeing him shrink before her eyes like someone wasting from a sickness.

The attacks on him made matters more urgent, but in fact he'd have felt as bad if no one had cared who he saw or what he remembered. The quiet resolve that motivated everything he did had been undermined; emotionally he was on his knees. The fear that he'd made a mistake with terrible consequences was racking him. Brodie wasn't sure she would heal his misery, but perhaps she could shorten it.

She could only see two alternatives. Either Deacon's suspect killed Chris Berry, in which case Daniel's failure to recognise him contributed to the death of the Sykes boy, or someone else did. In which case Chris was murdered not by a stranger for his strong young body but by someone he knew for reasons which would have made perfect sense to him had he lived to explain them.

Brodie didn't have to find either the reason or the killer. That was Deacon's job. If she could show that the runner's death was unconnected with that cluster of ten-year-old crimes then the lonely end of unloved, unwanted Kevin Sykes, street-kid, social outcast and whore, more brutalised by his life than by his death, was—what, exactly? A coincidence? Brodie didn't know, only that it wasn't Daniel's fault. If he was right about the man on the pier he had nothing to reproach himself for. Brodie wanted to give him that more than anything. If she could restore his self-belief, Deacon could take all the time he needed to find the actual killer.

Chris Berry. If he wasn't a random target then he was the key to what happened. His family could help her get into his life, see events from his perspective, begin to infer what he might have known. So could his friends. Brodie closed her office and headed for *The Attic Gym*.

THIS TIME THE DOOR at the foot of the area steps was locked. Brodie stood back and looked up at the building, rising two storeys above her. There was at least one flat up there, and since the windows weren't dusty she assumed it was occupied. If the gym was Ennis's baby there was a sporting chance he lived over the shop, and that there was a private entrance at the back.

Brodie walked up Fisher Hill until she found an entry. Behind the houses were a series of iron stairways serving the first-floor flats. She had counted her way along: now she counted back and, finding a paved yard filled to capacity by a black van with the words *The Attic Gym* inscribed on the side, climbed to the door and rang the bell.

It wasn't Ennis who came to the door, it was Nathan Sparkes. He seemed startled to see her, the dark eyes widening in the pallor of his face. But when she asked for the coach he dipped his head and stood back to let her in. "I'll call him."

He left her in the hall and disappeared through a door. She heard feet on another stairway, presumably leading to the gym. Feet again and Nathan was back. "He'll be up in a minute."

Brodie tried to put him at his ease. For all his height and strength, what was watching her warily was a little boy wondering if he was in trouble. "I didn't get the chance to thank you properly last night," she said.

He shrugged awkwardly. "Thank George. I wouldn't have known what to do."

"Between you, you got my friend out of a death-trap. I suppose you've seen it?—there's nothing left."

Nathan nodded without meeting her gaze. Suddenly Brodie knew what the problem was. He wasn't used to talking to women. Girls his own age, and his mum, of course, but mostly his time was spent with other men. He worked with them, trained with them, competed against them. Women were an alien species and he hadn't yet worked out if they were dangerous.

The door opened and George Ennis came in. "Mrs Farrell. Is everything all right?"

"More or less," she said, "thanks to you two. Daniel's keeping his head down for the moment, but he asked me to say how grateful he is." Brodie had no reservations about bending the truth any time it served her purpose. "He could have died last night."

"It was a sheer fluke," said Ennis, showing her into the sitting-room. She thought he'd been cleaning down in the gym: he'd changed before he came up but she could smell the faint tang of disinfectant. "Nathan and I had been for a run—we couldn't settle to doing anything else. On the way back we passed *The Rose*. A couple of people stopped us to say how sorry they were about Chris and asked us in for a drink.

"There was only one topic of conversation in the whole place, of course, but that was understandable. But even as we stood there the mood of the place started changing, getting mean. When I realised what was coming I sent Nathan to get Mr Hood away from his flat. It's only a couple of minutes from *The Rose* to here at the speed Nathan runs, and the van was in the yard—I thought he could reach the shore before anyone else. While he did that I called the police."

"Thank God you were there," said Brodie, "realised what was happening and knew what to do."

"I was a policeman for a lot of years," shrugged Ennis. "Which meant that when I told the station there was going to be trouble, they believed me."

"Even so," said Brodie, "they weren't able to reach Daniel's house ahead of the mob. If Nathan hadn't got there first he could be fighting for his life in the hospital burns unit right now."

She leaned forward earnestly. "Mr Ennis, I came here to thank you—both of you—and also to apologise for my manner earlier. But there's something else I need to discuss with you. Would you think it impertinent if I asked you about Chris? Daniel's troubled about what happened. That he wasn't able to help, of course, but also that he hasn't been able to help

Jack Deacon. Everyone in Dimmock reckons to know why Chris was murdered, and quite a few think they know who did it. And maybe they're right. But there are other possibilities, and if I knew more about Chris maybe I could work out why the man Daniel saw doesn't seem to be the man everyone's blaming."

George Ennis sat back, away from her, the craggy brow lowering over his pale blue eyes in a prelude to refusing her request. She hastened to stop him. "I realise this is difficult for you. Would you rather talk to Daniel? Whatever's happened since, in the early hours of Monday morning he earned the answers to a few questions."

Ennis pursed thin lips. Brodie saw Nathan glance at him but he didn't return the look. At length he said, "You're right, of course. Your friend risked his life for Chris, and the fact that he couldn't prevent a tragedy doesn't detract from that. Of course I'll answer your questions. What do you want to know?"

Brodie wasn't entirely sure herself. "I suppose, what kind of a lad he was. I know he was eighteen, that he worked for his father and that he was a top-class fell-runner. That's about all. What was he like as a person—cheerful or dogged? Did he run because he enjoyed it or because he refused to be beaten? Did he play other sports? Did he have a lot of friends or a few good ones? Did he go on holiday to Ibiza with his drinking buddies, or did he prefer museums and art galleries and history? Talk about him—I'll stop you if I need more detail."

After a moment Ennis nodded. He collected his thoughts and then began. "To tell you about Chris I have to start by telling you something about me. Why I set up the gym, what I had in mind.

"It goes back those ten years, to the first murders. I was at a crossroads in my life—I could go on as a CID officer or take my pension and do something else. I hadn't considered leaving the force until then. But when you've worked a murder case for thirteen months only for your prime suspect to walk away, you start seeing things afresh. I hadn't the heart to go on.

"Then there were the boys. I interviewed a lot of teenage boys in those months. I knew as I was doing it that in due course I'd see a lot of them again, in custody themselves next time. This is a nice town in many ways, but not for young people. Not now, and less so ten years ago. There was nothing for boys who were too old for woggles and too young to have family responsibilities. They spent their time on street corners and in amusement arcades, and moved into the local pubs as soon as they were old enough.

"The gym wasn't an original idea. Other people, a lot of them former police officers, were trying to involve young men in worthwhile interests at that time—renovating cars, outdoor pursuits, community service. I didn't know about any of those things, but I did know about physical fitness. I was a good boxer in my day and not a bad runner, and I'd always done a bit of coaching. I looked into the possibilities and, when the time came, I took the pension and bought this place. It took me six months to knock it into shape, work out what to do with it, then I opened for business."

He smiled at the young man who had lowered himself carefully onto the arm of the sofa. "I remember the first day I saw Nathan and Chris. Chris's mum brought them down. They'd been caught joy-riding—neither of them took the car but they hadn't the sense to stay out of it either. They were fourteen years old. She bought them each a three month subscription and said if they wasted a penny of it they'd have to answer to her.

"They were typical adolescent boys, their bodies growing faster than their brains, their hormones shouting louder than their common sense. They'd fallen in with some older boys who thought shop-lifting was clever and joy-riding was fun. They resented Mrs Berry's interference, were sullen with me. I told them not to come if they weren't prepared to work, they'd already made me as much money as they were going to. But they were afraid Mrs Berry would box their ears if she had to stand on a milk-crate to do it.

"So they tried out a few different disciplines. Because there were two of them they got competitive: trying to run further and faster than one another, trying to lift more weight. Before I knew it they were waiting on the doorstep when I opened up. At some point they made the transition between trying to beat one another to trying to better themselves, and then they were genuine athletes."

Even the memory sparked a certain pride in his eye. "I tried them on a variety of programmes. They were terrible boxers—hadn't the self-control, kept trying to finish the fight rather than win it. They were better at track and field events, but what they were really good at was keeping going in adverse conditions. The track steeplechase only scratched the surface—they could have finished one and run a better one right after. Strength, stamina, endurance and mental resilience: they were natural cross-country runners.

"I put them in for the Three Downs that first year. They were fifteen, for pity's sake—men of thirty should have been running over the top of them. But they weren't. Nathan finished eighth out of a field of sixty. Chris finished twelfth, on a sprained ankle. The next year he won it.

"So what was he like? He had guts, Mrs Farrell. He never gave up. Nothing was too hard for him or hurt too much. You showed him a goal and he could shut out everything else. He was a born champion. If he hadn't had the physique for running he'd have found something else to excel at. He was never going to be ordinary."

He was telling her what had impressed him as a coach. Brodie wanted to hear what kind of a boy Chris was, what kind of a man he was going to be. If he was solemn, or up for a night on the tiles. If he laughed a lot or took life as seriously as he took his sport. If the training and the competitions and being the best fell-runner around left time for socialising, for gambling or for romantic entanglements. Nobody killed Chris Berry because he was fast across country. He just might have died because he'd made some bad acquaintances, some bad debts or some bad choices.

She turned to Nathan, still as edgy in her company as a cat in a room full of rocking-chairs. "You must have had good times together. Running hard, training hard—drinking hard?"

But he shook his head. "You can't drink and run."

"So what did you do to relax?"

Nathan shrugged. "Get a video. A disco, maybe, if we weren't competing at the weekend. Normal stuff."

Brodie nodded. "Did he have a girlfriend?"

"Sure. Her name's Lindsay. Last week her name was Jill."

Brodie chuckled. "No danger of him getting too serious too soon, then."

"He was serious about running. Girls are like beer—they can get in the way. It's all right having the odd one, but you need to keep on top of the job."

But it was too soon for Nathan to be making even wry jokes about his friend. His voice caught and he stumbled to the window, stood looking up at the looming bulk of the Firestone Cliffs.

"I'm sorry," Brodie said softly, "I don't mean to upset you. I know you're hurting. You had a close friend for most of your life, now he's gone. All the things you did together you're going to be doing alone. It'll be hard for a while, but the worst will pass. You'll always miss him, but it won't always be like a knife in your side."

She'd been trying to comfort him. But the boy fled the room, choking back a sob.

Brodie put one long-fingered hand to her mouth, regarding Ennis over the top of it and speaking through the fingers. "I'm trying to make things easier for Daniel and what I'm actually doing is making things worse for you and Nathan. Maybe I should go now."

He didn't try to dissuade her.

"It's just— Look, you're a policeman…"

"Was," Ennis said quietly.

"All right, you were; but you know how these things come about. Something terrible happens, and everyone's so desper-

ate to deal with it they jump at the obvious answer. But obvious isn't always right. I'm worried that because it looks like
an open-and-shut case, because Jack Deacon thinks he knows
who did this, everyone's taking an awful lot for granted. Maybe they're right—but if they're not the man who killed Chris
must be feeling pretty smug by now."

Ennis frowned. He was twenty years older but there was
something about him that reminded her of John. An inner calm,
a quiet intelligence, a personality that made its impact without
trying too hard. Even six months ago, comparing someone to
her ex-husband would have been the kiss of death. It was a
mark of her recovery from the divorce that now she could remember what attracted her to him in the first place. He was a
good man, a kind man, an honourable man. He'd just had the
misfortune to meet someone he loved more than his wife.

Now George Ennis looked at her with the same astute,
troubled eyes and said, "Mrs Farrell, what are you suggesting? That we look for this other man together?"

Until that moment it hadn't occurred to her. But it made
sense. He owed it to his friend as she owed it to hers. "Why not?
Look, we want the same things. We want to know what happened. We want Chris's killer behind bars. If it's this—this—"

"Neil Cochrane," supplied Ennis softly.

"Right, if it's this Neil Cochrane then OK, it's not the perfect result for Daniel but he can start coming to terms with
the fact that he made a mistake. And once he's in custody people will relax. When they have a proper target for their anger
they won't have to use it up on Daniel."

"And what do you think Jack Deacon's going to say when
he hears I've got involved in his investigation?"

Brodie shrugged. "He won't like it, any more than he likes
it when I trample on his toes. But you're a private citizen now,
you're entitled to do things that you couldn't do as a police
officer. Asking questions on another detective's manor is one
of them. He won't like it, but he'll put up with it. I think he'll
understand why we're doing it."

Ennis eyed her askance. "We're still talking about Jack Deacon, are we?"

Brodie laughed. "OK, maybe that's optimistic. But as long as we don't obstruct his inquiry there's nothing he can do. If we make any progress, we'll tell him and maybe he'll have the grace to thank us. If we don't he can have the pleasure of rubbing our faces in it. Either way we're not going to get under his feet. I'm looking for a man he doesn't believe exists. How can that jeopardise his investigation?"

Still George Ennis looked deeply unhappy. "I don't understand why you're so sure there is another man."

"I'm not," admitted Brodie. "Even Daniel isn't confident any more. At the time he was. He saw the killer, and he didn't think it was Neil Cochrane. The second murder shook him to the core. I want to set his mind at rest. Of course I want to see a man who enjoys sodomising teenage boys and then beating them to death in jail, but principally I want to help my friend. He's hurting, and he's in danger, and he will be until this is resolved. And if Jack Deacon's looking for the wrong man it's going to take too damn long."

"Forgive me, but—what do you think you can do about it?"

Brodie bridled at the doubt in his voice. "Deacon's chosen to tackle this inquiry from one angle; well, I'll approach it from another. I don't think Chris was a random victim. I think his death was a consequence of something in his life, something he knew or was involved in. If so then other people may know about it, even if they don't know they know. His family and friends may know things whose relevance they haven't suspected because everyone thinks Chris was waylaid by a pervert. If his friends have different pieces of the jigsaw, maybe all it'll take is for someone to put them together. I'm going to try. If you're offering, I'll be glad of your help."

There was a long silence. She tried to read Ennis's expression. He didn't like it, but then he used to be the man at the hub of the investigation whom everyone else was trying to second-guess. Naturally his sympathies lay with Deacon.

But he wasn't blind to her argument, and he knew that if she proved Deacon wrong the policeman would be too busy reeling in his catch to waste much time in recrimination. Brodie couldn't tell what Ennis thought of the central idea, that maybe the farmer from Menner Down wasn't guilty of Chris Berry's murder. But he didn't have to buy into it, had only to acknowledge the possibility and recognise that vital time could be wasting. It wouldn't do Chris any harm if he helped her and they were wrong. It might aid the killer if he refused to help and she was right.

Brodie hadn't much more to offer by way of persuasion. She murmured, "If someone's going to be asking about Chris, I dare say the people who cared for him would sooner it was you than me."

George Ennis drew a deep breath and finally nodded. "God knows what we can achieve. But if you want me to talk to his friends, I can do that. I'm not sure I believe in this other man of yours. It is hard to identify people from a snatched glance, I'm not surprised Hood didn't recognise Cochrane and I wouldn't take that as proof that Cochrane wasn't there. All the same, if there's even a chance that he's right we can't ignore it. If we look for another man and fail to find one, that'll be something in itself."

Brodie nodded in relieved agreement. This was something she meant to do, but she had no illusions about how difficult it would be or how unpopular it could make her. Having Chris Berry's coach along for the trip would make it easier. "That's how I see it. If we can get at the truth, what that truth is will be of secondary importance. Whether it's Cochrane or someone else, we all want the right man to pay for what he did."

"What if it was Cochrane?" said Ennis. "Will Hood accept that?"

"He'll have to," said Brodie bleakly.

ELEVEN

WHAT BRODIE WANTED was to bring Chris Berry's friends together. "Could you invite them to a wake here this evening?"

George Ennis looked astonished. "None of us is in the mood for a party!"

Brodie was determined. "Then tell them it's a prayer meeting. But don't mention me. They mightn't come if they expect to be questioned, but once we start talking about Chris they'll stay."

Ennis was doubtful but seemed unable simply to refuse. He spread one hand in an oddly helpless gesture, then went into the hall and made the phone-calls. Through the shut door Brodie heard Nathan's voice raised in a plaint. Ennis responded sharply and the voices sank to a mutter. More calls followed.

When Ennis returned alone, Brodie said, "Is Nathan all right?"

He shrugged. "Not really. They were very close. He's hanging on by his fingernails."

"There are counsellors," she said. "If you think he needs help."

"I think he just needs time."

Probably no one knew Nathan Sparkes better than his coach so perhaps he was right. Brodie hoped so. "Who did you call?"

"Everyone we could think of who was more than a casual acquaintance. School-friends Chris stayed in touch with; kids from the coffee-bar in Bank Lane; people from the gym, of course, and others he knew through running. And Lindsay. But I don't think she'll come. The poor kid was crying on the phone."

"I'm sorry to involve you in this," Brodie said quietly. "All I can say is, if it leads to anything it'll have been worthwhile."

"Of course it will," said Ennis, but his heart wasn't in it.

"How many are you expecting?"

"Maybe a dozen." He looked critically at his sofa and his one chair. "We'd better do it downstairs."

"I'll need you or Nathan to brief me on who's there—their relationship to Chris, how long they knew him, that sort of thing."

"Not a problem."

JACK DEACON DIDN'T get home for breakfast. He didn't get home for lunch, and by the time he remembered he'd promised to help Daniel with his bank it was mid-afternoon and the place would be closed. So he got on with his work.

At four-fifteen the phone rang. Dr Roy had preliminary results of the post mortem on Kevin Sykes. "Do you want the good news or the bad news?"

Deacon breathed heavily. Hari Roy was an excellent forensic medical examiner but he had an odd sense of humour. Deacon put it down to his university education. Deacon didn't have a lot of time for education. "There's some good news?"

"Yes," said Dr Roy, "or possibly no, depending on how you look at it. Kevin Sykes may not have been murdered. Not by the man who killed Chris Berry; conceivably, not by anyone."

Deacon scowled. He'd seen the damage himself. You can commit suicide in a variety of imaginative ways but not with a blunt instrument. "What are you talking about?"

"There are fragments of car paint in the head-wound. I don't think he was beaten with a wheel-brace, I think he was hit by a car."

They'd been over this already. "There were no leg injuries," objected Deacon.

"I think he was lying down at the time. In fact, I think he was dying at the time. There was enough heroin in his system to take out a horse."

Deacon's scowl eased from irritable to puzzled. "You think someone shot him full of heroin and then ran him down?"

"Or," said Roy, "he shot himself full of heroin and passed out, and a car drove clean over him because the driver never recognised him as a human being. You saw him: with that coat pulled over him, in the dark and the dirt anyone could have taken him for rubbish. Whoever ran him down may not know how he dented the front of his car, or what the sticky stuff on it is."

Deacon was nonplussed. He hadn't considered that the death of Kevin Sykes might fall outside the pattern. "Accidental death?"

"That's not a forensic conclusion," said Roy. "But if you want my personal opinion, I think it's the likeliest explanation."

Deacon's brain churned, amending what he thought he knew in the light of this fresh information. So he was never going to connect Neil Cochrane to the death at the brewery. But Roy was right: that might be good news. Cochrane could have an alibi for Monday night—he didn't seem to have but he could—without it getting him off the hook as far as Berry was concerned. Far from derailing the inquiry, this just might simplify it.

It also meant that the men in the cells downstairs had torched Daniel Hood's flat for no good reason. Not that there was ever a good reason for arson, Deacon thought quickly—even in the privacy of his own head his respect for the law was absolute. But they'd done it because they thought his indecision had led to another death. Deacon would enjoy telling them they were going to prison for a misunderstanding.

And the other person who'd be interested in Dr Roy's conclusion was Daniel. Deacon rang his own number but got the machine. Daniel must have given up waiting and gone to tackle the bank manager alone, trusting to his ownership of the world's most honest face to achieve as much as a signed statement from a senior police officer. Deacon glowered. It would probably work. A man with no charm of his own, he mistrusted it in other people. He knew it was a potent weapon, and he couldn't charge anyone for possession.

BY SEVEN-THIRTY everyone had come who was coming. There were eight of them: fewer than Ennis had hoped but enough if one of them knew Chris had made an enemy.

Brodie passed round coffee and biscuits, introduced herself but offered no explanation for her presence. The young people were confused. Some of them thought they were here to drown their sorrows, some for a short memorial service. Coffee and ginger-nuts puzzled them all.

But they each obediently took a cup and for a while just sat together, sharing their shock and grief. Then they began to talk about the young man whose passing they were here to mourn.

At first Brodie just listened. Nathan, who was perched beside her, murmured the names of the speakers and explained how they had fitted into Chris's life. They were remembering aloud, little anecdotes from their shared lives, moments of kindness, of bravery, of triumph, and, as the mood relaxed, of comedy too.

They were all young—late teens, a couple in their early twenties—and for most it was their first experience of irrevocable loss. To start with they didn't know how to talk about it: all the vocabulary they had were clichés. But as they grew easier with the process they discovered that what you really remember about someone is the times they made you laugh.

But that was never going to explain why Chris Berry died. Brodie realised she would have to declare herself if she wanted to achieve anything. She took a deep breath and prayed they wouldn't walk out before she'd finished.

"Please don't feel offended, or angry—or if you are, be angry with me, not George. This was my idea. He agreed to help because we all want the same thing—the man who killed your friend. I don't know that this will help, but it may.

"Everyone thinks they know who killed Chris and why. They may be right, but I'm not convinced. It may have been someone else, hiding behind the events of ten years ago. If so he's going to get away with murder unless someone comes up with an alternative explanation.

"You don't have to know that someone wanted Chris dead, you don't have to know that they killed him. You don't even have to believe there *was* a someone else. But if you saw or heard anything odd, that bothered Chris or he was unwilling to talk about, that may be the reason. If someone was gunning for him, he may have known who. He may have said or done something significant, something that would point the police in the right direction. You must want that even more than I do."

They heard her out in silence. It wasn't politeness: she'd rendered them speechless. They thought they knew what had happened, and appalling as it was they'd started coming to terms with it. Now a woman they didn't know from Eve was telling them they'd got it wrong—that everyone had got it wrong—and one or more of them knew what had happened instead. They stared at her open-mouthed with disbelief.

But it wasn't the first time Brodie had stilled a room. She wasn't embarrassed. The secret was to keep talking until someone else was ready to. What she said mattered less than the fact that someone who had something useful to contribute wouldn't have to break a stunned silence.

Her voice was quiet and conversational. "I didn't know Chris. But I met his mum once. If she'd been any prouder of him she'd have exploded. But in some ways you knew him better than she did. There were things he'd tell you that his mum and wild horses wouldn't get out of him. You know what I mean: things you know you should be ashamed of and actually aren't. Making out with people precisely because they'd horrify your mother. Drinking too much; smoking a joint, popping pills, just to see what the hype's about. Losing at strip poker and reckoning it was worth it because of who was second worst.

"Come on, it's not *that* long since I was eighteen—I know about lager roulette. I know about behaving badly for no better reason than it looks more fun than behaving well. You're not going to tell me you never do stupid things just for the hell of it? That Chris never did?"

Finally one of them interrupted her: a girl in her late teens, long fair hair scraped back, scrubbed cheeks, eyes still puffy from crying. But the voice was ribbed with anger and the refusal to hear the dead boy slandered. "You got one thing right—you didn't know Chris. We did. Don't you dare tell us he brought what happened on himself."

Brodie spared Nathan a questioning glance. "Tiff Willis," he murmured, "she's a runner too."

Brodie nodded. "I'm sorry, Miss Willis, that's the last thing I want to suggest. Nothing Chris did or didn't do could justify what was done to him. It was murder. There can't be any mitigating circumstances.

"But the fact is, almost nothing comes from nowhere. Most events have a history, and most victims of violence know their attackers. Chris may have known his."

"*We* know Chris's attacker," rasped a young man with ginger hair and the upper body development of a thrower. "The freak with the sheep."

A tall black youth remembered the name. "Neil Cochrane."

Brodie nodded. "Quite possibly. And that's the line CID are following. If it was Cochrane, they'll get him. I just want to be sure that we aren't missing something because of this man and what he did ten years ago."

The gathering thought about that, and if they still resented her suggestions, her very presence here, at least they could see merit in her argument.

Tiff Willis said disdainfully, "If you think we can tell you about a secret life Chris was leading as an international drug-smuggler, you're wrong. He was a runner—an athlete. It doesn't leave you time to get into much trouble."

Brodie dipped her head encouragingly. "I can see that. But some trouble comes to your door without an invitation. Did he *seem* troubled in the last few weeks? Was he spending time with people you wouldn't normally see him with?"

There was a soft mutter of discussion. The black youth—Nathan Sparkes said softly, "Joffe Matthews"—said, "He was short of money. But he always was. We all are."

"Did he ask you for a loan?"

Joffe chuckled. "Hell no—he knew better than that! But he was pricing parts for that car, said he couldn't afford the scrapyard prices let alone the list price."

Brodie flicked a grin. "Chris ran a car?"

George Ennis explained. "He and Nathan bought it together. It's a bit elderly, but at the level they were competing at it's a nightmare depending either on lifts or on public transport."

"So he was hard up," said Brodie. "Any reason? Had he been spending much recently?"

"Mrs Farrell," murmured Joffe Matthews, "are you *sure* you remember being eighteen?"

There was a general ripple of amusement. Brodie didn't mind them baiting her as long as they kept talking. "I remember my first car. You didn't park where you were going, you parked at the top of the nearest hill." A chuckle and a general softening of the atmosphere were her reward.

Tiff Willis seemed to have known the dead man as well as any of them, and—in the absence of his girlfriend—to have cared as much. She wasn't beguiled by Brodie's easy manner, still resented discussing her friend with a stranger. But Brodie doubted if anyone here was more likely to come up with useful information. Because she knew Chris well enough to know personal things about him, and cared enough to share them even when she'd rather not if she thought she could help catch his killer.

But she couldn't give Brodie what she was looking for, thought she was looking for something that didn't exist. "He wasn't spending more than usual. But he used up his savings buying the car and running it cost more than he bargained for." Her gaze, faintly censorious, settled a moment on Nathan. "I don't think anything else was worrying him. And though I saw him all the time, it was always with one of us, or Lindsay, or someone else I knew."

Her voice hardened. "As for drugs—you really don't know anything about athletics, do you? The authorities test everybody, for everything. You don't need to win, or to have a reputation. It doesn't have to be steroids: you drink the wrong kind of herbal tea and they know about it. If Chris was doing drugs, any kind of drugs, we'd all know about it."

Brodie wasn't surprised but she was disappointed. She'd wanted there to be more to the dead youth than met the eye. But it seemed that Chris Berry had been exactly who he appeared to be. In desperation she trawled the back-waters of her brain. "What other kinds of trouble can a young man get into? Was he a gambler—could he have owed money that he had no way of raising? Was he playing away on the romantic front? Could he—?"

The hard chair clattered on the floor as Tiff sprang to her feet, narrow face suffused with anger. "That's my *friends* you're talking about," she shouted, "and one of them's dead and can't defend himself, and the other's too upset to be here. Lindsay hasn't left her house since this happened. She hasn't left her room. Her mum says she hasn't eaten anything and she doesn't think she's slept. She and Chris were doing fine together, and if that ruins your theory, too bad. If it leaves your friend feeling guilty about his mistake, that's too bad too.

"Chris isn't dead because of anything he did. He's dead because there's a dangerous animal living in the hills, and one night it came down into town and snatched him off the street. And it wasn't the first time, and it wasn't the last. Your friend *should* feel guilty. Maybe he couldn't have prevented Chris's death, but he could have made sure it was the last."

Only by clenching her teeth could Brodie hold back her own anger. Perhaps she was asking too much of these people, but she was damned if she'd let them ignore the facts. "Daniel Hood risked his life for Chris. Do you understand what that means? He *risked* his *life*…"

"I know he got a bit wet," spat Tiff, as offensively as possible. "But when the chance came to actually do some good he was too damned scared to. You can call that by any name you like, but he saw Chris's murderer and that man is still at large. So don't talk to me about looking for the truth. I know what you're looking for, Mrs Farrell, and you won't find it here."

With that she turned on her heel and stalked out. After a moment, casting an uncertain glance at Ennis, Joffe Matthews hurried after her. Brodie heard their voices, then she heard the front door open and shut. Joffe came back and, with an apologetic shrug, resumed his seat.

"Tiff and Chris," he mumbled by way of an explanation— "well, going back a bit they were an item. She—I mean, we all—but her more…" The sentence petered out.

Brodie folded her long hands as if in prayer and waited for the anger to subside. "I'm sorry," she sighed at length. "I didn't come here to upset you. Maybe Tiff's right—Tiff and the police and just about *everyone* else in Dimmock. Does everyone think I'm barking up the wrong tree with this?"

After a moment's discretion there was a chorus of assent. When she looked at George Ennis he nodded too, wryly.

"It wouldn't be the first time," she admitted disconsolately. "Well, like I said, the truth is what matters. If Inspector Deacon was right all along, I'll have to settle for that."

But her instincts rebelled. She didn't think it was obstinacy. She didn't think it was because Daniel needed her to find a different answer. She was bothered by how well most of the pieces fitted and how determinedly the last few refused to; and how no one else seemed to think that significant.

A last desperate idea occurred to her. She knew she was scraping the bottom of the barrel. She knew she'd cause offence when she voiced it and was sorry for that. These people were trying to help, didn't deserve to be hurt again.

But ideas can't be unthought: either she said it aloud or she didn't, in which case she'd never know if it had legs. "Oh God," she groaned, "you're going to hate me for this. But I have to ask. Is there any chance that Chris was attacked by a rival? Another runner, someone whose only hope of a Three Downs title lay in nobbling him? That he'd have settled for breaking Chris's leg but the fight got out of hand and he ended up dead?"

She'd knocked the wind right out of them again. They were too stunned even to object.

George Ennis had said next to nothing in the last half hour. But now he'd heard enough. In his quiet voice the fury was unmistakable. "I'm going to give you the benefit of the doubt and assume that's ignorance talking. Because if I thought you knew what you're suggesting I'd ask you to leave.

"These people are athletes, Mrs Farrell. Of course they want to win, but not at all costs. Nobody here, nobody I know, would injure another runner in order to win a race.

"You think it's about winning?—about taking home a plastic trophy and a gift voucher at *Spikes R Us?* It isn't. It's about testing yourself against athletes you admire to see how you measure up. If you're strong enough, if you're fast enough, if you've trained hard enough. Finding that you are and have is the best feeling in the world. Winning any other way doesn't mean a thing."

Brodie nodded slowly. "But—"

"But?" snarled Ennis. "You think I'm wrong? You think you know these people better than I do? All right, Mrs Farrell, ask yourself who stood to gain by putting Chris out of competition? The man who followed him across the finishing-line most often, yes? Nathan, Mrs Farrell thinks you murdered your best friend for a bit of silverware. What do you say to that?"

He didn't mean to be cruel, she told herself, it was exasperation talking. His emotions were tatters. But the words hit Nathan Sparkes like a blow. She heard him gasp, saw his lips struggle with denials he couldn't voice and shouldn't have had to. Then his eyes filled; and all the time his anguished gaze was on George Ennis as if he couldn't break free.

Brodie was on her feet with her arms around him before any-one else could move. His strong young body was so rigid it shook. "It's all right," she murmured softly, "it's just reaction. The stress of the last few days has set up so many chemical in-terfaces you're on a hair-trigger. Everyone here is in pretty much the same state. Including George," she added, casting him a fierce look over the boy's shoulder, "which is why he thought that was clever. Come upstairs for a minute, wash your face and get your breath back." She steered him away.

She was livid with the coach, but actually she knew that En-nis too was barely getting through each day. The fact that he'd spent his working life watching other people go through this was no protection when it was his turn. He couldn't keep from hitting out. It wasn't deliberate, it was built in at a genetic lev-el. Men can't feel hurt without wanting to hurt someone else.

But that was scant comfort to Nathan. Brodie was suffi-ciently detached to recognise what was happening but the boy wasn't. He shook as if he'd been whipped. He kept whisper-ing, "It isn't true! I didn't..."

"Of course you didn't," she assured him, "and nobody in that room thinks you did. Including George. It wasn't you he was getting at, it was me. It's just, right now his aim's off."

"Chris was my *friend!*"

"I know that. My God, you've practically got it tattooed on your forehead! It was a stupid thing to say, stupid and hurt-ful; and when you're both feeling better he'll want to apolo-gise. I know it's hard, but try to understand that George is suffering almost as much as you are. Try to forgive him. You can't afford to lose one another as well."

Brodie left him in the sitting-room with a can of lager from the fridge, not drinking but cooling his brow on the tin, and went quickly downstairs. But it was too late. The party was over, the last of the guests hurrying away. Ennis watched her covertly, waiting for the explosion.

Instead she sat down on the weights bench and regarded him levelly. "Of all the monstrous things to say! I know you're grieving for Chris, but what about Nathan? It's too late to help the boy in the morgue, but the one upstairs needs your kindness. He doesn't need to be accused of murdering his best friend."

"I was making a point," said Ennis in a low voice.

"And I took it. I'm not complaining about your treatment of me. Maybe what I said was stupid, but you could have put me straight without reducing a vulnerable young man to tears in front of his friends."

Ennis glanced at the stairs. "Is he all right?"

Brodie snorted in despair. "Don't ask me! Go and ask *him!*" She snatched up her handbag and left.

THERE WAS A MESSAGE on her answering machine when she got home. Even if he hadn't given his name she'd have recognised Jack Deacon's tone—gruff, surly and defensive, as if she knew where he'd buried his mother. He'd called half an hour earlier and left a number where he could be reached. It wasn't the police station or a mobile so she presumed it was his home.

He answered within a couple of rings, but muzzily, as if he'd been asleep. Brodie supposed that right now he was napping as and when he could.

But he remembered why he'd called her. "Some news on the Sykes post mortem. Good news, I suppose. There's no reason to connect the two deaths, which lets Daniel off the hook."

Brodie just breathed lightly for a moment, tasting the relief. And she knew to multiply that by a factor of ten for Daniel. Even if he was wrong about what he thought he'd seen, the mistake hadn't cost anyone his life.

Then she started thinking. "You mean, it was a coincidence? You've got two murderers at large in Dimmock?" It seemed excessive for a small town.

"It doesn't look as if Sykes *was* murdered," grunted Deacon. "The FME thinks he was probably hit by a car. I'll have to find the driver to be sure but he may not even know about it: there was so much junk in the kid's veins he couldn't have been standing up at the time. The doctor reckons he'd have died even if nothing else had happened to him."

"I see." Brodie was fighting the urge to be happy. Whatever the immediate cause, whoever was and wasn't to blame, a seventeen-year-old boy had died in a gutter because no one cared enough to help him out of it. Any way you looked at that, there was no cause for celebration. She said, "I'm sure Daniel was relieved when you told him."

"I haven't spoken to him," said Deacon.

Brodie felt a spark of anger behind her breastbone. With just a little fanning it would burst into flame. "You haven't *told* him? For pity's sake, Inspector…! He's been tearing himself apart since that boy was found. I've been buzzing round like a blue-arsed fly trying to set his mind at rest! Now you have proof that nothing he did had any bearing on Kevin Sykes' death, and you haven't even told him? Trust me: if he's asleep he'll want to be woken."

From the puzzlement in his voice, even before she heard his answer Brodie knew they were in trouble. "Mrs Farrell, are you under the impression that Daniel's still here? He was here this morning, but some time during the day he left. He didn't leave a message, but I assumed he'd come back to you. That's why I called—I thought you could tell him."

Brodie felt the blood draining from her face, her muscles stiffening in fear. "He isn't here. He hasn't *been* here. The last I saw Daniel was when he left with you. Are you telling me you don't know where he is, and it's hours since you did?"

TWELVE

WHEN DEACON LEFT him, at first Daniel couldn't sleep. His mind was ablaze with the night's events. He'd lost everything he owned, he had nowhere to live, and people he didn't know hated him enough to try to kill him. They blamed him for the death of a seventeen-year-old derelict, and Daniel hadn't even the scant comfort of knowing they were wrong. He thought they were probably right. He lay for hours, staring at the white ceiling of Deacon's spare cell, not moving, not weeping, tormenting himself.

Eventually exhaustion intervened and he slept. His dreams were full of fear and the stench of smoke, and he woke with a start, sweating, three or four times while it was still dark.

But the next time he woke it was day and the house was still empty. Even the cat was gone. He padded round till he found a clock, and it was a quarter-to-ten.

He didn't want to eat. He washed, and made the bed, then he looked at the clock again and it was five-to-ten. The day stretched ahead of him, empty and implacable as a desert. He was alone with his regrets, and the eye of his conscience beat down on him like the sun.

He kept going over and over it: what he could have done differently, where he might have gone wrong. He couldn't find the point where he'd lost the thin silver thread that was the truth, the place where if he had it to do again he could do it better. But still two young men were dead.

The simple, brutal reality battered his heart and frayed his spirit. His actions had cost lives.

He couldn't bear it. He didn't know how to go on knowing that: how to face the next day, the next hour. Guilt enclosed him in a cloying, choking cloud. The limewashed walls of the stone building crowded in on him. He needed air. He couldn't stay here with the quiet and the guilt, he had to get out.

He thought a walk would steady him. He pulled Deacon's front door shut as he left, only to remember he had no way of opening it again. It didn't matter. He couldn't stay there alone. He headed for the open spaces of the Firestone Cliffs.

It was a stiff climb up the steep path but that was what he needed: something to stretch his muscles and occupy his mind. At first it seemed to help. Daniel didn't know enough about biology to understand that his anxiety was due in part to the adrenalin flooding his bloodstream, and that physical exertion would mop it up. But by the time he reached the sheep-cropped turf atop the bluff and felt the chill wind cooling the sweat under his clothes he was regaining a sense of perspective.

Then he saw a woman watching him. She was walking a small dog and watching Daniel. Her face was closed, defensive, but her eyes knew and despised him.

Her look broke his stride. At half past ten on a Wednesday morning they were the only people up here, and he'd still managed to find someone who hated him. The whole town must know what he'd done. Everyone he met from now on, people he knew and people he didn't, was going to look at him with that mixture of fear and disgust. Like a slug on the path, his proximity made their skin crawl. He had forfeited the right to their human understanding.

He felt himself flush. He knew what he should do. He should bid her good morning, pat the dog and go about his day. Whatever she thought, he'd done his best. He didn't deserve her odium, could refuse to accept it. That was what he should do.

But he couldn't. It was too difficult. Unmanned by her silent resentment, he turned back the way he'd come.

The defeat weighed in the hollows of his eyes. All his adult life he'd fought to be stronger than he was, to be braver, to face trouble with dignity and courage. But a middle-aged woman walking a dog had demolished him with a look. He walked faster as the path descended. Soon he was running.

After that the people he met stared at him because he was tearing down a steep, rough path at break-neck speed. But he thought they recognised him too. Their eyes whipped him on. Once he missed his step, rolling in the dust. But as soon as he found his feet he resumed his headlong flight.

He didn't know where he was going. He ran blindly until he could run no more, when he slowed first to a panting jog, finally to a halt.

He bent double, fighting for breath. When he straightened up he found himself surrounded by startled people. Mere chance had brought him to the bus station. A blue and cream single-decker was changing its display as it waited in the rank.

If it had been going to Bognor or Brighton, the course of future events would have been different. But the bus was heading for Guildford, across the Three Downs.

Spelled in electronic dots, the words transfixed Daniel. He felt a curious exultation constrained by an odd sense of inevitability, as if he'd found the answer and any moment now would know what the question was. He wiped his face on his sleeve. Then he hunted through his pockets for loose change. He knew he was going to do something extraordinary before he knew what it was.

And the answer was, Because then no one can accuse me of being afraid to do what's right. And the question was, Why would a sane man go looking for a murderer?

He couldn't remember Neil Cochrane's face. He knew he'd seen it—Deacon had gone to considerable lengths to ensure that he saw it—but he had no recollection at all. So perhaps he had not actually looked at him. Deacon thought he had but Deacon could be wrong. He'd been waiting for the Inspector to speak to him—why would he have been looking at a man he didn't know? Then they were past, and Daniel had only known later that he was supposed to be taking advantage of the situation.

But if he never saw Cochrane he couldn't be sure he wasn't the man on the pier. He hadn't recognised the photograph, but that was different. He'd said from the start he should see the suspect in person. And it turned out Deacon had been listening, but when the moment came Daniel was looking the other way. Somehow it figured.

There was no point holding an identity parade now. If he recognised Cochrane the man's lawyers would cite the meeting in the corridor as reason enough for their client to look familiar to the witness. Deacon had taken a gamble and lost.

But Daniel had lost too. He'd lost the chance to know if his error had set a murderer free to kill again. And he was desperate to know. Desperate enough to take a gamble of his own.

The bus driver was in his seat, the engine coughed to life. If Daniel thought about this any longer his decision would be academic—he hadn't enough money for a taxi. He sprinted across the tarmac, up the steps and onto the bus.

IT DROPPED HIM AT the point where the three downs met. A plaque identified it as the start and finish point for the famous race. The bus driver indicated the lowering swell to the northwest as Menner Down but claimed never to have heard of Manor Farm. From the bleak looks Daniel thought some of his fellow passengers knew but none would tell him. He climbed down and looked for a house where he could ask.

There were houses scattered across the hills. The nearest was half a mile in the wrong direction. Instead Daniel took the road that skirted Menner Down, trusting he'd chance on a farmhouse or cottage before long.

But he walked for twenty minutes and saw no houses and no people, only sheep. Slowly the adrenalin and the dream of atonement it had fed began to dissipate and common sense to reassert itself. He thought about returning to the main road and hitching back to Dimmock.

But for a moment back there he'd scented redemption, and he was loathe to give it up. He hadn't known he needed other people's approval until it was lost. Restoring his credibility was worth an hour of his time and a few blisters.

It was even worth the risk involved. He knew that if Cochrane caught him he might beat his head in with a wheel-brace. But he didn't intend to confront the man, only to snatch a look at him. He thought one glance would tell him if Neil Cochrane was the man at the pier. Legally his testimony might now be tainted, but if he could tell Deacon one way or the other it had to help. Help stop a killer, and silence the clamour of accusation in his head.

Before he could do any of that he had to find Manor Farm. He walked, growing weary, and found neither the farm nor anyone to direct him until he turned a bend in the lane and there was a man laying a hedge.

Farm work isn't a spectator sport. Usually the only people around are other farmers, and if they're prepared to help they do and if not they pretend to be busy elsewhere. The man with the bill-hook looked at Daniel as if he were a stray tup.

Daniel nodded. "Hedging," he said inanely.

The man's eyes narrowed until they vanished in a net of creases carved into the wind-tanned skin. "No fooling you."

Daniel chuckled tiredly. "Sorry. I'm lost. I'm looking for Manor Farm."

The man pushed his cap back an inch and stared off into the middle distance. He was so tall that Daniel couldn't see where he was looking. Finally he grunted, "You're lost all right."

Daniel wanted to get this done. He wanted to find Cochrane's farm, find a quiet corner where he could wait until the man crossed the yard, and once he was out of sight again quit these alien hills. Almost he was past caring whether Cochrane was the killer or not, if he could just be sure. "Do you know where it is? Or should I ask someone who isn't so busy?"

The man gave a snort that might have been laughter. "It's

a good step from here. You could walk it, or you could wait a few minutes 'cause I'm going that way myself."

There was a Land Rover parked in a gateway, a border collie snarling through the windscreen. Daniel leaned gratefully against the bumper. "I'll wait."

Hedging is slow, painstaking work. It was soon obvious to Daniel that the job would take hours. But the sun was at its zenith so perhaps the labourer meant to knock off for lunch.

"You looking for Neil, then?" the man asked without looking round.

Daniel should have known that if he started seeking directions someone would ask him why. He stumbled for an answer. "I don't know him. I just—need to see him."

But the man was more interested in his hedge than Daniel's business. "Pass us the mallet." He hammered in another pair of hazel stakes, kept weaving. Finally he straightened up. "That should hold it. All right, boy, you want that lift now?"

As the Land Rover climbed higher Daniel was glad he hadn't proceeded on foot. It was bleak, rough and isolated. The lane deteriorated as they went, first to a single track, then to a cart-track with grass growing up the middle, finally to a mere stony path.

"He doesn't get many visitors," ventured Daniel.

The farmer sniffed dourly. "Even the Jehovah's Witnesses have given up on Neil."

"Do you live nearby?"

"Not far."

"You know him, then."

"Much as anyone."

Daniel tried to draw him out. "A bit of a hermit, I'm told."

"You could say."

When the lane was just a gap between field-stone walls, a structure weathered the same colour as the hill firmed against the backdrop and became a barn, a low cottage huddled beside it. Daniel glanced awkwardly at his companion. The last thing he wanted was to be dropped in the farmyard with Neil Cochrane staring out of the kitchen window. "I'll walk from here."

"That's OK," said the man at the wheel, "I've got business here myself."

This wasn't going according to plan. Daniel had thought he could establish, once and for all, whether Cochrane was the man he'd seen without the farmer ever knowing he'd been here. Now it seemed he was going to meet him face to face. At least they wouldn't be alone. And the man on the pier had not got as good a look at Daniel as Daniel had at him. If Cochrane wasn't the killer he certainly wouldn't recognise him, and he might not even if he was.

Which wasn't enough to blind him to the danger he was in. He was a mathematician, used to thinking in terms of percentages. But a sixty percent chance he could get away with this was still a forty percent chance that he couldn't. That Daniel's face, glimpsed for a moment on a dark and violent night, had burned itself into the killer's brain as the killer's had into Daniel's. That Cochrane would know him, and know he had nothing left to lose. The answer to his question could be the last thing Daniel would ever know.

Time ran out. The Land Rover stopped in the yard and the driver got down. "You try the house, I'll try the barn."

Daniel climbed out slowly, looking round. So this was Manor Farm. It was hard to believe anyone lived here. The low stone house had a few rags of curtains at the windows but the barn had lost part of its roof to a winter storm and grass was growing through the cobbles of the yard. The name was scandalously misleading. Probably it had once been Menner Farm, like the down.

No wonder, Daniel thought, taking in the desolation, that Neil Cochrane was everyone's favourite murder suspect. Living alone, like this, would have been all the proof some people needed. The same people who'd burned him out, for what they no doubt considered equally good reasons. Someone was to blame for what had happened, and this time he was the outsider.

Surrounded by the ruins of the man's existence Daniel suddenly saw what Deacon had seen: that to people who knew neither of them, he and Cochrane had enough in common to seem like natural allies. The recognition shocked him to the core. This was how people saw him? Not just odd but suspect? Dangerous? He was used to being alone. He'd always thought it was from choice. Now he felt not so much a loner as an exile.

He tried to put the thought behind him. He needed to concentrate on what he was doing. He couldn't afford to be taken by surprise, not for a moment. He needed a plan.

There was no one in sight. He could make a run for the lane, and maybe Cochrane would never see him. Or maybe they'd meet on the track, unwitnessed. Coming here had left him with no risk-free options. Going through with it, finding out what he had been so desperate to know, might entail no greater danger than taking off alone into these barren hills. There was still that sixty percent chance that when Cochrane answered his door he'd see a stranger. In which case he'd ask what he wanted, and Daniel would need to say something. He couldn't think of a single reason for coming here except the real one.

He knocked at the kitchen door, waited a moment, then knocked again. If the man came he'd—ask about puppies! Yes. Cochrane kept sheep, he was bound to have sheepdogs, if he had dogs he probably had puppies. If he hadn't he'd send Daniel away. If he had—well—maybe Paddy would like a puppy…

A minute passed and still no one appeared. Perhaps Cochrane was out on the hill and the house was empty. In that case, Daniel thought, daring to hope, they'd have to leave. He could come back another time, when he'd worked it out more carefully; with back-up, in a car; or not at all. If he got away from here in one piece it might be a long time before he played at private detectives again. He turned back to the Land Rover, ready to leave.

Behind him the plank door groaned open.

Too late to run, impossible to hide. He filled his lungs and turned to face the man who just might need him dead.

"Found what you were looking for?" asked the man who'd brought him here.

Daniel shut his eyes a second and let the pent breath go. "No," he said then. "I thought you…"

His eye travelled through the doorway into the kitchen. The place was derelict. Not just squalid—a man living alone can exude squalor as if from his pores—but a ruin. He blinked. "I don't understand. Why did you bring me here?"

"You were looking for Neil Cochrane."

"He doesn't live here. Nobody's lived here for years."

"He comes here. When he has things to do he don't want to do at home. Nobody knows about this place, see. There's only an old trod up to it, you saw that. No mains water, no electric, no phone. It don't even appear on maps now. To find it you'd have to know to look."

Teaching is a great way to learn. Daniel had learned as much from his pupils as he'd ever managed to teach them, and one thing was the art of hearing what wasn't being said. Those synapses concerned with interpreting unspoken messages were firing now. He was being told something, and it wasn't what the man was saying or even what he was implying.

Daniel moistened his lips. He looked at his companion as if for the first time. A big man, tall and rangy, still quite strong enough in his mid-fifties to break Daniel across his knee.

It took him a second to find his voice, and then it was low and as hollow as a rotten log. "I've been pretty stupid, haven't I?"

The man nodded, watching him curiously. "I guess."

Daniel felt as if someone had not so much pulled the rug from under him as excavated the ground. He hadn't suspected, not for a moment. Now he was desperately trying to work out how bad a mistake that had been.

But it was too late even to wonder. Running wasn't an option. The man who killed Chris Berry had kept pace with a champion fell-runner. Daniel didn't fool himself he could cover ground faster than that with the hounds of hell on his heels. Most of the exercise he took was mental.

So maybe he needed to think more than he needed to run. Facing a man who was bigger, stronger and, despite his age, fitter than him, on his own territory and in a situation he had himself created, mental agility was Daniel's only advantage.

He made himself look the farmer in the eyes. "You're Neil Cochrane. Well, I'm Daniel Hood."

Cochrane's shoulders filled the door. "Sonny, I know who you are."

THIRTEEN

JACK DEACON HAD promised himself an early night. He'd
barely been home since the murder of Chris Berry three days
before: the food was going stale in his fridge and the cat was
thinking of sub-letting the place.

Also, he was not blind to the fact that useful work might be
done round his living-room fire this evening. With the ruins of
his own home still smoking on the shore, Daniel Hood might
be more co-operative. And if he wasn't, if Deacon couldn't
shake his story with all evening to do it, with the man buried
in one of his sagging armchairs and sipping his Scotch, it was
maybe time to look at the alternatives. Like, perhaps Hood was
right. Perhaps Neil Cochrane didn't murder Chris Berry.

For Deacon even to think that way was an evolutionary advance comparable to the opposable thumb. And now he was
prepared to listen to his witness, the witness had disappeared.
Daniel might not have been the answer to a detective's prayer,
but he was still the only one who'd seen Berry's killer and
Deacon couldn't afford to lose him.

All hope of a quiet night abandoned, Deacon put every officer he could find onto the streets, into the pubs and clubs
and anywhere else that casual malice might spawn a genuine
threat. When the attempt on his life failed, had those pillars
of the community whose primary function was supporting the
local hostelries turned to abduction? Deacon hoped that if he
trawled enough public bars he'd learn what had happened to
Daniel Hood.

Or rather, half of him did. If some kind of plot had been
hatched, he'd find out who had taken Daniel and where he

was, and soon after that he'd have them in custody. But the other half of him hoped fervently that he'd got this wrong and that wasn't what happened at all. The only reason anyone could have for taking Daniel was to get information out of him. They could have had him for twelve hours by now. You can do a lot of damage to someone in that time, particularly if he hasn't got the information you want.

The alternative was that Daniel had left Deacon's house of his own volition and gone about his own business. Deacon called the bank manager at home. A man whose house had burned down trying to obtain funds without any form of identification would be sufficiently unusual that Mrs Carter should remember. But she was sure Daniel Hood hadn't got as far as the bank.

He questioned his neighbours. No one had seen Daniel leave the house, but if a mob had gathered at his door someone would have noticed. So maybe he…went for a walk? It was a stupid thing for a hunted man to do, but Deacon had known Daniel was not entirely rational. He might have gone out simply to prove he wasn't afraid to.

If he'd wanted fresh air, he might have gone to the shore or the cliffs. Deacon despatched teams to begin house-to-house inquiries along both routes.

By nine-thirty he had established that Daniel Hood, walking alone, had taken the path up the cliff a little after ten that morning. He was seen walking up and, a few minutes later, running down. No one seemed to be chasing him but he appeared distressed.

The path came out on Edgehill Road which, hugging the underside of the cliff, would have taken him into town the back way. But no one else recalled seeing him. It might simply have been that, by running out of puff and dropping back to a walk, he became less conspicuous. Or something might have happened to him about then.

The bus-station was at the end of Edgehill Road. Deacon got a list of the services leaving between ten-forty, when

Hood was last seen, and eleven-fifteen, by which time he would have been in town if nothing had stopped him. Then he got the names and home numbers of the drivers.

Eight local services and four regional ones left the terminus in that thirty-five minute slot. Deacon could have spent another hour contacting and questioning twelve drivers, except that he got lucky. The second number on his list was the driver of the Guildford bus.

Yes, he remembered Daniel. He had to scrape his fare together in coppers and scraps of silver, and then he wanted directions to Menner Down.

Deacon's heart thumped within him. Menner Down: was that all he said?

No, he was looking for Manor Farm. The driver didn't know where it was, and no one on the bus volunteered the information. He stopped at the Three Downs and Hood got off.

A meddlesome little ant was tramping up and down Deacon's spine, setting up an itch in that part of his central nervous system which recognised when he wasn't getting the full story. It really didn't make any difference but he wanted to know. "You knew who he was, then."

He seemed to hear the driver shrug. "I couldn't have told you his name. But yes, I knew who he was. I live in Dimmock. Everyone knows who he is."

Deacon nodded slowly. "You know who lives at Manor Farm, too, don't you?"

There was a brief pause this time. "Sure."

Deacon considered. He was a policeman, which meant he was responsible for people's deeds, not their consciences. But he couldn't let it go. "Three nights ago Daniel Hood risked his life trying to prevent a murder. Last night, by way of thanks, the good citizens of Dimmock burned his house down, and would have done it with him inside if he'd been there. And this morning, when he got on your bus in a distressed state with nothing to his name but small change, though you knew who he was and where he was going you made no attempt to stop him. You didn't even contact us. You let him off your bus in the middle of nowhere, and no one's seen him since. When he turns up dead in a ditch, you can be proud that you got him where he wanted to go."

He heard the man sniff. "I'm just a bus-driver. I don't ask people if their journeys are necessary. I take their fares and I give them a ticket. I let them out at the stop nearest their destination. That's the extent of my interest in their lives."

Jack Deacon wanted to reach down the phone, grab the man by the throat and shake him. But he recognised the impulse as unreasonable. No one had made Daniel Hood go to Manor Farm, only his own meddlesome ant. All the time Deacon had known him, he couldn't meet a mystery without trying to solve it or be aware of a threat without confronting it. If Deacon was going to be angry at anyone it should be himself. He'd kept playing the guilt card until Hood believed it, blamed himself for a boy's death. Of course he did: it was what Deacon wanted. He should have known then that Hood wouldn't settle for regrets, that he'd try to atone for them.

His hand on the phone was rigid with fury. He ended the call before he said something he'd rue later. Then he phoned the police station, and six minutes after that he and Charlie Voss were on their way to Manor Farm.

BRODIE SAT BY THE phone, willing it to ring. It wouldn't. She kept telling herself that no news was good news but she wasn't convinced. If Daniel was safe, wherever he was and whatever he was doing he'd have let her know before now. She picked up the phone to make sure it hadn't inexplicably died, but the dialling tone was steady. No fault, then, just no calls. Brodie sat beside it and waited.

DANIEL HADN'T wanted this encounter, certainly hadn't planned to make a fool of himself like this. Despite that he

had achieved what he came here for. He had seen the face of
Neil Cochrane. And he hadn't seen it before.

He no longer had any doubts. In the craggy, creased, auto-
cratic face before him he could see the man, ten years younger, whose photograph he had been shown but not the one he'd
seen on Dimmock pier three days before. They might be of
an age, of a generally similar appearance, but they were two
men. Which meant Daniel was not responsible for the death
of Kevin Sykes. Having that load lifted from his shoulders was
a benediction. He felt himself grow light, shriven of guilt.

Cochrane said gruffly, "And I'm damned if I know what
you've got to smile about."

Daniel couldn't help it. "Don't you see? Half Dimmock believes you killed one boy on the pier and another at the old
brewery. The police believe it. I know they're wrong. When
I convince them you'll be off the hook."

"That's good," nodded Cochrane phlegmatically.

Daniel didn't understand his manner. "Come to the police
station with me. Then Inspector Deacon can stop trying to pin
the guilt on you and start looking for the man I saw."

Cochrane came out of the house and shut the door behind
him. Daniel had to stop himself shooing the man along like
a sheep. His own sense of urgency was such that he couldn't
believe that Cochrane wasn't already racing down the cart-
track spitting stones from under the Land Rover's wheels.

The farmer looked down at Daniel through narrowed eyes.
"You'll recognise him again, will you?"

"I think so. When the police find him. Which they won't
do," he added pointedly, "until we make them go and look."

Cochrane curled a thin lip at him. "Slow down, young feller, there's time enough. Not much in life is as urgent as people think."

But Daniel's mind was buzzing. "You don't understand.
For the last two days people have been telling me I made a
mistake that cost someone's life. Now I know I didn't, I have
to tell them!"

Cochrane sniffed. "Two days isn't very long. Everyone I know has suspected me of murder for ten years. It's of little consequence to me if they go on thinking it another hour or two."

"But—" Daniel got a grip on himself, knotting his fingers behind his yellow head. "All right. You're used to being blamed for something you didn't do. I'm not. I want to put the record straight. If you don't care about proving your innocence, will you help me prove mine? I've already had my house burned down. I'd like this sorted out before anything else happens."

Cochrane squinted at him. "You got another house?"

Daniel stared. "Of course not."

"Then what can happen? You've already lost everything you own. And nobody's going to find you up here."

The countryside is different to the town. Obviously: one has pavements while the other has trees, you can get tradesmen and take-aways in town but let your kids run wild in the country. But these are superficial matters. The real difference between urban and rural life is one of mentality. Townsfolk crave order: if something goes wrong they want to know whose job it is to fix it and when it'll be done. Country people, on the other hand, are self-sufficient. If something goes wrong, mostly they fix it themselves, when it suits them. Time obeys other clocks. Today means today or maybe tomorrow; now means when there's nothing better to do.

Daniel gave a little snort that was mostly amusement. "Thanks for reminding me. Just for a moment there I thought things could get worse."

Cochrane chuckled too, darkly. He looked Daniel up and down. "Describe this man you saw on the pier. He was a big feller—my size?"

"As near as I could judge."

"What did he look like?"

"He looked like you," said Daniel. "Your age, your height, your build. Even his face. I can see why people would think it was you—but it wasn't. I'd stake my life on it."

"And you never saw him before."

"If I had, he'd be behind bars by now."

Cochrane gave that some thought. A flicker of annoyance crossed his rough-hewn features. But the truth of what Daniel was saying was self-evident: if he'd known who the killer was he wouldn't be here.

Another thought occurred to the farmer. "So there's this big strong feller on top of the pier, armed with a wheel-brace and standing over the body of the boy he's just brained with it. And you're shouting at him and waving your torch at him, and I dare say you threatened him as well, did you?"

Daniel hadn't enough detachment to share in his dour amusement. He said simply, "I did everything I could think of. It wasn't much; it wasn't enough. I should have been able to stop it. I was right there…"

The humour faded from Cochrane's long face. "Did you think what you'd do if he came down to shut you up?"

Daniel shook his head. "It happened too quickly."

Cochrane nodded thoughtfully. "Events do that to a man. Sneak up on him and pounce when he least expects it. When he thinks something's in the past, only it rears up and grabs him by the throat again."

Daniel thought he understood. "After ten years you must have believed it was history. And though the police never caught the killer, the killings stopped. People knew that you were still around so they must have known they'd made a mistake."

Cochrane raised an eyebrow. "You reckon? They just thought I was smart. They thought I'd got away with murder. They tried burning my house down, once. I set the dogs on them."

Daniel wished they were having this conversation on the road to Dimmock, but since he seemed incapable of galvanising the farmer into action he might as well ask what had puzzled him. "Why was everyone so sure it was you? If there'd been any evidence the police would have charged you. Since there wasn't, why were they so certain they knew who the killer was?"

Cochrane's eyes narrowed till they vanished under the shaggy brows. "One of the boys did some work for me. I had some local lads up picking a field of beets. Paid them fifteen quid each, I did. Then one of them gets himself killed and the police are all over me. Did I make advances to him? I did not, I said, in farming you get paid when the job's done and not before."

"That was it? That was all?"

Cochrane watched him. "What did you think—I left my Farmers Union card at the scene of the crime? They were clutching at straws. Some of the stuff they can do now, the science stuff, they couldn't do then. They had to do it the old-fashioned way: find a suspect and hammer a confession out of him."

Daniel caught his breath. "They beat you up?"

"No; but they tried to make me think they were going to. I told them, you can do what you like, it won't alter a thing. I don't have to prove I didn't kill that boy, you have to prove I did. They didn't have a case and I knew it as well as they did. In the end they let me go.

"But that bastard Ennis made damn sure everyone in Dimmock knew who he suspected. That town's treated me like dirt ever since. It don't bother me—I didn't have any friends there before. But I don't reckon to owe them much either."

"Ennis retired. Inspector Deacon's in charge. But you know that—he paid you a visit after Chris Berry was killed."

"Oh yeah," growled Cochrane. "Seemed to think he'd catch me washing blood off my wheel-brace. Damned fool. How did he think I had my wicked way with an eighteen-year-old fell runner who was damn near as big as me and twice as fast?"

It had always been the biggest obstacle to belief. But it applied to whoever killed the athlete. "Somebody did. Took him by surprise, I suppose, overpowered him before he could put up a fight."

The farmer snorted disparagingly. "It don't make no sense. If he was overpowered, how come he got free again? None of the others did."

"The others were younger. Smaller."

"It ain't a question of size when you've got a chain pad-locked round your ankle!"

This was the first Daniel had heard of a chain. Of course, Cochrane was here ten years ago, had every reason to re-member the details. Daniel shuddered. "Is that how…?"

"So I heard," grunted the farmer.

"I read the article in *The Sentinel*. It said one of the vic-tims had cuts on his leg, but…" His voice petered out as the picture resolved from the mental static. "Oh dear God."

"Animal in a trap'll do that," said Cochrane. "Gnaw its own foot off. It reckons it's better to live on three legs than to die."

"They were *children!*" whined Daniel. "And one of them was desperate enough to try to amputate his own foot? What with, for heaven's sake? Whoever kidnapped him was hard-ly likely to leave a knife handy!"

Cochrane shrugged. "Maybe he found a bit of glass or something."

"I doubt he'd have left him a beer-bottle either!"

"I don't know what it was. Something with a sharp edge, just. There's all sorts of garbage lying round on a—"

He stopped dead, and for a moment thought he'd stopped in time. Daniel Hood was still preoccupied with the image be-hind his eyes, of a terrified youth trying to saw through his leg because the alternative was worse. He wasn't an interro-gator, trained to pick up every slip and nuance. Cochrane had survived hours of interviews with trained interrogators be-cause he knew how careful he had to be. This young teacher with the troubled eyes behind his bottle-bottom glasses had tempted him into an indiscretion precisely because he seemed harmless.

But maybe the error was of no consequence. He'd strangled it at birth: he hadn't actually said anything. Hood would have to know what he was about to say in order to recognise it as a slip, and he didn't seem to be paying that much attention.

But Cochrane needed to be sure, even if the process of

making sure planted the very suspicion he had to erase. He said nothing more but went on looking at Daniel until Daniel felt his gaze. "What?"

"Nothing. You looked a bit shaky there."

Daniel had never been robust. He'd grown from a small pale child to a small pale youth and finally a small pale adult. He was used to people asking if he'd been ill, and it wasn't twelve months since he was offered a half-price admission to a museum. Until he was sixteen he'd entertained faint hopes that a late spurt of growth would leave him towering over classmates, shaving twice a day and fighting off selectors for the county rugby squad. Then he'd accepted what nature had been trying to tell him, that his genes didn't code for substantial and he'd better find other ways of being happy.

These days his lack of stature didn't concern him, but he still wished he was tougher. His eyes would fill, his stomach turn and his knees buckle faster than anyone he knew, including women. He didn't know if it was a physical thing, entirely outside his control, or if he just thought too much and empathised too much in which case it was a self-inflicted injury. He found it a damned inconvenience.

He smiled thinly. "I'm all right. I just— For a moment it got to me. I'm not very good at detachment. I let things haunt me even when there's nothing I can do about them."

He took a deep breath and straightened his shoulders. "Sorry, what were you saying? That there's all sorts of garbage lying around on a farm?"

And that was it. He'd heard what Cochrane hadn't said, and any second now he'd recognise its significance. When he did he'd understand his own error. He knew Cochrane was innocent of Chris Berry's murder. He'd thought that meant the farmer had no secrets to guard.

Cochrane sighed too and leaned back against the Land Rover. His gaze crossed the mossy yard to the barn. "I never told you about this place, did I, or why I brought you here?"

"Not really."

"My father bought it forty years back. He wanted the land and the house came with it. There was a tenant once but it's been empty for years. The barn's useful for storage—gear I only use a couple of times a year can be left here out of the way. Nobody comes. I don't think anyone remembers it's here."

"So—why are we here?"

"So we won't be disturbed."

Before he had time to react to that, Neil Cochrane's fist came from nowhere and smashed across his face, spilling him onto the cobbles, his wits cartwheeling in one direction, his glasses in another.

The yard was bathed in spring sunshine, but for Daniel it vanished in a mist of colour of ox-blood shot through by fireworks. He didn't exactly lose consciousness. But the force of the blow left him floundering, physically and mentally. He didn't feel himself hit the ground. For a minute he was quite literally unsure which way was up.

Trying to catch his breath he choked on bubbling blood. He tried to get up, because whatever was going on he'd be better on his feet than face down in the dirt, but his balance was shot. He pushed himself as far as his knees before the wheeling stars unbalanced him and he felt himself slide sideways towards the ground.

Strong hands gripped him. He shook his head numbly, trying to clear his vision, but the other man's face remained out of focus, indistinct. He tried to ask what happened but though his broken lips formed the question-mark he couldn't formulate the question. He had the idea it had been some kind of accident.

The farmer peered into the white and bloody face before him and saw the pale eyes roll with concussion. "And the answer to your next question," said Neil Cochrane softly, "is no. The police never found this place before, and I doubt they'll find it now."

FOURTEEN

CHARLIE VOSS DROVE. Jack Deacon spent much of the journey talking to Constable Huxley on his mobile.

A mobile phone was a bit wasted on Constable Huxley. Deacon held the instrument at arm's length. He'd have got much the same result by switching it off and opening the car window.

"What times did you do the drive-bys at Manor Farm?" he asked, and immediately removed his ear from the fall-out zone.

"Eight-fifteen and eleven-ten this morning," boomed the response, "and again at two-fifty this afternoon. I came off duty at four, and Constable Vickers was out there again shortly before five."

"Any sign of activity?" Again the rapid switch of phone from head to wing-mirror.

"I observed him for seven or eight minutes on the first occasion," reported Constable Huxley. "From the nearest public road, about two hundred yards from the farmyard. He appeared to be feeding his animals."

"Did he see you?"

"I think so, sir," said Huxley stolidly. "Either that or he was celebrating some kind of victory."

"Did you see him again mid-morning?"

"Yes, sir. He was putting tools in the back of the Land Rover."

Deacon's tone hardened. "Tools like a wheel-brace?"

"No, sir. Tools like a bill-hook, a sledge-hammer and some wooden stakes—that kind of tools. Hedging tools."

Deacon, a city-dweller to his boot-soles, was impressed.

But none of the victims had suffered injuries which could be attributed to a hedging kit. No slashes, no stakes pounded through their hearts, and the head injuries that were consistent with an iron bar could not have been inflicted with a sledge-hammer. It sounded more like farm maintenance than murder. "Did you follow him?"

"No, sir. I waited ten minutes, but he still wasn't ready to leave so I continued with my rounds."

"And at two-fifty?"

"At two-fifty I observed him returning to the house. He parked in the farmyard, gave me a wave and went inside."

"Would you say he was in a panic, at all?"

"No, sir. Sir?"

"Constable?"

"Has something else happened?"

"Hood's missing," Deacon explained briefly. "He was last seen mid-morning, heading for Manor Farm. But you saw no sign of him?"

"No, sir."

"But Cochrane left the farm in the middle of the morning."

"Yes, sir. But he was back there by early afternoon."

"How long does it take to…?" He left the sentence unfinished, cleared his throat. "Constable Vickers, you said." He rang off, called the station and got patched through to the area car. "Vickers, have you been round by Manor Farm recently?"

"About five o'clock. There was no one about. I thought I'd go back about ten."

"Meet us there now."

Voss waited until he'd rung off. Then, keeping his eyes on the road, he said quietly, "Even if Hood found him, that doesn't mean Cochrane hurt him. He had no reason to. Daniel's the one who keeps insisting Cochrane didn't do this."

"Unless he changed his mind when they met face to face."

"In which case we were wrong. We should have held an identity parade on Monday morning."

It wasn't meant as a criticism, Voss really did mean "we"

as in CID, but Deacon knew the call had been his. If Hood was dead, the responsibility was his too. He gritted his teeth and said nothing.

Charlie Voss, glancing at him sidelong, saw the anger and also the fear behind it. He said quietly, "We don't know what happened. It may not be what we're thinking. Daniel may be safe."

Deacon was least able to accept kindness when he needed it most. "Nobody's seen him for ten hours, sergeant! Wherever he is, I don't think he's safe!"

"Then what do you think? That Cochrane kidnapped the one man in Dimmock who *didn't* think he was a murderer, and raped him and bludgeoned him to death, and drove off with the body in the back of his Land Rover on a day when he knows we're watching him? It makes no sense, sir. If he was that reckless you'd have caught him ten years ago."

Deacon stared at him. "So what are *you* saying? It's a co-incidence? Daniel convinced himself the only way he'd know the truth was by confronting Cochrane. So he came up here and vanished, but it's still just a coincidence? He's fine, he's just keeping out of sight and not telling anyone. Last night he wouldn't sleep in Hastings because it might look he was running away. But today he's crawled into a hole in the ground and pulled the grass over the top of him—and he knows what we're going to think, what his friends are going to think, and he doesn't care? *That's* what I'm supposed to believe?"

Voss gave up looking for a silver lining. "No, I don't believe that either. We're going to find him dead, aren't we?"

Manor Farm appeared in the headlights; as Voss braked the lights of the area car appeared in his mirror. This was neither a discreet surveillance nor a card-making exercise: it was a murder inquiry, and both cars sped up the concrete lane as if there was just the chance they could prevent another tragedy.

But the farmyard was as Constable Vickers had left it four hours before: empty and quiet. There were no lights showing in the house or buildings, and no response to Deacon's fist hammering on the door. He tried it and found it locked. He tried it again, with his shoulder this time, and found it open.

"Charlie, with me. You men, check the outbuildings. Watch your backs. If you see or hear anything, call me."

"Sir?" It was Constable Vickers. "What are we looking for?"

"We're looking for whatever's here," said Deacon tersely. "It might be Hood, it might be his body. It might be signs of a struggle. Just—don't miss anything." He stalked into the house with Sergeant Voss on his heels.

They found nothing. They quickly checked every room in the house, and then went back to do a more thorough search. There were no signs of a struggle, or the clean-up that would have been necessary to conceal one. Deacon glowered at Voss as if it was his fault.

Constable Vickers was calling in the farmyard. "Sir? Down here, sir. We've found something."

A moment before, when they had nothing, Deacon had been angry and frustrated. Now he felt his heart sink through his belly. "Damn." He went downstairs and headed for Willis's torch.

They caught up with the constable just inside the barn. "What is it?" asked Deacon. "A body?"

"In a manner of speaking," said Willis.

"Either it is or it isn't!" snapped Deacon.

"It is," said Willis. He shone the torch. "But it isn't Daniel Hood's body. It's a dog."

They stood together looking down at the shaggy black and white fur, clotted with blood, flat as an empty glove, and at first there was a sense of anticlimax. Then the significance of their discovery dawned on them: what it means when a shepherd shoots his dog.

Voss put it into words. "He isn't coming back."

THE MIST IN HIS head came between Daniel and any kind of action. He couldn't have fought off Neil Cochrane, but he might have given him the slip except for the mist. It infiltrated the connections between his brain and limbs so he couldn't rely on them. He could think, at a fairly basic level, but he couldn't initiate the simplest actions.

Cochrane's face loomed level with his own. Daniel wasn't sure if he was kneeling in the dirt too or if he'd lifted Daniel to his feet. He was getting no feedback from his body.

He could just about put a simple thought into words. His swollen lip got in the way but he concentrated on making himself understood. "Mistake," he mumbled. "You're making a mistake."

"You reckon?"

Daniel could hear the words but he couldn't make sense of them. He felt his wits failing. He knew he was in deep trouble but he didn't know why. He said roughly, "Let go of me," and tried to shake himself free.

There was that in Neil Cochrane's gaze which might, in other circumstances, have seemed like compassion. "All right." He released his grip on Daniel's arms.

Daniel knew he had to put some distance between them, his life depended on it. He tried to back away from the farmer. But the sky cartwheeled around him, so did the buildings, then his knees turned to string and the last thing he saw was the mossy yard rushing towards him. He didn't feel his cheek collide with the cobbles. He didn't know anything more.

TIME PASSED. He wasn't sure how much. Sometimes Cochrane was there, sometimes he wasn't. Daniel hardly cared which. He was sick and disorientated, and his face ached.

At first he hovered on the borders of consciousness, his senses washing in and out like a tide. But after a time he started to feel steadier and, finding himself alone, thought this was a good time to leave. He hauled himself to his feet and set off doggedly for the barn door. But something stopped him before he'd gone two metres. When he'd worked out what he crawled back to the bed of straw he'd started from and hunched around his misery, defeated and afraid.

The chain muttered as the links slid together. It was pad-locked around his ankle. Even if Cochrane had been careless enough to leave something sharp lying around a second time, even if Daniel had been able to find it, he knew he hadn't the courage to save himself that way. He thought he was going to die here. And he still didn't understand why.

He must have slept. The fear and nausea were not enough to deny his body the respite it needed. When he woke his head was clearer. His immediate surroundings were an island of light in the deep shadow, and Neil Cochrane was standing over him with something in his hand.

Daniel yelped in panic and scrambled crab-wise in the straw, retreating as far as the chain would allow. Cochrane fol-lowed. But it wasn't a wheel-brace he had. He dropped Dan-iel's glasses onto his heaving chest.

After a second, moistening his lips, he put them on. The inside of the barn sprang into focus. The light was coming from a hurricane lamp hung on a beam. Beyond the barn door dusk was gathering in the yard.

All he could think to say was, "I *know* what I saw. It wasn't you."

Cochrane nodded. "That's right."

"Then…?"

"I didn't kill Chris Berry. I didn't kill the boy at the brew-ery. I *did* kill three boys ten years ago."

There was no ambiguity in that. It was either a lie or a state-ment of fact, and Daniel didn't think Cochrane was lying. Fear knotted up his stomach.

Cochrane moved closer. He lowered himself into the straw at Daniel's side. "I want to tell you about it. Then we'll de-cide what happens next. At least"—he flickered a graveyard grin—"I will."

FIFTEEN

"IT'S NOT IMPORTANT that you understand why I did it," said Neil Cochrane. He was sitting on the straw beside Daniel with his knees drawn up to his chest and his arms bridged across them, and his gruff voice had taken on an odd rhythmical cadence as if he were repeating a liturgy. "It's important you understand that I stopped. And, how hard that was."

Daniel was, physically as well as metaphorically, at the end of his tether. He couldn't put any more distance between himself and the madman so he had to deal with him. He could hear the quake in his own voice but he made himself finish. "You had to stop. The police knew who you were."

"The police!" He couldn't have got more scorn into the word with a trowel. "They knew nothing. They could prove nothing. Yes, they thought it was me; but there wasn't any evidence.

"That was half the pleasure, you know? Leading them by the nose. Knowing that they knew, and that they couldn't prove it. It didn't matter how often they pulled me in, how long they questioned me or how much time they spent searching my house. They were looking in the wrong place. They don't even know this place exists."

Daniel's voice was only a breath, but there was just enough anger in it to show that he knew the answer. "So what was the rest of the pleasure?"

Cochrane looked at him sidelong, knowingly. "Now, how do I explain that to the likes of you? It was only after I split your lip I was sure there was any blood in you."

Daniel gritted his teeth. "God in heaven," he swore, "you're not claiming that buggering little boys makes you a bigger man than me?"

Momentarily surprised, Cochrane frowned at him. "You watch your mouth, sonny."

"Or what?!!" demanded Daniel, reckless with despair.

"Or I'll make you wish you had," rumbled Cochrane.

"You're going to kill me!" yelled Daniel.

The farmer considered. "I never said that."

"You have to. I know what you did."

Cochrane shrugged. "Everyone in Dimmock reckons to know what I did. Hear me out, and then we'll talk about what happens next."

"I won't be your apologist," spat Daniel. Even as he said it he knew he was probably cutting the only life-line he would be thrown. "I'm not going to tell your story to the Sunday papers. I'm not going to tell them you had an unhappy childhood and it really wasn't your fault and—"

Cochrane struck out, a casual swipe with the back of his hand that sent Daniel reeling in the straw. "Shut up," he said mildly, "and listen."

He hadn't meant to start with why. He didn't owe anyone an explanation. But he couldn't tell the story without at least touching on the reasons.

"They say rape isn't about love, it's about hate; not sex but violence. I can only speak for myself, but I didn't hate those boys. It wasn't love either, but by God I admired them. They're perfect at that age: smooth and untouched. No past, only promise—they can be anything they can dream of. And I wanted them. I wanted them so bad I could scarcely breathe.

"Don't think I didn't fight it because I did. I fought it till it filled the whole of my head, till I couldn't think of anything else. I was already a middle-aged man, I'd never known I had that in me—either the wanting, or the stomach to do something about it. It seemed to come from nowhere. Suddenly I was aware of these beautiful young boys everywhere, and thinking how I could get them alone, and what I'd do to them if I did.

"And sure I knew it was wrong. Leastways, I knew I'd be damned if people found out. But then, people round here never had a good word for me beforehand. I didn't reckon their goodwill was worth having if it meant denying what every cell in my body was crying out for. But I was afraid. I knew what would happen if I was caught. I didn't want to go to prison. Men in prison have families, they have sons, they know there's no one looking out for them while they're inside. You go into prison for something like that, you better not count on coming out. Not all of you, anyhow. So I fought it."

He sighed. "That boy who came to lift my beets: Jamie Wilton, his name was. The minute I set eyes on him the fight was over. It was only a question of when, and how, and what then.

"I wasn't stupid. I didn't look at him when he was about the place. But afterwards… I'd heard them talking, see, about what they did of an evening. This boy belonged to some sort of youth group. I found out when it met, and what time it finished, and I let him get half way home one wet night and then I chanced along and offered him a lift. He was glad to see me. Reckoned to know me, see."

Cochrane paused for a moment, remembering. Possibly savouring. "I kept him for six hours. I knew that when I was finished with him I'd have to kill him. I made it quick. Poor little sod was crying his eyes out, swearing he'd never tell, but anybody'd have said the same in his position. I stove his skull in with the first blow—there wasn't time for him to feel anything. I left him at the pier. It was on his way home from the church hall, see. I wanted the police to think he'd been there all along."

He looked at Daniel then as a man might look at his priest, as if his confession somehow made them co-conspirators. Daniel felt his insides clench in resentment. But if he was alive because Cochrane needed someone to tell it would be madness to stop him. He kept reminding himself that listening wasn't the same as condoning.

Cochrane had expected more in the way of reaction. He

watched Daniel, head on one side, waiting. Then, disappointed, he shrugged. "So now I'd done what I'd dreamt of doing.
I'd had him, and I'd killed him, and as the weeks went on I
realised that I'd got away with it. And the funny thing was, as
soon as I felt safe the wanting began again. I tried to resist,
told myself I'd been there, done that, it wasn't worth the risk
just to do it again. But when the chance came I could no more
have walked away than flown."

He stretched out his legs, making himself comfortable.
"Peter Krauss. Funny name: foreign, I guess. I brought him
here too. Kept him for three days." He nodded at the giant tu-
bular toast-rack to which he'd attached Daniel's ankle while
he drifted in and out of consciousness. "Used that same chain,
the same padlock, and bedded him down in that last cubicle.
They're calf-racks, in case you don't know, left over from the
last tenant here. Never used them myself, except for the boys.
But it seemed kind of appropriate. What else were they except pretty young animals with a purpose to serve?"

"They were human beings!" blurted Daniel, the words torn
from him by grief. "They were people's sons; but for you
they'd have grown up to be people's fathers. They were desperately scared young boys, and you abused them and then
you killed them. And you dare tell me you felt some kind of
passion for them? You thought of them as cattle! You fed on
their terror."

He caught his breath and watched for Cochrane's big fist
to swing at him again. But Cochrane only shrugged. "I don't
expect you to understand. Another farmer might. We value our
beasts, take a pride in doing them well, but we don't lose sight
of what it's all in aid of. They're bred to be used. That boy
was here to be used. When the time comes, the beasts go to
the market and he went to the pier."

He chuckled, bleakly. "The second time, that bloody town
went daft. You'd have thought the Hellfire Club was meeting
every night in the Temperance Hall, not just little old me
scratching an itch every few months. You could hardly move

for police patrols and Neighbourhood Watchers and God knows what else. I thought I'd better lie low for a bit. Another five months passed.

"Then fate took a hand. I don't remember anyone try to hitch a lift with me before or since. He said he was heading for London because he'd fallen out with his da, and he'd left a note behind saying as much. It was like he was sent, and I'd have been crazy to send him back. I brought him up here."

A shadow passed across the granite features. "Gavin. That was his name: Gavin Halliwell. He was nothing to look at. A scrap of a boy, he didn't look like he'd had a square meal for months, I could have picked him up in one hand. But by God he had gumption. He didn't beg, he fought me. Every time. I had to knock the stuffing out of him every single time.

"I found myself half-hoping he'd escape. He *deserved* to, you know? He deserved better than to be spitted and then have his brains beat in by an old goat with no self-control. But if I'd let him go I'd have spent the rest of my life in jail, and that was never an option. And—I was enjoying him.

"Then I came up here one morning and found him lying in his blood. He'd been groping around under the calf-racks and come up with a bit of glass. God knows how it got there—it could have been there for years. He'd tried to cut his foot off. But the glass wasn't sharp enough to cut bone and he passed out."

Cochrane's lips compressed to a thin line. "That was the end of it. Not the police, not the idiots in town—that. I'd taken these boys because they were fresh and perfect and I wanted them; and two of them I'd smashed to pulp and the third I'd made desperate enough to butcher himself.

"I put him down there and then. I didn't feel to have any choice, but I didn't want him waking up still in chains. I knew it wasn't safe to go to the pier again so I left him at the dump. I felt badly about that, too—he deserved better. But I promised him it would end with him. There wouldn't be any more. I couldn't afford to let him go but I hoped it would be some consolation that he'd bought other boys' lives with his courage."

"Oh yes," hissed Daniel, "that must have made all the difference. To him, to his family…"

Cochrane rose in an abrupt movement and stood over the younger man, staring down at him. The meagre yellow light of the oil-lamp chased anger and disbelief around his face. "I can't make you out," he said roughly. "Do you *want* to die? You *know* what I'm capable of. You're not much more than a boy yourself, if I took the padlock off you still couldn't get past me. I could kill you as easy as scragging a chicken for the table. I could do other things first. You *know* that. And you sit there, not only passing judgement on me but telling me about it! *Do* you want to die?"

Daniel was shaking; he knew it was audible in his voice and hardly cared. "None of them wanted to die. They had all their lives ahead of them. Wives, children, careers—you didn't just kill them, you robbed them. *And* you desecrated the bodies. There may be lower forms of life around but you need to turn over stones to find it."

Cochrane snatched his hand back and Daniel flinched. The farmer frowned. "You *are* afraid of me. Of course you are. Then why are you trying to provoke me?"

Daniel swallowed. "Mr Cochrane, I know you can kill me. I can't stop you. And yes, I'm afraid. But since nothing I can say will alter what you're going to do, you might as well know that I despise you with every fibre of my being. I want you to be aware of that when you're smashing my head in with your wheel-brace." It took him two breaths to get that out.

Cochrane shook his head, deeply perplexed. "You remind me of that boy—Gavin, the last one. You've nothing in the world to fight me with, you know you're going to lose, and you still won't give in. I've known plenty of tough men, and I wouldn't have said you were one of them. But you are, aren't you? If I sawed you in half you'd have the words 'You can't make me' running right through."

Absurdly, perhaps half hysterically, Daniel wanted to laugh. He still believed at his heart's core that he was going

to die here. Cochrane couldn't afford to let him leave. He believed he was going to die and he didn't think there would be
anything heroic about it. He was telling Cochrane what he
thought of him because (a) he didn't think he had anything to
lose and (b) he wasn't sure he'd get another chance. He was
glad to have got it out without breaking down. If Cochrane
wanted to see him reduced to a sobbing, quivering jelly beg-
ging for mercy, he'd probably get his way. But for now, for
just this minute, Daniel still had command of himself. "Are
you finished?"

The killer looming over him shook his head slowly. "No.
I'm just coming to the important bit.

"I'm not a man of many virtues, but I gave my word and I
always meant to keep it. You can say it was in my interests
too—that bastard Ennis was getting too close for comfort, if
I'd made the least mistake he'd have had me. But I'm not sure
how much difference that made. I'd been careful, I'd have
gone on being careful—I think I'd have gone on getting away
with it. Only I gave my word, so I stopped.

"They call it Cold Turkey, don't they, when it's drugs.
That's how it felt—like I'd been high on something for
months and now I'd had my last shot. Knowing was like ice-
water in my veins. Knowing I couldn't do it again, I wanted
to more than I ever had before. I was crazy with wanting. I
found myself looking at people I knew—the apprentice at the
abattoir, the boy who was seeing practice with the vet, even
Motson's boy down the agricultural suppliers and he's got a
face his mother couldn't love.

"But I'd given my word, to a boy who died for it, and I kept
it. Somehow. I never stopped wanting, but I got that I could
want without thinking I could have."

He took a deep breath. Like the shadows crowding in, the
anger in which he moved poured into the mould of his body
and boiled behind his eyes. The light of the little lamp seemed
to fail before the strength of it, and Daniel felt icy fingers doing piano practice on his spine.

"I stuck it for ten years," said Neil Cochrane, his voice that particular quiet that is the only possible alternative to ranting fury. "Ten years. And then, when it was all in the past, when people had all but forgotten why none of them liked me, when my life was nice and simple with no secrets and no surprises, it started again. Someone was taking pretty boys. And not just taking them, not just killing them, but doing it *my way*. If he'd carved my initials on the bodies he couldn't have made it plainer!

"And then I had not that bastard Ennis but his damned rottweiler scratching at my door. Wanting my Land Rover, wanting my trailer, ransacking my house again. And questions, questions. Where was I, what was I doing, who saw me, how could I prove it?" His gaze slashed Daniel's face like broken glass. "Do you know the stupid part? When I had something to hide I had a story ready to tell. They couldn't shake me; I damned near convinced myself. When I hadn't done nothing I hadn't a thing to say for myself. I sounded like the worst kind of liar—a stupid one."

As a boy Daniel had been afraid for much of the time. Small, short-sighted and academic, he attracted bullies as a jam-jar draws wasps. He learned to hug the shadows, to have nothing and want nothing so as to offer no provocation to those who would take whatever he had. And mostly what they took was his self-esteem.

Finally something changed. One day he'd had enough. He was tired of being a victim, of keeping his head down and handing over his bus-fare to save bigger boys the trouble of mugging him. He realised he'd rather be mugged sometimes than afraid always. He started standing up for himself.

And the funny thing was, it was a sham. Underneath he was still scared. But if he could keep the secret, fake courage served as well as the real thing. People who used to bully him left him alone. And the longer he kept up the act, the less of an act it was. And though he still got the occasional bloody nose, he never emptied his pockets again.

Now he was afraid again. Death had him by the hair. He heard his breathing ragged in his throat and strove to control it, to free up those faculties which might yet help him. There were two things he was good at. One was thinking, the other was talking. He needed to control the panic in order to do either.

He said, "So you weathered the accusations when they were true, but you're going to prison this time when they're not? Where's the sense in that?"

Cochrane's eyes burned like coals. "Who says I'm going to prison?"

"Well—what do you *think's* going to happen? They can't prove you killed Chris Berry because you didn't. I could have proved you didn't, only now you have to kill me because you've told me what happened ten years ago! All you had to do was keep quiet and let me convince Inspector Deacon of your innocence. You'd have been safe for the rest of your life.

"Instead of which you drag me up here and start telling me things you should have taken to your grave! *Why?* You've told your story to someone you daren't let repeat it, and you've thrown away the best defence you could have had. And when I'm missed, you'll be the first person Jack Deacon will look for."

Cochrane nodded. "But he won't find me, and he won't find you. I could disembowel you outside in the yard, and no one would hear you scream and only the crows would find your carcass. You're mine, Daniel Hood."

"I could have saved you!" yelled Daniel in exasperation. "And now I can't. Deacon'll find this place eventually. You're going to spend the rest of your life behind bars because—because— Damn it, I don't even *know* why! All you had to do was drive me back to town and it was over. You were a free man. Now, maybe you shouldn't be, but if that was preying on your mind you'd have confessed years ago. You kept it together for ten years and then you threw it away. For nothing. You're going to destroy us both, for nothing."

Cochrane was looking at him, and there was enough light from the hurricane lamp for Daniel to see the muscles working at his cheeks and temples. He bent forward, thrusting his rugged unshaven face into Daniel's. "Look at me, damn you! I'm fifty-three years old. Ten years from now I'll be sixty-three. I can't do it all again. I can't spend another ten years burying something that won't stay buried. I haven't the time and I haven't the energy.

"Have you ever smoked? Done drink or drugs? Got in too deep with bad women? Dear God," he swore disgustedly when Daniel kept shaking his head, "I was right—there really isn't much blood in you. Well, *imagine* how it would be having to give up something that had you hooked like that. People try for years before they finally stop smoking. It's expensive, it's dirty and they *know* it's killing them, and they still can't quit.

"But I did. It was the most important thing in my life—you know that, you know what I was prepared to do for it, what I was prepared to risk—but I gave it up because I promised. I gave up the most special thing in my life, the thing that defined who I was, and I couldn't even boast about it."

The coals kindled again. "And then someone comes along and thinks he'll take what I set aside. What I still crave every day. More than that, he thinks I'll protect him. That was no coincidence—he thought he'd be safe if he could send the police after me. And it worked a treat. Give him his due, he's a clever sod. He knew how to get at Deacon. He did his homework, picked out the details that would make it look like I was back in business, then he went out to have himself some fun.

"And after ten years of self-denial, of living like a hermit because anything else would be too dangerous, I'm public enemy number one again! I've got policemen watching me and vigilantes trying to drink enough courage to take me on."

He thought he saw a glint of laughter behind Daniel's glasses. He couldn't have been more wrong, but he thought he was being mocked. His voice hardened. "That amuses you? The idea of a lonely middle-aged man chewing his fingernails to the knuckles to keep from doing something no normal person would want to do in the first place? Only to have someone else take what he so desperately wants and leave him with the bill? That strikes you as funny, does it?"

Daniel shook his head. "No."

But Cochrane didn't believe him. "You're laughing at me. Who the hell do you think you are, laughing at me?" Hands like the grab on a JCB gripped Daniel's shirt-front and lifted him bodily. "I'll wipe the smirk off your face, my lad. Let's see how funny you find it when you're dancing to *my* tune."

With a jerk he tore Daniel's clothes open from throat to navel and forced the sleeves off his shoulders, pinning his arms. His skin cringed in the cold air. Cochrane thrust him back against the straw wall, one hard hand around his throat, the other between them, flat against his chest.

The blood froze in Daniel's veins. He'd thought he was as frightened as he was likely to get. He'd been wrong about that too.

He wanted to say, Don't hurt me. But the words stuck in his throat. He was at the mercy of a man who'd been fighting his darkest desires for ten years. If that fight was now lost he couldn't imagine that the star-burst of Neil Cochrane's self-destruction would leave him standing.

He wasn't going to prison. He wasn't going to wait for the police so he had nothing to stop him doing whatever he wanted one last time.

SIXTEEN

THERE WAS NOTHING to be learned at Manor Farm. The man had gone and wasn't coming back. For a decade he'd weathered the worst that police suspicions and public opinion could do to him, and clung obstinately to his rough downland acres. If he'd left now there was a reason.

"I guess Daniel found him," Charlie Voss said quietly.

Deacon nodded grimly. "He wanted to know if he'd made a mistake. I guess he knows now."

"You think Cochrane killed him?"

"I think Cochrane killed him eventually."

"Then where's the body?"

Deacon shrugged. "He took him wherever he took the others. If any of them had been here we'd have found some trace. He must have taken them somewhere else."

"Them, yes," agreed Sergeant Voss. "He knew we'd come here and he meant to brazen it out. This time it's different. He didn't go looking for Daniel, Daniel came looking for him. Cochrane answered a knock at the door and there he was.

"Cochrane could have sent him packing, but if he had Daniel would have gone back to Dimmock and Cochrane would be here. Instead of which both men have disappeared and the dog is dead. Cochrane isn't coming back. Sometime this afternoon he decided he was never coming back. He fed the stock, destroyed his dog, shut the front door and left."

"Daniel recognised him," said Deacon. "He knew the game was up."

"Then why go somewhere else? He could have killed Daniel and left him with the dog. He could have shot himself, if that's what he intends. Why go somewhere else to do it?"

"He needed time. He knew we were watching him, he didn't know how long he'd have before the area car came back."

"It doesn't take that long to shoot a dog, a man and yourself," objected Voss. "One barrel each: you'd only have to reload once. You wouldn't have to reload at all if you were going to make a run for it."

"He didn't want to shoot Daniel," said Deacon gruffly. "Daniel's what he wanted the time for. He didn't go looking for him, but he couldn't resist when he turned up here. He doesn't shoot any of his victims. He rapes them and then he beats their heads in. For that he needed a little more time and a little more privacy than he could be sure of here."

Charlie Voss hadn't been doing this as long as Deacon, but he'd been doing it long enough that he could discuss horrendous deeds without batting an eyelid. He could reduce them to cyphers and solve them like a jigsaw, as an intellectual exercise, without really confronting the fact that these were actual events which overtook real, flesh and blood, terrified people. It was a necessary defence: you could agonise over the violated or tackle the violent but there wasn't the capacity in one human soul to do both. Voss was a policeman, not a priest. It was his job not to feel for the last victim but to protect the next. Professionalism required a degree of detachment.

But Daniel wasn't just a victim, someone whose file he was intimately familiar with but whose face he might not recognise in the street. Voss knew him, was talking to him only yesterday. It was impossible to think of him as just a name on a crime report. Voss knew how Cochrane treated his victims, but until now they had been strangers. He no longer had that comfort.

But he couldn't let the image of Daniel Hood's torment shatter his concentration. "So where did he take him?"

"If I knew that," growled Deacon, "I'd have nailed him ten years ago."

Voss was thinking. "Cochrane knows that. Wherever he is, he must feel pretty safe."

"Yes. So?"

"Two of the three boys were missing for days. He wanted his money's worth before he killed them. If he feels safe—if he doesn't think we can find him—maybe Daniel's still alive."

STILL THE PHONE was silent. At ten o'clock Brodie could sit beside it no longer. She wrapped Paddy in her duvet without waking her and carried her upstairs to Marta. Then she drove into town.

It wasn't that she expected to find him sitting on the pier gazing disconsolately at the wreckage of his home. She didn't expect to find him at all. But she needed to be doing something. Even pointless activity was better than none.

She parked at the pier, meaning to check the ruins of the concert-hall, but someone emerged from the shadows to challenge her.

"Can I ask what you're doing here, miss?" Then the young policeman recognised the face in the beam of his torch. "It's Mrs Farrell, isn't it? Sorry—I'm just watching for any unusual activity." He didn't have to say what he meant by that.

"I don't suppose you've heard anything?"

He shook his head. "Sorry, miss. But half the station's out looking for your friend. Mr. Deacon'll find him, don't you worry."

"They tried Cochrane's farm?"

"First place they went. There was no one there."

"No one?"

The constable knew what he was telling her, was pretty sure she understood too. "The place seemed to have been abandoned."

Brodie caught her breath. Finding Daniel alive and well would have been the jackpot, but finding Cochrane would have been a prize worth having. But Cochrane had gone? She could only see one way to read that, and she turned away with tears pricking her eyes and stumbled back to her car.

She drove like an automaton, barely aware of her surroundings, not caring where she went, no longer even looking for him, just driving and punishing herself.

So it was Cochrane all along. Daniel had seen him, he just hadn't recognised him. It was always the likeliest explanation. She should have told him that instead of speculating on alternatives. In a very real sense this was her fault. No one could bully Daniel, no one could make him do something he didn't believe in or not do something that he did, but he listened to Brodie. He valued her opinions. With his faith in himself shaken, more than ever he'd been open to her views. And instead of helping him face facts she'd confused him with fairy-stories. With his mind in turmoil, torn apart by hopes and fears, finally he'd lost his grip on reality and gone to Manor Farm to seek answers from the one man who knew them. She couldn't be more responsible for Daniel's fate if she'd sent him there herself.

For half an hour she drove in a kind of daze, dull and bereft. Eventually she started to recognise where she was, and she was on Fisher Hill. There was a light on above *The Attic Gym*. Brodie slowed the car, drawn there. She couldn't see what good it would do—if George Ennis had had any idea where Neil Cochrane took his victims he wouldn't have sat on the information for ten years. But she couldn't make herself drive past.

She parked in the side-street and went up the back way to the flat. She moved mechanically, without haste. She really had no idea what she was doing here. Perhaps she just needed someone to tell to make it real, and if she went home and told Marta she'd fall apart utterly. Telling a man she'd only known a few days would be easier.

She didn't expect anything from Ennis, unless maybe a cup of tea and a hanky. But he would understand better than most. They weren't friends: mere circumstance had brought them together and only now did they have something in common; but if she made a fool of herself she would never have to see him again. It all made her feel that this was where she needed to be. By the time she discovered it couldn't help another fifteen minutes of this endless night might be gone.

THINKING, AND TALKING. In his present extremity they were all Daniel could do; but then, they were all he could ever do. He forced the words to come.

"Is this it?" he gasped, and even though he was choking he managed to barb his tone with contempt. "Is this what it was for? Ten years of denying yourself—of denying your very nature—and you're finally tempted beyond endurance by a twenty-six-year-old maths teacher? And I thought I was a sad case.

"That boy you're so fond of whining about. The one you loved so much he tried to cut his foot off? You talk as if it was some kind of a gift to him, that he was going to be the last. But he was always going to be the last. You'd had enough. It wasn't doing for you what you thought it should, the police were closing in and it wasn't worth the risk any more.

"That's the truth of it, isn't it? You'd played with the toy until you were sick of it. Every time you did it you saw in those boys' eyes what you'd turned into, and it wasn't the rampant monster of your imagination but a despicable, pathetic man who had nothing to bring to a relationship of equals, for whom young boys were not the first choice but the only option. It was them or the goddamned sheep!"

Neil Cochrane stared at him in astonishment, too amazed to react to the insults. He thought he'd heard it all from young men desperate to escape: threats, tears, appeals to his better nature, even professions of regard. No one had tried bawling him out before. Perhaps that was what you got for abducting a teacher.

And it worked. Daniel's desperate tirade acted on the farmer like a stun-gun, seizing his muscles and disrupting his mind. For a moment he quite forgot what he'd intended, and by the time he remembered he was too angry to do it. Incandescent with rage, still holding Daniel by the throat he drove his other fist hard into his face. Then again, and again.

By then Daniel was dead weight. Cochrane let go and he slumped into the straw, his face a bloody mask and his eyes shut.

Cochrane stepped back, shuddering, trying to master himself. He wasn't shocked at what he'd done; he'd done much worse. He was shocked that he'd allowed himself to be taunted into doing it. He thought of himself as a phlegmatic man with one ungovernable passion. But for one vital minute Daniel Hood had taken control of him. Cochrane didn't understand why Hood wanted to provoke him, couldn't see that he'd brought another helpless, obstinate young man to the point where anything seemed better than letting events take their course. But he knew it had been deliberate, and that he'd done what was required of him by pounding Daniel senseless. That troubled him. He didn't reckon on being anyone's puppet. He stood back, staring down at the tumbled figure, limp as a rag doll in the straw.

THIS TIME WHEN Daniel stirred it was dark beyond the ambit of the hanging lamp. So he'd lost more time to the hard fists of the big man leaning over him. If Cochrane kept hitting him like that he was going to suffer brain damage. But then, while the alternative was the wheel-brace, it was probably a gamble worth taking. He was still alive, and he might not have been.

Cochrane leaned closer, and Daniel felt the big hands sitting him up against the straw and touching his face. In revulsion he raised an unsteady arm to defend himself; without rancour Cochrane batted it away and continued wiping the blood from Daniel's face with his handkerchief.

When Daniel could see him Cochrane sat back on his heels, sucking on his teeth. "You want to tell me what that was all about?"

Daniel vented a weary sigh. "Diversionary tactics. I'm just trying to survive here."

"By pissing me off?" Cochrane's voice rose incredulously.

"Seems to have worked," whispered Daniel, shutting his eyes again. "For the moment."

Cochrane shook his head in a kind of wonder. "Do you understand what I've been telling you?"

"Of course I understand," mumbled Daniel. "I just don't buy it."

"Don't buy *what?*"

"The whole redemption thing. The idea that, because of a promise to a dying boy, you turned your back on the cities of the plain and lifted up your eyes unto the hills." He wiped his mouth on the back of his hand. "Hell's bells, a religious conversion was about the only thing you left out."

Cochrane felt no further urge to hurt him, not in any way. If that was what Daniel had been hoping for, he'd succeeded.

"Redemption," said the farmer, tasting the word. "Is that what I was talking about? I suppose it is. You sacrifice something that matters to you, do your penance, and when it's done you're entitled to look to the future." His voice hardened. "Except after ten years of sacrifice someone snatches the future away. I did it all for nothing. Through no fault of mine, I'm back where I started, with policemen poking through my belongings and strangers hating me from a safe distance. Because somebody used me as a stalking-horse. I've been fighting this same battle for ten years, and now I'm back in the same damned trench!"

Daniel was watching him from under gathered brows. It wasn't compassion, much less sympathy, but he was beginning to comprehend the man's bitter sense of injustice. He looked for the right words. "You can't expect me to understand what you did. But stopping was an achievement. You can't turn the clock back, repair the damage you did, but stopping was the next best thing. I don't know about redemption but it was something to set against the harm you'd done.

"Then someone with his own agenda took that from you. The sense of atonement, of closure. He made a bonfire of your hopes to fuel his desires. I understand your anger."

Neil Cochrane searched Daniel's smeared face intently. He hadn't been this close to another human body for ten years and it took an effort of will to ignore the sensations it awakened. "Do you? Maybe you do."

"What I don't understand," said Daniel, "is why you didn't take what I offered. I believed in your innocence. You should have let me go on believing. You'd have been safe. I'd never have known any better."

"You would," said Cochrane, his voice low. "You'd have worked it out. I got careless. You weren't a policeman, I didn't think you were any danger to me, and I got careless. I don't think you noticed, but it was there in your head. You wouldn't have forgotten, or decided it was none of your business. Sooner rather than later you'd have wondered what it meant, and worried away at it until it came unravelled. I couldn't let you go."

Daniel licked swollen lips. "Are you going to kill me?"

Murderers, even psychopathic murderers, can seem as normal as the next man. It would be handy if those who'd done what Neil Cochrane had done moved in an aura of evil, because then they'd be easy to find and easy to stop. If Cochrane had looked wicked or insane Daniel would not be here now. He didn't. For most of the time he seemed no odder than his lonely lifestyle explained.

But the look behind his eyes was not normal. Like the facets of a fly's eye it comprised individual fragments that did not add up to a cohesive whole. Something was missing. He saw the same world other people did, comprehended it well enough to make it work for him, but there was no empathy. He didn't feel for other people. He knew the difference between right and wrong, but didn't feel the urge to be better rather than worse.

Three young boys had sat in the straw here, and asked the same question, and met that barren gaze for a reply. It wasn't that Cochrane was incapable of emotion, more that all his feelings were for himself. What he needed, what he wanted, what angered him. He'd looked on those boys as a hungry man looks at steak.

Dazed, afraid, chained and helpless, Daniel's situation was not so different to theirs. Like him they must have hoped against reason that somehow they could survive. That an opportunity for escape would arise, or a search party would stumble on this ruin in the hills. So they'd endured what he'd done to them and waited for the split-second when they could snatch back their lives.

But the moment had never come. Cochrane ended the waiting with a wheel-brace. Now Daniel wanted to know if his own story was going to end the same way. He thought he was ready for the answer, whatever it was.

But Neil Cochrane wasn't ready to give it. His intense but still oddly detached gaze, unplumbable depths hidden by impenetrable shallows, scanned Daniel's face as if what he saw there puzzled him. "You want to live?"

It was the sort of question that could be answered only very briefly or at immense length. Daniel said softly, "Yes."

"How much?"

Chills gripped his spine. "What?"

"How much do you want to live? What are you prepared to do to survive?"

Daniel swallowed. He knew the answer, he just wasn't sure it was what Cochrane wanted to hear. But how was he to judge? He couldn't second-guess a mind like that. For all he knew the truth *would* set him free. He said, "Almost anything, but not quite."

Cochrane went on staring at him for perhaps half a minute. Then, incredibly, he laughed. "I don't know if you're a brave man or a fool, Daniel Hood."

Daniel's voice shook. "Neither. I'm a frightened man who sees no point in lying."

"All right. Then, what *wouldn't* you do? Remember, this is your life we're talking about."

There was a danger that he could give Cochrane a target to aim for. But he knew too much about suffering to overestimate his capacity for it, so the list was short. "I wouldn't hurt someone else. I wouldn't let you hurt someone else."

"Who?"

Daniel blinked. "Anyone."

Cochrane raised a sceptic eyebrow. "You'd die to protect a stranger?"

Reduced to a sentence it sounded absurd: gallant and foolish and improbable. But Daniel knew both his strengths and his weaknesses, even if he wasn't always sure which were which. He knew this was something he could do, and that saving himself at another's expense wasn't. "Yes," he said simply.

Cochrane was nodding slowly. "A killer?"

His heart stumbled. "What?"

"The man you saw. The man who wasn't me. Would you tell me who he was?—if you knew."

"I don't know."

"But if you did."

"I'd tell the police."

"Yes. But would you tell me?"

He was determined on an answer. Daniel felt his gaze penetrating like knives. Finally he had to say something. He whispered, "No."

There was no common ground between them: a man who felt nothing for other people and one who would, if need be, lay down his life. It would have been easy to discount as hyperbole. But Neil Cochrane was unaccountably impressed by Daniel Hood. He didn't understand him, but then he didn't understand anyone except on the most superficial level. He didn't know why Hood in particular troubled him.

He sniffed. "Suppose I let you go. Would you tell the police about me?"

The answer was obvious, which meant Cochrane was testing him. "Yes."

"You'd tell them everything I told you?"

"Yes. Of course I would: you *must* know that. Whatever I

say now, you must know that if you let me go I'll tell the police what happened. Everything that happened."

Cochrane shook his head in disbelief. "And you think that, knowing that, I'm going to let you walk out of here?"

Daniel's voice was barely audible. For just a moment he'd dared to think there could be a way out of this. The disappointment was unbearable. "No."

"Turn round."

Daniel's eyes flared. "What?"

"You heard me. Turn round." When Daniel still didn't move Cochrane dragged him to his feet and shoved his face against the straw wall. "Keep still. This won't take a moment."

When someone with the power of life and death over you issues an instruction, the natural instinct is to obey. Daniel knotted his fingers in the straw, pressed his hot cheek against its spiky roughness, squeezed his eyes shut and waited, shaking with fear.

He could hear Cochrane behind him. The man seemed to be looking for something. "Here we are," he said mildly. "Now—"

But Daniel wasn't a dumb beast, waiting at an abattoir with no hope beyond the skill of the slaughterer. He was a man, and he wanted to live, and he didn't care if he angered his murderer. He'd made a credo of facing his enemies: he turned in defiance to face Cochrane.

He met the knotted end of a wheel-brace coming the other way.

SEVENTEEN

GEORGE ENNIS SAID, "Of course we looked for a bolt-hole. At the farm, out on the downs, even here in town. But we never found where he took them."

"He has Daniel there now," said Brodie.

Ennis breathed in and then out. "Then he's dead."

"No!" She wouldn't let herself think that. "You don't know that. He's alive until we find out different."

Ennis knew what he thought: that when Daniel Hood went alone to Manor Farm he gave himself up to a power neither he nor Cochrane could control. To Ennis he was already a shape on the ground with a chalk-line round him. But he could see the state Brodie was in, saw no reason to make it worse for her. "All right, then he's alive. Jack Deacon's looking for him, and he has all the information I ever had. I don't know how you think I can help."

"Neither do I!" wailed Brodie. "But someone has to."

Only when Ennis offered his handkerchief did she realise the tears were coursing down her face. Embarrassed, she took it and dried her eyes. "I'm sorry. I don't know what I'm doing here. I couldn't think where else to go."

"I'd help if I could."

"I know." She pulled herself together with an effort and a watery smile. "How's Nathan now?"

"Nathan? Why?"

"He was pretty upset last time I was here. You were having a go at me and he thought you were having a go at him."

"Oh. Yes." He seemed to have forgotten. "He's better now. Calmer."

"It must have been a terrible shock. At that age you think people live forever. Losing a close friend like that—"

"Yes," Ennis said again. "Look, I'm not sure how much good it'll do, but sitting and waiting is the hardest part. If you want we could join the search. We might get lucky."

She knew he didn't think so. He was humouring her, trying to help her through this. The tears welled again. "That's very kind of you. I could go alone?" The question-mark expressed the hope that he wouldn't take her at her word.

"No, I'll come. If we stumble on something there ought to be two of us." Also, he didn't think she should be driving. He shepherded her to his van. Extricating the big vehicle from the yard behind the gym took time and skill.

"Nathan must be a pretty good driver," said Brodie.

Ennis glanced at her. "Why do you say that?"

"For you to trust him with this last night. Most eighteen-year-olds have their hands full with the family hatchback."

Ennis shrugged. "You do what you have to when someone's in danger. It's only a van: if he'd put a dent in it, too bad. Machines are easier to fix than people."

He drove not to Menner Down where Deacon was concentrating his search but to the adjacent Frick Down. "We can broaden the search without getting in Jack's way."

Brodie nodded anxiously. She didn't dare speculate on the chances of success. If she had she'd have known they were minimal. She didn't look at Ennis for the same reason: it was in his face that he believed Daniel was already dead. But he was right, it was better to be doing something than nothing. Brodie threw herself into the search with the unreasonable dedication of the desperate.

But after they'd been threading the darkness for forty minutes, quartering the hillsides by lanes and tracks that twisted and doubled back and had them lost within half a mile of the main road, she knew they were never going to find Daniel this way. If he was alive he was a captive somewhere; if he was dead in a ditch they would drive past in the dark and never know. "We're just wasting time," she said hopelessly.

"Do you want to go home?"

But she couldn't bring herself to quit. It felt like abandoning Daniel to his fate. "Soon."

So they just drove, not even looking any more, going through the motions. At some point they crossed from Frick Down onto Chain Down. Further on they could see the lights of many vehicles.

"Jack's lads," said Ennis.

Brodie found the sight oddly comforting, asked him to stop so they could watch. They couldn't see the cars, only the wash of headlights along hedges as they twisted and turned. Brodie counted eight of them. "They're doing their best, aren't they?"

"Of course they are," said Ennis. "They're looking for a murderer."

The breath caught in her throat. "I thought they were looking for Daniel."

The man beside her winced. "If they find one they'll find the other."

But Brodie knew what he'd meant, and her heart stumbled. She was acting like a fool. Everyone else knew her friend was dead. She said wistfully, "I wish Daniel could see this. He thinks Jack Deacon hates him."

Ennis chuckled bleakly. "Jack Deacon hates everybody. It doesn't stop him being a damned effective police officer."

He went to start the van again. Brodie's hand caught his wrist. "Look."

He followed her gaze but couldn't see anything new. "What?"

For a moment she didn't answer. She wanted to be certain she wasn't imagining it. She watched the little fireflies sketch the meandering of the lanes, and for another minute she really wasn't sure.

Then she was. "They're all heading the same way. George—they've found something!"

CONSTABLE VICKERS who found the body hurried back to his car to call it in. Then he took the blanket from the boot and spread it gently, and settled down to wait for Detective Inspector Deacon to find him.

A minute later his blanket groaned and sat up.

BY THE TIME Deacon arrived Daniel was more or less conscious. Vickers had bound his bloody head with half the First Aid kit before calling for further instructions. The duty sergeant in Dimmock told him to proceed carefully to the hospital. Deacon told him to stay where he was.

Three false turns later he finally found the area car. Vickers tried to make his report but Deacon wasn't interested. He brushed past to where Daniel was sitting on the verge, huddled in the blanket, enough bandage round his head to turban a Sikh. "Where is he?"

Daniel looked blearily at him. One eye was bloodshot and he thought Deacon was leaning to the left. Actually it was him that was tilting. "Who?"

Deacon's fists knotted as if clinging to his patience by a feat of physical strength. "Cochrane! That is who you were with?"

Daniel thought for a moment then nodded, carefully. "I don't know where he went. I don't know when."

"What happened?"

"I thought he was going to kill me." Daniel's voice was a low monotone, drained of emotion. Partly it was concussion, partly anticlimax. He'd expected to die, not to wake with a thumping headache. "He hit me with that wheel thingy. When I woke up he'd gone. But the chain was unlocked so I started looking for civilisation. This is as far as I got." He flicked a tired smile. "I don't know how long it took. I kept passing out."

Deacon looked around but the only lights were the cars. "Where were you? A house?"

"There was a house," agreed Daniel. "Empty—derelict.

And a barn. That's where he kept me. And yes," he added, answering the next question, "it's where he kept the others too."

An expression perilously close to triumph washed across Deacon's face. "I *knew* it! Where? Tell me where."

"I don't know," said Daniel wearily. "Not far. I might be able to find it in daylight."

But Deacon couldn't wait. He stuck one arm behind him, snapping his fingers. Voss, who was fast learning to read his mind, put a map in his hand and he leaned down to read it by the light of a headlamp.

After a moment he straightened up angrily. "Where are we?"

Constable Vickers indicated the spot with a tactful fingertip. Deacon looked again. "There isn't a building within a mile of here. You think you walked a mile?"

Daniel shook his head. "No."

"Then it's not on the map." He slapped the offending item down on the car bonnet. "That's how he got away with it. He evaded us for ten years because some bloody map-maker didn't think it was worth recording a derelict farmhouse! He killed four boys, three of them while we were looking for this place."

He caught Voss's expression then, and it wasn't critical—because an ambitious Detective Sergeant doesn't criticize his superiors in public, even by the look on his face—but it was guarded. "Well?" demanded Deacon sharply.

"Nothing," said Voss quickly. "Nothing."

Deacon knew better. The hint of surprise behind Voss's eyes was nothing to the sensation in the pit of his own stomach. He knew what Voss was too polite to ask. His own conscience was asking the same thing. "You want to know why we trusted to the map. Why, when it mattered so much, we didn't come and look on the ground."

"Well—yes," admitted Charlie Voss.

Deacon clasped his fingers behind his head, tightly enough that the knuckles turned white and ached. He looked away over the dark landscape, dotted by an occasional distant light.

His voice was bitter, and beneath that Voss heard despair. "Because every investigation is a compromise between time being spent and progress being made. We had everyone available looking everywhere we could think to look. There was no reason to suppose there *was* anywhere else. The map said not. Nobody mentioned a derelict property. We thought we'd done a thorough job, and he was keeping them somewhere else. In town, maybe, or an hour down the coast.

"How do you set about finding a derelict barn that's not on the maps and isn't visible from the road, when you don't even know it exists? Follow every ploughed-out lane on the Downs? There are hundreds of them. Every time two farms become one, half a dozen lanes fall into disuse. At first there's a wired-up gate; then the gate gets used somewhere else and a wire fence goes up; then the stone walls are robbed out to repair a more important boundary. Grass grows over the tyre-tracks, and within a few years there's nothing to see. If we'd thought to look, maybe we'd have found it. But we'd have had to take people off other leads that seemed more promising at the time."

At least he was defending himself to someone who understood the practicalities of police work. When the Press got hold of this they'd want an explanation too—only none of them would have experience of organised searches, for evidence or missing persons, where the manpower was never enough and the time was always too short. They wouldn't know, as Voss did, that it takes hours—*hours*—for a crack team to thoroughly search one room. Menner Down stretched across fifty square miles. If you couldn't trust the maps…

He looked back at his sergeant. Voss wasn't judging him. He knew how easy it was to make a mistake, and how much one mistake could matter. If Deacon had known the look of compassion, he'd have recognised it now. He said, with a kind of quiet despair, "A helicopter would have found it."

Voss nodded sombrely. Then he shrugged. "It was ten years ago. Did you even have helicopters…?"

"Of course we had helicopters," snapped Deacon. "At least, we could call on them. For emergencies. Accidents, people in danger, missing children. I don't know if I'd have been given one to fly a search-grid over Menner Down on the off-chance an old barn had disappeared from the map."

Voss risked a tentative grin. "I'm not sure you'd get one for that today."

Deacon breathed out, nodding slowly. There had been a chance to stop Cochrane ten years ago; he hadn't realised; but maybe no one else would have done either. Not Divisional HQ, not the Assistant Chief Constable (Crime), not even the Press. Perhaps it had been a mistake on his part; but perhaps it was just the wonderful twenty-twenty vision afforded by hindsight.

Daniel was getting left behind. "Four?"

"Four?" echoed Deacon, puzzled.

"You said, he killed four boys."

"That's right, you couldn't know. The boy at the brewery wasn't one of Cochrane's after all."

"Neither was Chris Berry," said Daniel.

WHEN THE LANE SNARLED up with cars Ennis stopped. Before he had the handbrake on, Brodie was out of the van and running. It was too late to stop her, and anyway there didn't seem any reason to. The height of the van meant he could see over the tops of the cars, over the heads of the gathered officers, to the focus of their attention. And it was sitting up and arguing.

Brodie didn't know whether to hug Daniel or box his ears.

Jack Deacon couldn't remember the last time he felt the urge to hug someone, and he didn't now. He was keeping his hands off Daniel's throat only by concentrating on more urgent matters. He was setting up road-blocks.

Concussion destroys the sense of time, but certainly an hour must have passed and it was unlikely Cochrane was still on the downs. But Deacon couldn't take it on trust. If by chance he was it would be possible to cut him off before he vanished into the wider countryside because all the lanes of the Three Downs funnelled together into half a dozen roads. A car at each would prevent the Land Rover leaving.

The police-cars struggled to turn and then sped off in directions indicated by Deacon's stabbing finger. George Ennis left too: the van was in the way and he knew Brodie would want to go with her friend. When Deacon had calmed down enough to see that he ought to be in hospital.

There was a lot of engine noise, a bit of shouting, the flare of headlamps, then suddenly there were just the three of them—Daniel, Brodie and Deacon.

The policeman stood with his arms crossed on his chest, looking down at the young man hunched on the verge, his face grey between the bruises and the blood. He shook his head. "Daniel, what in hell am I going to do with you?"

Daniel had been hurt and he'd been frightened. But he wasn't frightened now. "You're going to listen to me, Inspector. Because you're not looking for a murderer any more. You're looking for two."

At BRODIE'S INSISTENCE he told his story in the car on the way to Dimmock General. There was a brief hiatus while he was in Radiography, and he finished the telling while having his head stitched up.

There was no fracture but he'd taken a beating and the doctor wanted to keep him overnight for observation. Since his own bed was ashes he raised no argument, knowing he'd sleep as soon as his pounding head hit the pillow.

But Deacon wasn't ready to let him sleep. He wanted to know everything Daniel knew. He wanted to go over it again and again until he had every detail nailed in his mind. Neil Cochrane killed Jamie Wilton, Peter Krauss and Gavin Halliwell. And he didn't kill Chris Berry.

"You believed him?"

"Yes," said Daniel. "I know he wasn't the man on the pier. And if the rest of it wasn't true, why would he say it?"

"Why say it anyway? What did he have to gain by confessing to three murders? What did he want you to do with the information?"

But Daniel couldn't help him. "I thought he wanted me to be his biographer. But he never asked. Then I thought maybe he just wanted to put the facts on record. He thinks he can stay ahead of you, but if he's never caught he never gets to tell his story. What he did, how he stopped doing it, how it wasn't him when it started again. He's bitter about that. Outraged. He hoped I could tell him who it was."

"Was that the reason?" wondered Brodie. "He thought you could tell him who'd squandered ten years of his life, but only if he explained why it mattered so much?"

"Maybe," Daniel nodded slowly. "He was deeply offended that someone had used him like that. He was much more upset at what had been done to him than at what he'd done. I was glad I couldn't help him."

Deacon raised an eyebrow. "Oh?"

Daniel cast him a furtive glance. "If I'd known who it was at the pier, I'm not sure I could have kept from telling him. I said I wouldn't let him hurt anyone else, but... He really wanted that name, you know, if he'd thought I had it... I don't know what he'd have done to get it."

Brodie stood up abruptly. "It's time we left you to rest," she said pointedly. "Mr Deacon, can I impose on you for a lift? I left my car in town."

Deacon hadn't finished questioning Daniel, except that he rather suspected from Brodie's tone that he had. "So how did you get to the downs?"

"In George Ennis's van. We were out looking for Daniel too."

She'd succeeded in surprising him. "Ennis?"

"I'll explain while you drive me home."

"So you were both right," she said as Deacon drove. "You were right about Cochrane being a murderer. Daniel was right about him not killing Chris Berry."

"You mean, I should have listened to him sooner," said Deacon ungraciously.

"Maybe he should have listened to you too. He wouldn't have got his head beat in if he had."

"But he didn't get his head beat in, did he?" said Deacon pensively. "Not actually. I wonder why not."

"Because he can identify the killer. The other one."

"Why should that matter to Cochrane? Even if we find the man, what good does it do him?—he's going to be either in prison or on the run. It's academic what happens to the other guy now."

"He doesn't think it's academic," said Brodie. "He thought it was worth blowing a cover that served him for ten years. Cochrane doesn't see how he can carry on here now; so his first priority is making sure that the man who put him in that position pays the price. That's why Daniel's still alive: so when you find the killer you'll have the means to convict him."

Deacon gave a disheartened little snort. "He has a touching faith in my abilities."

"He knows how good you are at this. He knows how close you came to him. If you'd had a witness ten years ago you'd have got him. He's hoping you'll be as dogged when you get your teeth into the man who killed Chris."

"*If*," he said heavily. "*If* I get my teeth into him. If Cochrane didn't kill Chris Berry I have no idea who did. And I've no idea how to find out."

Jack Deacon wasn't a man whose soul benefited from confession. But something about Brodie Farrell prompted him to candour. He wasn't trying to impress her: lies would have served better than honesty if he had been. He had no illusions about himself. He knew that, on the thinking woman's wishlist, men like him came just below cystitis. He had no class, and no aspirations to it. He wouldn't even describe himself as a rough diamond: anyone chipping away at his rocky exterior would end up with only blisters. He was nothing other, and certainly nothing more, than he appeared to be.

But if he had had the power to attract women, Brodie Farrell was the sort of woman he'd have liked to attract. Perhaps because she was the sort of woman he had least experience of. Apart from other police officers, the only people policemen meet are criminals, victims and barmaids and Brodie was none of these. There was a strength about her, a self-possession, which he admired. She looked life in the eye and dealt with both the good and the bad. Deacon envied her cool aplomb, and never suspected that every trait he admired in her was the result of two years' dragging herself back from the brink of despair. As much as Daniel, she was the product of her own efforts, the realisation of her own blueprint.

Brodie didn't know what was going through his mind. But she recognised a compliment when she heard one, and Jack Deacon opening his heart to her certainly qualified. She liked him better than he might have guessed. She smiled at the troubled, irritable side of his face. "Do you have to get back? Or have you time for a coffee?"

He drove home with one foot on the accelerator and the other one kicking himself. His face was set in hard, bitter lines and his eyes were smoky with self-loathing.

"Memo," he said to himself savagely. "When a beautiful sophisticated woman asks you in for coffee you say yes. If she offers you meths, you say yes!"

EIGHTEEN

BRODIE WATCHED him go with a smile. She thought, If I ever need to blackmail you I'll threaten to tell people you're shy. Then she went inside.

They let Paddy sleep. Marta made some supper. "Daniel—he's all right?"

"Yes, he is. He got knocked about a bit but he'll be fine."

The tall Polish woman nodded thoughtfully. "So he was right."

"About what he saw? Yes, he was."

"So who *did* kill the runner boy?"

"We don't know, Marta. Daniel doesn't and the police don't. If they come up with another suspect he can tell them if they're right. Until then I don't see what any of us can do."

Marta sniffed. "I know what I can do. In the morning I give you your child back, and Daniel can have my spare room."

IT WAS MIDNIGHT before Brodie fell into bed. In a state of nervous exhaustion she didn't expect to sleep. But she did. For eight hours straight, and when the alarm went off she was dreaming about George Ennis's van.

There was nothing particularly odd about that. In her time she'd dreamed about walking statues, space travel and the Isle of Wight, so it was only when the dream refused to fade, kept intruding on her waking thoughts, that she began to think someone was trying to tell her something, and it was her.

Brodie didn't believe in precognition. She did think that sometimes, in the middle of the night when everything was quiet and the demands on it were minimal, the brain set about spring cleaning—solving problems, resolving concerns, tidying up left-over anxieties—and that dreams could be an expression of that. They couldn't predict the future. They might cast light on past events and present worries.

But a van? She didn't have unfulfilled yearnings for a truck-driver. She didn't ache to throw off her responsibilities and hit the road. She had, as it happened, made love in the back of a van and had found it more uncomfortable than erotic. So what was she trying to tell herself? To what was she trying to draw her own attention?

But the harder she chased the faster the spectre fled; the quicker she turned, the more rapidly the shadow behind her dissolved. Annoyed, she shook her head and tried to catch up on some work.

At ten-twenty Marta phoned to say she and Paddy had been in a taxi to collect Daniel from the hospital, he'd fallen asleep on the sofa and now Paddy was sitting on the floor beside him in case he woke up needing to hold someone. Not for the first time Brodie wondered how on earth she and John, two essentially ordinary people, had managed to produce a child at once so innocent and so knowing.

She wanted to talk to George Ennis, partly to thank him for his help the previous evening, partly to apologise for running out on him, most of all to make sure he knew what Daniel had discovered. That he'd been right ten years ago. That Neil Cochrane was the killer he believed him to be.

Jack Deacon might have called him. They'd worked the case together, no one understood better than Deacon the frustration of their failure or the horror when it returned to haunt them. But Deacon would be busy. Ennis needed to know that he'd been right ten years ago, but failing to prove it hadn't cost any more lives.

Brodie thought he'd probably call her after Deacon called him. When she hadn't heard from him by eleven, she shut the office and walked up Fisher Hill to *The Attic Gym*.

There was a car parked out front, a silver hatchback with

eight-year-old plates and a dented wing. Nathan Sparkes was working out in the otherwise empty gym, brow lowered in concentration, beating the stuffing out of a punchbag.

He didn't notice her come in and, reluctant to distract him, she headed upstairs to the flat. He wasn't just exercising his muscles, he was exorcising his ghosts. In his own head that wasn't a punchbag he was hitting.

He must have glimpsed her out of the corner of his eye, or heard her step on the stair, because he stopped punching and staggered back, panting. Brodie turned to say, "It's all right, it's only me." And then she saw his face, and his hands.

So Ennis reckoned he was all right, did he? Calmer? The boy was fragmenting before her eyes. His face had fallen to a death-mask, sallow skin stretched taut over the high bones, hollow-eyed. Driving himself to exhaustion wasn't ridding himself of his demons, it was laying him open to them. They had a bit in his mouth and were riding him. He couldn't stop any more, didn't know how to. He threw himself back on the bag, pock-marked with blood from his ungloved knuckles, and his eyes were stricken with the knowledge that, however hard he hit it, it wouldn't hit back.

Brodie hurried to him, put her arms around his shoulders. His vest was saturated, the sweat cold on his skin and pooled in the hollows of his collar-bones. He hadn't got like that in a few minutes. He could have been standing there, battling his hags, since the place opened.

"Nathan, stop it. Stop now. Please, Nathan—you have to stop."

By degrees her voice, authoritative and insistent, penetrated the darkness in which he'd cocooned himself. There was no strength left in his arms, the well-oiled machine running on fumes alone. The punchbag hardly moved when he hit it. Slowly his eyes slid back into focus and he saw where he was and what he was doing. Brodie saw them flicker with confusion and despair.

His knees buckled under him. Brodie would let him fall:

she went down with him, still holding him, steadying his head against her. She heard his racked breath turn to sobs.

She wasn't far from tears herself. "Nathan, this is *crazy*," she insisted, her voice cracking. "You *can't* believe Chris would want to see you like this. You mourn lost friends, you don't immolate yourself over them. What happened was a tragedy. But so is this, Nathan. So is this."

His strong young body went to butter in the compass of her arms, melting into the contours of her. She held him tight. She couldn't think what else to do for him. "What is it? Why are you doing this?"

"My fault," he whined into the shoulder of her jacket. "My fault."

Brodie shook her head. "Everyone feels that way when they lose someone. Something dreadful happens and every-one tries to blame themselves. You think if you'd done some-thing different Chris would still be alive. If you'd been with him, if you'd stayed in instead of going to the pub, or…"

She wasn't helping. The sobs were turning him inside out. It was as much as he could do to form a few words. "The car," he stammered. "The damned car…"

She struggled to understand. "You had it that night? That doesn't make it your fault! You couldn't have imagined—"

But that wasn't it. He pushed her away, rocking back on his heels. His ravaged face was streaked with tears, the eyes swollen with guilt. "I trashed the wing. Four hundred quid's worth. I hadn't the money to get it fixed."

He swallowed. Brodie didn't try to help. He needed to get this said, to tell someone what was tormenting him. When he was able he went on. "We argued. Chris said it was my prob-lem, he wasn't going to bail me out. But I hadn't got the mon-ey so I kept on at him to pitch in." His breath was coming faster, the words tumbling over themselves.

"So it was off the road when the day came that it mattered? If you hadn't bent it, or if you'd got it fixed, he'd have been driving instead of walking and would never have met his killer?" It crossed Brodie's mind to wonder why the thing, still dented, was obviously road-worthy now. But pinning the details down mattered less than getting through to him that he was not responsible for his friend's death.

"Nathan, that's exactly what I'm saying. There are things in all relationships that we'd regret if the worst happened. Every action we take could conceivably lead to disaster. That doesn't make us responsible. There was no way you could guess that not having the car that particular night would lead to Chris's death. You don't even know he'd have been driving. If he'd had a couple of drinks he'd have left it and walked home, wouldn't he? And the same thing would have happened. You're not to blame, Nathan. You have to stop crucifying yourself."

Upstairs a door opened and closed. The woman and the boy, both on their knees, looked up.

Brodie breathed a sigh of relief. She was saying all the right things but she wasn't sure Nathan was hearing them. If he wouldn't believe her, perhaps he'd believe his coach. Both hands occupied, she raised her chin in greeting. "George. Can you—?"

But Nathan stiffened in her arms. He gave a little plaintive cry and shoved himself away from her, rolling to his feet in a fluid motion that a moment earlier he had not seemed capable of. Brodie was surprised enough to let him go. "Nathan?"

He ignored her. His eyes locked with Ennis's for a second, then he spun and ran. He crossed the gym in a couple of strides, fumbled briefly with the door and was gone.

Ennis came down the stairs two at a time, his eyes ablaze. "What was that about?"

Brodie rose to her feet, spreading her hands in a gesture of confusion. "Beats me."

"What did he say?"

"He was telling me about the car. He blames himself for not getting it fixed. He reckons if he had Chris wouldn't have been walking on the seafront at two in the morning. I told him no one can read tea-leaves that well, it wasn't his fault, but he was in no mood to believe me. He'd beat himself stupid on that damned punchbag. Did you see his hands?"

But Ennis wasn't worried about bloody knuckles that would heal in a few days. He was worried about losing another of his golden boys. There had been nothing he could do to help Chris. But Nathan was teetering on the edge of undoing, and there was just time to snatch him back, if he'd allow himself to be saved. "Come on," Ennis said roughly, "we have to find him." The black van was in the back yard. Despite the urgency it took vital seconds extricating it.

Brodie climbed up beside him, her eyes on his face. "You don't think he'd hurt himself?"

"I don't know," gritted Ennis. "A week ago I'd have said he could take anything the world could throw at him. Now?— I really don't know. He's been torturing himself over what happened. It didn't help that you kept raking over the coals."

That was unfair, but a worried man's aim isn't to be depended on. Brodie shrugged. "I was trying to help my friend. I'm sorry if I hurt yours."

He looked at her then and couldn't justify his anger. "No, I'm sorry. I'm doing the same as Nathan: failing to distinguish between reasonable actions and unforeseeable consequences." He twitched a brief smile. "I always seem to be apologising to you."

Brodie smiled too. "You don't have to. If I'd been through what you have I'd be behaving a great deal worse."

They reached the street. The silver car had been pointing down the hill and Ennis turned towards the seafront. He said quietly, "If you thought too much about it you'd fall apart. You get through by concentrating on one thing at a time. You don't let yourself look at the whole picture. You deal with the details, one at a time."

Brodie bit her lip. "Where do you think Nathan's heading?"

He spared her a sharp glance. "Well, that's the sea and the pier's just up there. Where do you think?"

As they reached the esplanade the silver car came into

view. Nathan had driven as far as the pier and pulled off onto the paved concourse. Once it had been populated by can-
dyfloss machines and Laughing Policemen, and people
counting out their pennies to pass through the turnstiles onto
the pier. Now the sweet-sellers were gone, the turnstiles were
gone and the policemen hadn't much to laugh about. All that
stood between Nathan Sparkes and the place where his friend
died were the notices forbidding entry and a plank barrier that
was more rot than wood.

When the van drew up behind him Nathan put his foot hard
down on the accelerator and the car took off like a race horse,
smashing the plank into matchsticks.

Brodie's jaw dropped and her eyes rounded in astonishment as the little car sped out along the wooden deck.

For a split-second Ennis hesitated. Then he pumped his
own accelerator and the van surged forward through the splin-
tered barrier.

For the same split-second Brodie couldn't bring herself to
believe what he was doing. Shock paralysed her mind and her
muscles. Then she shook free, grabbing for his arm. "George!
No. You'll kill us all!"

"It'll hold," he grated, still accelerating.

Brodie couldn't imagine why he thought so. The decking
had huge holes in it where timbers had fallen through. It
seemed to her that the vibration of two vehicles travelling up
it at speed would shake the rotton pier apart. "It may hold
him," she shouted, still clutching his arm. "But this thing
weighs twice as much as a car. If you bring it down about our
ears, Nathan will die too."

She'd managed to find the button he still answered to. He
took his foot off the pedal and the van coasted to a halt.

Brodie climbed down gingerly. She could hear the whole
structure rumbling as the car ahead wove between its gaping
wounds. She could feel the tremor in its bones. She stared at
George Ennis. "Is he *trying* to kill himself?"

Ennis stared back at her in rank disbelief. "Of course he

is. Why do you think he came here?" Then he was running, and even his feet rattled the deck.

"Oh God," whispered Brodie, stunned. She hadn't realised that was what was happening. She'd thought he needed to get away from them, to be alone, and came here to be close to his friend. She'd known the boy was in pain. She hadn't realised he'd despaired of finding any other remedy.

There was nothing she could do. Ennis, running hard, had a head start on her, and there wouldn't be anything he could do either unless Nathan took his foot off the accelerator in the next few seconds. Even so. Brodie couldn't just stand and watch. She headed after them at a cautious jog.

Two-thirds of the way down the pier the silver hatchback began to slow. Brodie slowed too, back to a panting walk, but Ennis kept sprinting, closing the distance. After a moment Brodie sucked in a deep breath and started to run again. She wasn't sure what Ennis would do when he caught up with Nathan but she didn't trust him to just hold the boy quietly until she arrived.

Ennis reached the car and snatched open the door. Brodie heard raised voices, one deep and angry, the other edged with hysteria, a keen. She had barely enough breath for her own voice to reach them. "Will you just calm down for a minute, the pair of you, and let's talk—"

Ennis looked at her, straightening in the open door. She just had time to think, That boy would have got a thumping if I hadn't been here; then the car jumped forward, spinning Ennis to his knees.

This time nothing interrupted its progress. Not the holes in the deck, not the jumbled remains of the old concert hall, not the rail beyond. The silver hatchback drove all before it and the note of its engine never wavered. Nathan's foot was hard to the floor when the car crashed through the rail and the weight of the engine-block took its nose down perpendicular. It hit the sea in a crash of foam and when the foam cleared it was gone.

NINETEEN

HORROR GLUED HER to the deck for perhaps ten seconds. Then Brodie, whose idea of vigorous exercise was trotting beside a five-year-old child, was running as fast as her muscles would power her. Not for the broken rail at the end of the pier but for the man lurching to his feet this side of the concert hall. There was nothing she could do for Nathan. She'd tried; perhaps she hadn't tried hard enough but anyway she'd failed. He couldn't have made that clearer. He'd given her a grandstand view of the consequences of her failure. Reaching Nathan now would take a crane, divers and cutting equipment, and too long.

But she could still save George Ennis. She knew what he'd do when he flung off the shackles of shock. He'd follow the car off the end of the pier, down through metres of roiling water to the bed of the Channel, and fight with the car for Nathan's life. And he wouldn't succeed, so he too would die. Brodie thought—because a crisis stretches time, leaving time for thought in the spaces between heartbeats—that if there'd been a chance she'd have let him try. He'd lost one of his brilliant boys, she'd have let him risk everything for the other. But she knew he'd be throwing his life away—for nothing, for the look of the thing, for a young man who was probably already dead and in any event had longed to be.

Ennis floundered on the deck with limbs denerved by grief. Brodie caught up as he staggered to the rail, gripping his arm above the elbow. "No! George, listen to me. He's gone. Nathan's gone. There's twenty feet of water down there, and a tide running at five knots. Even if you could dive that deep, the car wouldn't be there. You'd never find it in time. I won't let you throw your life away for nothing!"

"You don't know that!" he cried, dragging her to the rail. "There's air in the car, it wouldn't sink right away." Wild-eyed, he scanned the grey-brown water that hissed and seethed around the pilings. Apart from weed and a little floating refuse there was nothing to see. The waves had erased the ripples already.

"The door was open," Brodie said gently.

George Ennis stared at her. Then he threw back his head and howled like an animal. For a moment Brodie thought he meant to throw himself through the gap in the railing anyway, not in hope now but in despair. She clung on for all she was worth. "If you go," she hissed fiercely, "I'm coming too. And I can't swim."

For half a minute they stayed as they were, the moment frozen. Behind them Brodie heard voices and running feet, then a siren. All that concerned her was keeping George Ennis from following his last star westward to oblivion.

Finally she felt the terrible tension start to bleed from his muscles and knew that the worst was over. She went on holding him, as only minutes ago she'd been holding Nathan, while the strength drained from him and he sank exhausted to the battered deck, which groaned like a heart breaking.

When the police divers found the car it was empty. The body of Nathan Sparkes was recovered, hours later and a couple of miles up the Channel, by the crew of the Inshore Lifeboat.

"WHY DID NATHAN kill himself?" asked Jack Deacon. His voice was low but insistent and he waited for an answer.

Ennis slumped in the chair on the other side of his desk. This had been his office once and he'd sat under the window; and he'd asked questions no one had wanted to answer, and kept asking until he got a response.

He sighed and lifted his head as if it was heavier than always. "He lost his friend. Chris wasn't just someone he went running with: they were closer than brothers. They shared everything that was important in their lives. When Chris was killed, Nathan hadn't the strength to go on alone."

"Grief," said Deacon. "Just grief?"

Ennis raised an eyebrow and the blue eye under it glittered. "*Just* grief? Wars that killed thousands have been started by grief. Good men commit murder through grief. It's one of the most powerful forces in the library of human emotion. He was only eighteen. He hadn't learned that even things that hurt that much can be survived. He thought the pain would never stop and he couldn't bear it. That wasn't suicide, Jack. He was stopping the pain the only way he knew."

"They were that close?"

"Yes," said Ennis simply. "They'd known one another all their lives. Each was the other's main source of support—more than anyone in their own families. They were like two halves of one thing. That wasn't a bereavement Nathan suffered, it was an amputation."

"Were they lovers?"

Ennis was too tired to be angry. "Don't be stupid. They were about as queer as a pair of young tom-cats. That damned car wore out more springs parked on the cliffs than it ever did on the road."

Deacon thought for a moment. "You always call it that."

Ennis frowned. "What?"

"That damned car. Was it a lot of trouble?"

"It wasn't very reliable. They should have waited till they could afford something better. The time and money they spent on it could have been better used."

Deacon went and stood at the window, staring out, hands thrust deep in his trouser pockets. The next bit would be difficult but he couldn't avoid it any longer. He turned back to the room. "George, have you considered the possibility that Nathan killed Chris?"

He wasn't sure what he was expecting. Denial, certainly; probably fury, possibly the kind of savage fury in which friends say things which can never entirely be forgiven. But

Ennis didn't surge to his feet and start shouting. Instead his eyes dropped. His voice was low too. "Of course I have."

"When?"

"Since—" He couldn't put words to it. "In the last two hours. I've thought of nothing else."

Deacon kept his tone level. He didn't want to add any more to the man's suffering. He also didn't want him to dry up. "What do you reckon?"

With an effort Ennis met his gaze. His eyes were raw. "Jack, I don't know. He didn't say anything to me. But something was eating him alive, and maybe it wasn't—how did you put it?—just grief."

"Could they have fought?"

"They were eighteen years old, they fought all the time. I never saw it come to blows."

Deacon blinked. "It was a bit more than that. Someone beat Chris's head in with a wheel-brace!"

"Could it have been an accident?" ventured Ennis.

Deacon blinked at him. "You mean, Nathan accidentally took a swing at him with a steel bar? And when he saw what he'd done, instead of calling an ambulance he tipped Chris off the pier into the sea. Call me a cynic, George, but it doesn't sound much like an accident to me."

"It doesn't, does it?" murmured Ennis. "Jack, what can I tell you? I don't know what happened. I don't know why Nathan killed himself. I can speculate, but that's all it would be. And I'd much rather not. They were two good kids, young men to be proud of. I'd have been proud of them if they'd had four left feet between them. Now they're dead. You're satisfied that Neil Cochrane wasn't involved, so maybe Nathan could have told us what happened if he could have brought himself to. However it looks, if it was a squabble between him and Chris I know as sure as if I was there that neither meant to hurt the other."

Deacon shook his head doubtfully. "I think you're kidding yourself."

But Ennis was desperate for an explanation other than the

obvious one. "I knew them, Jack, and you didn't. I *know* Nathan never meant to hurt Chris. But they were young men, and athletes—they were used to challenging one another. Maybe—I don't know—it started as a bit of horse-play, then the adrenalin kicked in and they ended up fighting in earnest? Nathan got carried away, didn't realise what he was doing until it was too late, then he panicked. Either he knew Chris was already dead, or he didn't dare think anything else. He let him fall in the sea and ran like hell."

Deacon had already fallen for one convenient explanation, it would be a while before he succumbed to another. Yet the scenario had some merit. "It would explain one thing," he ruminated: "why Chris couldn't outdistance whoever was chasing him. Nathan was one of a handful of people who could give him a run for his money."

His hand brushed the older man's shoulder as he passed. He wasn't a New Man, didn't go in for bonding; even his cat had to settle for a nod when he came in. This was about as close as he ever came to empathy. He picked up the phone. "I'll get Hood in again."

"WHAT?" SAID Jack Deacon. He said it very calmly, very quietly, and somehow the word echoed around the room in a way it would not have done had he shouted.

Daniel had slept until noon but he hadn't woken fresh and ready to take on the day. Between dreams and memories he'd got very little rest, and he woke feeling sore, soiled and exhausted. Another bruising round with Deacon was the last thing he needed.

He gave a tired sigh. "I said, it wasn't Nathan either."

Elbows on his desk, Deacon steepled his hands in front of him and pursed his lips. His face remained a dogged blank. "You do know who he was? Chris Berry's best friend and running partner. He killed himself this morning. Shortly before that he was sobbing on Mrs Farrell's shoulder, apparently consumed by guilt. He told her he was responsible for Chris's death and then he drove his car off the end of the pier."

"I can't help any of that," said Daniel. "All I can tell you is, Nathan Sparkes isn't the man I saw on the pier at two o'clock on Monday morning. I spent fifteen minutes with him on Tuesday night. Do you think I wouldn't have mentioned it if he was the man I saw killing Chris?"

Deacon ignored him. "He's another runner. Did you know that? The only person involved in all this who could match Chris in a foot-race."

"I know," said Daniel. "It doesn't alter what I saw. Inspector Deacon, we've done this before. I told you it wasn't Cochrane. You didn't believe me, but I was right. After yesterday everyone accepts I was right. Now you're offering me another suspect, and I'm telling you it wasn't him either—but hey, maybe *this* time I'm wrong! I saw the guy well enough to know it wasn't Neil Cochrane, but maybe I *didn't* see him well enough to know it wasn't Nathan Sparkes! Let's go with that, see how long it takes for the wheels to fall off."

Deacon's left brow lowered and his right eye kindled. "Don't take that tone with me, sonny."

Daniel stood up abruptly. His eyes were bloodshot and puffy, but also angry. "Or what? Inspector, I'm tired of doing this. Of being your whipping-boy. I haven't done anything wrong. From the moment this began I've been trying to help. And the good citizens of Dimmock burned my house down, and you threaten me whenever you're stuck for a genuine villain. And I've had enough. I'm going home now. Solve your own damned case. If you come up with a plausible suspect, I'll take a look—though what the point is when you never believe what I say, I'm not quite sure."

He headed for the door, taking Deacon's stare with him. But with his hand on the knob he hesitated.

Deacon cleared his throat. "I guess not having a home to go to makes storming out a shade less satisfying."

Daniel flicked him a tiny, rueful smile. "It's not that. Marta Szarabeijka's putting me up. Only…"

"Yes?"

"You couldn't lend me a fiver for a taxi?"

Further up the corridor people who heard the noise supposed Detective Inspector Deacon had finally lost control and was ripping the arms off his witness. They thought if it went on much longer they'd have to do something about it.

But that wasn't the roar of unbridled fury they were hearing. In fact it was something much rarer. It was Jack Deacon laughing.

TWENTY

AT CLOSE OF PLAY Deacon took Charlie Voss out for a pint. Voss was not fooled for a moment. He hadn't been working for Deacon for very long, but still long enough to know that these evenings of impromptu hospitality were nothing to do with thanking him for a job well done. They were a way of wringing a bit more work out of him without it counting as overtime.

"Nathan Sparkes, hm?" rumbled Deacon by way of opening the conversation. "Who'd have thought it?"

Voss sighed. But he knew what was expected of him. "Not Daniel Hood, apparently."

Deacon gave a disparaging sniff and took a bite out of his beer. "Hood! You'd get more sense out of Randolph Hearst's sheep!"

"Damien," murmured Voss. "Randolph Hearst owned newspapers. Damien Hirst pickles sheep." He could have said nothing but it might have been a test.

"Well, pardon my ignorance," snarled Deacon. "I don't get in a lot of art galleries these days. The last armless nude I saw was crammed up a drain under the railway line. Once you've seen that, you kind of lose interest in poncey sculptures."

DS Voss knew his inspector hadn't brought him here to be unpleasant to him. He could do that without buying drinks. He wanted to know what Voss thought without having to ask. "But he does have a point, sir. He witnessed the murder of Chris Berry and he saw the murderer's face. We could ignore his evidence if we had reason to consider him unreliable, but we haven't. Anything but. The fact that he stuck to his guns when everyone was telling him it was Cochrane suggests to me he has a pretty clear picture of the man he saw. And it wasn't Nathan Sparkes any more than it was Neil Cochrane."

Deacon went on glaring at him over the rim of his mug. But he didn't contradict, or even argue. Voss thought he was telling him something he already knew.

AT ABOUT THE SAME time Brodie was serving supper for three. At first they tried to keep the conversation light, to steer it away from recent events. But actually there was nothing else worth talking about. And with three young men dead it seemed somehow disrespectful to avoid the subject.

Marta voiced the question that was troubling everyone, those round the table and those in the pub. "But if the boy didn't kill his friend, why did he kill himself?"

"He was upset," said Brodie. She heard how lame that sounded, shrugged apologetically.

"Sure he was upset," said the tall Polish woman witheringly. "Life's not easy, things happen, lots of things upset people. They don't go round topping themselves!" Between music students she watched a fair amount of daytime television. It was beginning to show.

"He was eighteen," said Brodie. "Things hurt more when you're eighteen. You feel them more, and you can't see past to a time when you'll feel better. The balance of his mind was disturbed."

"Is that what you think?" asked Daniel quietly. "You were the last one to talk to him. Was he really suicidal over losing his friend?"

"I don't know," admitted Brodie. "He was fraught, he wasn't making much sense. He certainly blamed himself for something. I took it for survivor guilt—you know, where the one who didn't die looks for a reason to blame himself.

"But God almighty, if people behaved like that nobody'd reach middle age. We've all lost someone at some time. Yes, you flay yourself over it. You think of all the things you could have done differently that would somehow have affected the outcome. But even at the time, deep down you know you're being unreasonable. It's a ritual you have to go through in order to forgive yourself and get over it.

"So yes, I think there was something more going on. Something was gnawing away at him, and not just that Chris would have had the car if he hadn't damaged it. It never did get fixed, but that didn't stop Nathan driving it."

"Perhaps Nathan had it on Monday night," suggested Daniel, "and that's why Chris was on foot."

"I thought of that. I asked Nathan, in the gym ten minutes before he died. He never really answered, which I think was answer enough. If that was what was preying on him, surely he'd have given some sign of it?

"And anyway, what if Nathan did have the car? It was a joint purchase: sometimes one would have it, sometimes the other. It was just rotten luck that Chris didn't have it the night it really mattered. Even when he was hurting most, at some level Nathan must have known that. After three days he shouldn't still have been flaying himself. Of course he'd always have regrets—but suicide? I don't buy it. He killed himself because he couldn't live with what happened, and that makes no sense if Chris was the victim of a random psychopath—either Cochrane, or someone mimicking Cochrane, or some other violent maniac."

"But it would make sense if Nathan killed his best friend," said Daniel softly.

Brodie met his gaze and nodded. "Yes."

"It still wasn't Nathan I saw."

"THEN MAYBE HE HAD help," hazarded Charlie Voss.

Deacon frowned. "What?" They were onto their second beer by now.

"Maybe it wasn't just Nathan and Chris. Could there have been a third man?"

Deacon spluttered into his glass. "Oh sure. The one thing

everyone's agreed on is that those boys were best friends—and Nathan topping himself out of remorse doesn't work if they weren't. But hell, if we can't find a theory that fits the facts let's make the facts fit the theory. So you reckon he got someone to help him brain Chris with a wheel-brace, is that it?"

Voss clung onto his patience. "No, sir, that doesn't fit either. Not with what we know of the two boys, and not with what Daniel saw. He saw an older man chase Chris out onto the pier, hit him with an iron bar, tip him into the sea and run away. He saw his face. He's adamant it wasn't Nathan Sparkes."

"Then why is Nathan dead?"

Sergeant Voss had those oddly clear green eyes that tend to go with red hair. They were intelligent and kind, and right now they were grim. "Because we didn't get to the bottom of this fast enough, sir. And we aren't there yet."

"AND IT WAS NOBODY you've seen before or since?" asked Brodie.

Daniel shook his head. "I'd have recognised him if he was someone I knew."

"Which rules out the staff at Dimmock High, a handful of local tradesmen. Some policemen, and that's about all." Feeling their eyes Marta had the grace to look apologetic. "You got to admit, Daniel, you don't got the biggest social circle in the world."

Daniel gave a wry smile. "You two, and Paddy, and a bad-tempered policeman who hates my guts. But I do know other people to see, and I'm as sure as I can be that I never saw that man's face before. He was a stranger to me."

"COULD IT GENUINELY, for once, have been a passing maniac?" asked Voss. Deacon squinted at him. "Just checking, sir," the sergeant added hurriedly. "But it must happen sometimes. We'd feel pretty silly if that was the answer, and we missed it and kept looking for something more meaningful."

Deacon gave it some thought but then he shook his head.

"There was nothing insane about this, and nothing random either. It was planned, meticulously. Someone wanted that boy dead, and wanted Cochrane to take the blame. He thought if we couldn't prove it before we wouldn't be surprised if we failed to prove it again. He thought that the next best thing to covering up the crime was hiding it in a ten-year-old file that we'd despaired of closing.

"He knew how we'd react to the murder of a teenage boy with a wheel-brace on the pier. More than that, Charlie—he knew how *I'd* react. It was unfinished business, mine as much as George Ennis's, and he knew I'd leap at the chance of wrapping it up this time. Despite any discrepancies in the evidence. Despite the only witness ruling out the prime suspect. Damn it," he smouldered, "he's been pulling my strings! If Daniel Hood wasn't a stubborn little son-of-a-bitch he'd have won. Even without the evidence to charge him, we'd never have looked any further than Neil Cochrane. Do you know how that makes me feel, Charlie Voss?"

It was a moment for tact if ever there was one. Oddly enough, detective sergeants who seek advancement are better not being seen out-thinking their inspectors. He said carefully, "It makes you feel like it's personal, sir?"

"ALL THE THINGS HE KNOWS," said Daniel slowly. "Don't they tell us something about him?"

"Like what?" Brodie was watching him warily. He had a habit of saying what she was thinking, and she thought he was about to do it again.

"Like, he was in Dimmock ten years ago. He followed the original case in some detail. Those aren't just the headlines he's remembered, they're the essence of what was happening. We know he wasn't the killer then, because we know who was. But he must have been pretty close to the action."

"How?" asked Marta, leaning bony elbows on the table.

"A reporter covering the murders would have that kind of detailed information," murmured Brodie.

"Tom Sessions was the reporter covering it for *The Sentinel*," said Daniel.

Brodie couldn't see Sessions as a killer either. "Others would come down from the London dailies."

"But how many of them are still in Dimmock today?"

Brodie considered. "So who else would know all the details?"

"The victims' families," offered Marta. "They'd remember everything that happened, everyone who was involved. Probably they still live in the area."

Brodie's eyebrows rocketed. "Hellfire, Marta, that's a bit sick."

Marta bristled. "Whoever did this *is* sick. It's the one thing we know for sure. You want to know who was around ten years ago and is still here now, who would remember the killings in more detail than the average reader of newspapers? Well, there were three victims, they each had parents, they would have brothers and cousins and uncles. Any of them could be the man you're looking for. I'm sorry if it's bad taste to say so, but you know what us damned foreigners are like…"

Daniel chuckled. Then the pale eyes behind his thick glasses went distant and still. The machinery of thought was grinding almost audibly.

"What?" asked Brodie.

"Marta's right," he said slowly. "We have to think the unthinkable. There's someone else who'd have all the necessary information, and enough understanding of how the police work to be able to protect himself. You said someone was pulling Jack Deacon's strings, Brodie. To do that he'd need to know him pretty well…"

"HE KNOWS YOU, sir," said DS Voss. "I don't mean that he has your name and rank as the officer heading this inquiry. He knows *you*. He knew how you'd react when it seemed Cochrane was up to his old tricks again. He knew if he threw down the right clues you'd follow them out to Manor Farm. And while you were doing that you wouldn't be looking for him."

Deacon's face was both dark and frozen, like a section of thundercloud somehow preserved for posterity. He wanted to shout at someone but Voss didn't deserve it. Voss was doing his job, making connections and inferences and not being misled by preconceptions. If Deacon had refused to be misled by preconceptions they might have reached this point three days ago. But whoever did this knew he'd go after Cochrane first. Knew that even the testimony of an eyewitness wouldn't stop him. Knew Deacon's weaknesses, in fact, better than Deacon knew them himself. Almost nothing that had gone before angered the detective as much as that.

He had to unclench his jaws to get the words out. "And if he knows me that well, I know him."

"Brodie?" It was Marta, growing anxious because the seconds were turning into minutes and there was still no sign of her friend returning from the inner space to which she had retreated. "Brodie! You still there?"

"What?" She blinked. "Sorry. What?"

"I thought you emigrated."

"No. Just thinking." Brodie managed a distracted smile.

But Daniel wasn't fooled. He said, very quietly, "You know who it is, don't you?"

"No! No," she said again, less emphatically, "I don't."

"Then, you know who it could be. Tell me. It doesn't matter if you're wrong. It won't go any further unless you're right."

Brodie felt a spark of anger at him. "Who says if I'm right or wrong? You?"

"I saw him," said Daniel. "I'll know him when I see him again."

"Then I am wrong," said Brodie, "because you've seen him lots of times. At least…" Her voice slowed and died.

"Yes?"

"Actually, no. *I've* seen him lots of times, but maybe you haven't. Maybe…" She thought some more. "No. That's ridiculous."

Daniel again: "Brodie?"

She had to tell him. She honestly didn't know what it meant, or if it meant anything, but she had to tell him. "It's almost as if he's been avoiding you. He sent Nathan to get you on the night of the fire, even though that meant leaving a novice driver to wrestle a big vehicle out of a tiny yard and then maybe to face a hostile crowd. He's a runner too: he could have come for you himself and left Nathan to call the police. But then you'd have met face to face.

"When I questioned him about Chris he wasn't going to answer, not for me. But when I suggested that he talk to you instead he changed his mind. Suddenly nothing was too much trouble. He'd do anything I asked, rather than have you asking.

"Last night, too. He helped in the search, but as soon as we knew you were safe he left. I thought he was making room for the police cars. But maybe he was afraid you'd see him. He thought you were dead—they all did. He didn't mind searching for a corpse. Dead men can't identify anyone."

All the expression had frozen in Daniel's face. When he had a voice again he said carefully, "Are you sure about this?"

Brodie nodded jerkily. "I'm sure of what I'm saying—that he fits the pattern. He was here ten years ago, was intimately familiar with the killings then. He knows Jack Deacon better than anyone: he'd know the mere suggestion that Cochrane was on the rampage again would make him rush off in pursuit, abandoning all the meticulous detective work and intelligent thinking he'd otherwise be doing. He'd know what strings to pull and what pitfalls to avoid. If old poachers make the best game-keepers, I dare say old policemen make pretty good murderers."

"George Ennis? *George Ennis* killed Chris Berry?"

"NEVER," SAID VOSS with conviction. He looked both shocked and offended, as if Deacon was having a joke at his expense. "You're kidding, right?"

Deacon ground out the words, "I have never been more serious in my life."

"But—damn it, sir, *why?* Chris Berry was his pride and joy.
Those two boys were his star athletes, the reward for the time
and effort he's put in on that gym. Their success was his triumph. The way he talks about them—I don't believe that's
an act."

"Neither do I," said Deacon tersely. "Whatever happened,
it tore him apart damn near as much as it did Nathan. But he's
older and smarter, and he did what he had to do to protect himself. But Nathan couldn't deal with it. He literally couldn't live
with what happened. He owed George too much to give him
up, and he could only see one other way out."

"George Ennis? George Ennis killed Chris Berry? And he
killed him with a wheel-brace so as to put you onto someone
else's trail?"

"I told you he was smart." Deacon's teeth were showing
but there was no humour whatever in the smile.

"I still can't imagine how it happened," said Voss.

"Me neither." Deacon got up and made for the door. "Let's
ask him."

They'd both drunk too much to drive. Deacon called for
transport. They were waiting for it when his phone rang.

It was Brodie Farrell. She sounded uncharacteristically
reticent, her tone uncertain, reluctant to state the reason for
her call. "I'm sorry to bother you this late, Inspector. It's
just… Well, we were talking about things—Daniel and Marta and me—and we came up with a…kind of…

"Listen, I expect we've got it all wrong. I don't believe it
myself, I wasn't sure I should call. But once we'd come up with
a name we didn't feel we should keep it to ourselves. But feel
free to laugh when I tell you who we were wondering about…"

"George Ennis," said Deacon flatly.

In any other circumstances the gasp at her end of the phone
would have given him immense satisfaction. "How—what—
how did you know?"

The police car rounded the corner. Deacon hailed it. "Because you, Chief Superintendent Fuller and a significant percentage of Dimmock's population have been right all along," he said bitterly. "It turns out I *am* a nasty suspicious bastard. I've just come to the same conclusion."

TWENTY-ONE

"I KNOW WHAT YOU DID, George, I know how you did it. I want to know why."

They weren't talking in Deacon's office this time. They were in Interview Room 1, with the tape running. Ennis had declined to have his solicitor present but Voss was there. Deacon was starting to feel slightly incomplete without the sergeant, though he couldn't have said why. He wasn't aware that Voss contributed much more than an attentive ear and a willingness to nod in the right places, but for some reason Deacon seemed to think more effectively when he was around.

They had gone to Ennis's flat and found it empty. He was downstairs, sitting in the gym in the dark. He must have been there for hours: when Deacon turned on the lights the floor round his feet was littered with photographs. He looked up at the sound of footsteps and smiled wanly. "Both my boys," he murmured by way of explanation. "Both my boys." The drifts of photographs were of Chris Berry and Nathan Sparkes, sometimes together, sometimes apart, covered in mud and smiles, holding trophies.

On the short journey here Deacon had built up a head of steam. Not even at what he believed Ennis had done, but at how he'd tried to get away with it. It was calculated and manipulative, and also arrogant. He'd used his knowledge of someone who respected him to try to get away with murder. Deacon had to keep reminding himself that wasn't actually the worst thing Ennis had done, because he wanted to bloody his fists on the man's face and that was why.

But when the lights went on and he saw George Ennis sitting in the wreckage of his dreams, the anger dissipated. Whatever he'd done, whatever he'd tried to do, all now was ashes. For the friendship they'd once shared, Deacon found he could spare a little gentleness. "Come on, George. Let's get this sorted out."

But if he was expecting a full and frank confession he would be disappointed. Ennis said nothing until they were going up the police station steps. Then he said, "I know what you're thinking, Jack. But you're wrong."

"Save it for the tape, George."

Taped interviews were introduced to protect the accused from coercion. There are people, however, for whom the presence of a machine faithfully recording their every word is an irresistible temptation. They have to fill the tape. Hard-eyed men who would hold their tongues under torture react to the tape-recorder as they do to a karaoke machine—they just have to play with the technology. Many an incautious word has been said to a machine that the person being questioned would have died rather than say to the detective.

But ex-Detective Chief Inspector Ennis was too familiar with the technology to fall into the trap. He waited to see how Deacon wanted to do this.

And the answer was, as directly as possible. "I want to know why."

Ennis shook his head slowly. He was gazing at the table top between his cupped hands, but he raised his eyes to meet Deacon's. "You think I killed Chris. You think I destroyed the most precious talent I've ever come across. Why? You tell me why. What possible reason could I have for killing one of the boys I've spent every spare minute of the last five years nurturing, knowing it would also destroy the other?"

Deacon sniffed. "You've been off the job too long, George, you've forgotten the routine. I ask why, and you tell me."

Ennis gave a little desperate snort, half a chuckle, half a sob. "I can't help you, Jack. I didn't kill Chris. He was my friend, my student, my protegé. As an athlete, and as a man,

I thought the world of him. It'll sound like a cliché but actually it's true: I'd have died for Chris Berry. I would never have
hurt him."

"George, you were seen! If I hadn't been so sure it was
Cochrane I'd have recognised the description. The mere fact
that Chris was running and not leaving his pursuer behind
should have been enough. You're the only man I know of our
generation who could do that."

"I dare say I could, but I didn't! I didn't chase Chris onto
the pier, and I didn't kill him with a wheel-brace. You might
as well believe me, Jack, because it's the truth. Hood? Good
grief, man, if you believed everything you'd ever been told
by a well-meaning eye-witness you'd have filled the prisons
with innocent men and set all the guilty ones free! Look. It
was the middle of the night, yes? Hood was on the beach, the
man he saw was on the pier. There's no way he could make
an ID in those circumstances. Whatever he thinks, you should
know better. I taught you better."

Deacon felt his eyes starting to burn and blinked. He knew
you couldn't see through a man's skin to where the guilt or
innocence showed, but he couldn't stop trying. He was desperate to know, and not for the lost youths now but for himself. He had to know if a man he'd trusted and respected and
occasionally risked his life for had used him. But if Ennis was
lying, he was doing it well.

Of course, this was a situation he understood. Even if he was
more familiar with the other side of the table, it held no fears
for him. He knew the limits of what Deacon could achieve in
the face of downright denial. That might have been all it was:
that the man believed he could claw his way to safety even from
here. But Deacon, who had been sure he was right only half an
hour ago, found himself wondering now if he had been wrong.

He spread his hands on the table. "We've known each other a lot of years," he nodded. "You were a damned good cop-
per; I always thought you were a good man. I still think that.

"Which means that one of those things happened which

can drive even good men to terrible acts. Trust me, George, tell me what it was. If it was one of those tragic misadventures that aren't really murder or even manslaughter so much as rotten bad luck, I'll understand. I'll help all I can. But I need to know what happened."

Ennis regarded him levelly. A little sympathy wasn't going to make him putty in anyone's hands, nor would silence seduce him. None of the standard CID tricks would serve here. The man knew them all. He'd invented some of them.

He breathed steadily. "I wasn't there, Jack, I didn't see what happened. Somebody killed Chris with a metal bar, I know that much. If you're sure it wasn't Cochrane then you'd better find out who it was. All I can tell you for certain, hand on heart, is that it wasn't me."

And the annoying thing was, Deacon believed him. In his years as a detective he'd believed a lot of lies, some only very briefly, some for quite a time. He still put a lot of faith in his own instincts. Until he found the evidence, instinct was sometimes all he had. "What about Nathan?"

There was a flicker of expression then, as if Deacon had kicked him. "What *about* Nathan?"

"He killed himself. Why?"

"Because he'd lost his friend and thought the world had come to an end. Because he was eighteen and didn't know that most pain fades after a while."

"Or because he was the one who killed Chris, and he couldn't live with that."

Ennis looked at him with disdain. "You have a witness, you have a description. If it fits me, it sure as hell doesn't fit Nathan. You want to take this to a jury, Jack, you'd better decide what story you want to tell them."

Deacon gritted his teeth. The effort of holding on—not to his patience exactly, he didn't have much of that at the best of times, perhaps to his self-command—sent a ripple along the powerful muscles of his jaw. He didn't like being lectured by anyone, least of all by a man who could still be a murderer, but he knew he could either vent his spleen or control this interview. He couldn't do both, not when the man across the table had won more of these confrontations than Deacon had.

Besides which, Ennis was right. He needed a coherent theory for what had happened, and this was one of those occasions when having one was infinitely better than having two. If he hoped to convince a jury there had to be no credible alternatives. Hood would tell them that he saw two men at the pier, the one who killed and the one who died, and that neither of them was Nathan Sparkes. One was Chris Berry, the other could have been George Ennis.

So Ennis was lying. So why did he sound like someone telling the truth?

"You want to talk about Hood, let's talk about Hood. He saw the murder take place. He's going to identify you as the murderer."

"Which begs the question," said Ennis, "why you wasted so much time chasing Neil Cochrane? Hood told you it wasn't Cochrane he saw but you thought he was wrong. You thought it was too dark for him to be sure. You thought, if you kept showing him men's faces, sooner or later one of them would look familiar. Yes, maybe it'll be mine. But if he could have been wrong once he can be wrong again. You can't base a case on a witness you've already dismissed as unreliable.

"Jack, I'm telling you the absolute, God-honest, cross-my-heart-and-hope-to-die truth. I didn't kill Chris. How could I have?—I thought the world of the boy. Of both of them. Let's be honest here: I loved them.

"Oh, don't look at me like that," he said wearily. "I know it's a dirty word in your vocabulary, but most people have a bit more room in their hearts than you. I'm fond of all my kids—what I do wouldn't be worth the effort if I wasn't. But those two were special. Either of them would have made the last eight years worthwhile; together they were a coach's dream. You could train decent, determined, hard-working athletes for a lifetime and never handle champions like them.

They were eighteen. If they'd lived to be twenty they'd have been national heroes. If they'd lived to the next Olympics they'd have won medals.

"And yes, I loved them. In the last five years I put as much into their upbringing as their parents did. I spent more time with them. I taught them how to reach into their hearts and souls, how to reach down into their very bones, to be the best that they could be. And I watched them do it. I watched them hit the pain barrier again and again, for me. They strove, they suffered and they won—for me. They spilt blood, sweat and tears for no better reason than that I asked them to. You'd need a heart of stone to have boys like that around you and *not* love them. I'd have needed to be you."

It was meant as an insult, and Deacon felt it as one. He wasn't in touch with his feminine side. The only thing he ever wanted to feel was other people's collars. So it shouldn't have bothered him that George Ennis, a man who might yet prove to have murdered one teenage boy and caused the death of another, considered him cold and uncaring. If someone had accused him of being warm and affectionate he'd have denied it vigorously. Still somehow he felt diminished by Ennis's scorn.

The problem was, they knew one another too well. For years that had been a strength, an asset. Now it was a weakness to be exploited. The older man knew how to unsettle him, even without seeming to try. In the same way that he would have known where to direct Deacon's attention if he needed to hide his own involvement in a young man's death.

Deacon felt a flush rising in his cheeks. He opened his mouth with no idea what was going to come out of it.

Charlie Voss said softly, "If you didn't murder Chris, was it an accident?"

There isn't a lot of furniture in an interview room. There's a table, and usually four chairs drawn up to it; and the tape-recorder hissing quietly as it consigns the words to its mechanical memory; and there's a clock. Voss's murmured intervention momentarily stunned all three of them. Ennis froze, Deacon gaped, and the clock seemed to miss a beat.

Deacon recovered first. Puce with disbelief, he stared at his sergeant as if he'd caught him poking lighted matches through the evidence cupboard keyhole. *"What?"*

Voss didn't look at him. "Mr Ennis? Is that what it was—a terrible accident?"

But Deacon wouldn't let him answer. "What the hell are you *talking* about?" he demanded furiously. "An accident? He chased him up the pier and beat his head in with a wheel-brace! Exactly which bit of that is the unforeseeable conse-quence vital to the whole concept of Accident?"

Voss was watching Ennis's face. He knew he'd struck a chord: he wasn't sure yet what tune to expect. He knew he should pursue his line of questioning. But Deacon was his in-spector, he couldn't send him out of the room. He couldn't even ignore him for very long. He said in a low voice, "Mr Ennis, this could be the last chance to set the record straight."

Deacon was on his feet, his chair crashing behind him. He read the time onto the tape and stopped the interview. "A word with you outside, Detective Sergeant Voss."

Voss's eyes pleaded for more time. "Sir—"

"Now!"

When he was angry, Deacon could lift someone by the la-pels and slam him against the wall without laying a finger on him. In the corridor Voss felt the concussive wave of his fu-ry and for a moment thought he'd been struck. He struggled to organise his thoughts. "Sir—"

"Don't you Sir me!" snarled Deacon, nose to nose with the younger man. "Are you *trying* to get him off the hook? Be-cause he used to be a policeman—is that it? Well, lots of peo-ple used to be policemen. Some of them used to be policemen until they started pissing me around!"

"Didn't you see his face?" said Voss. "That meant some-thing to him. He was going to say something."

"Probably he was going to say, Thank you very much, Sergeant Voss, I hadn't thought of that! What are you *talking* about, an accident? We know what happened. Hood saw what happened. There's no way it could have been an accident."

Charlie Voss couldn't see how either. But he'd seen something in Ennis's expression that was more than just a desperate man clutching for a lifeline. He'd got a bleep on the radar, and if he didn't yet know what it meant he thought it was a genuine contact.

He said, "The more he talks about his runners in general and Chris in particular, the less likely it seems that he did that. You know the man a lot better than I do: do you believe it? That they fought over something so massive, so insurmountable, that Ennis saw no alternative but murdering a kid who was like a son to him? And not in the heat of the moment, a sudden loss of temper, a thrown punch and somebody's head bounces off the corner of the mantelpiece. No. He had to plan it, carefully, in order to leave the clues that would send you after Cochrane. Do you believe he's capable of that—of planning this murder and then carrying it out in cold blood?"

"I'd rather believe that than think it all happened by accident!" snapped Deacon. "Damn it, Charlie, you're playing right into his hands. He's responsible for the violent deaths of two decent young men—that's only one less than Neil Cochrane! Maybe I don't know the whys and wherefores, but I'll bet good money that when I put him in a line-up Daniel Hood will ID him. The fundamental, rock-bottom, nothing's-going-to-alter-it truth is that he committed murder. I want him to go down for murder. I don't want him persuading a jury that in some obscure way he was as much a victim as Chris Berry was."

"Then you do believe it," pressed Voss, half expecting Deacon really would hit him this time. "That Ennis is capable of the brutal premeditated killing of a boy who respected and relied on him."

"I believe," grated Deacon, "that almost anyone is capable of almost anything if you push the right buttons. When I know beyond question that George Ennis murdered Chris Berry, I'll find out why."

Voss nodded, defeated. "You want to put him in a line-up?"

"Yes," said Deacon. "Right now. Send a car for Daniel."

TWENTY-TWO

IT WAS THREE O'CLOCK in the morning. The police car on the gravel drive woke every occupant of the big house in Chiffney Road except the one it had come for. Used to sleeping through the sound of shingle, Daniel woke with a start when Marta shook his shoulder.

Brodie met them in the hall, pulling on her dressing-gown. "What's going on?"

Constable Vickers explained.

Brodie frowned. "You can't hold an identity parade in the middle of the night! Where do you find seven passers-by of broadly similar appearance to the suspect?"

The task had fallen to Sergeant Voss, who had applied himself with characteristic inventiveness. He took out a van and came back with a Leading Fireman, a nightclub bouncer, a male nurse, a printer from *The Dimmock Sentinel* and graveyard shift operatives from the local utilities. He even brought a spare—a supervisor at the continuous process carpet factory in Pettifer Lane—in case the witness happened to know any of the others. They were all between forty-six and fifty-eight years old, and between six foot and six-foot-four in height.

Deacon gave Daniel his instructions. "Take as long as you like. Nobody here has anything more important to do. Look at each man closely before you make a decision. When you've done that, if you recognise any of them I want you to tell me where you know him from. If you think one of them is the man you saw on the pier when Chris Berry was killed, it's important to be honest about how sure you are. If you're positive, fine. If you're not sure, don't try to help by pretending that you are." He sniffed disparagingly. "Of course, I don't need to tell you that, do I?"

Daniel was too tense to smile. He just nodded.

Deacon glanced at his sergeant. "You can send the spare man home now."

Voss headed up the corridor at a jog. "I'll be right back." He meant, Don't start without me.

But Deacon was on tenterhooks and wouldn't wait. He'd been disappointed twice: he wasn't a superstitious man, except today he believed in third time lucky. He turned to Daniel and nodded. "When you're ready."

Given his choice of where to stand, George Ennis had slipped into the line-up second from the left. Deacon said nothing but he knew that wasn't random. The door was on the left. A nervous witness was prone to picking the first face he saw; someone who didn't recognise anyone might choose the last in desperation. If he could restrain himself till he came to the second man, the average witness would do as he was told and check them all out before saying anything; in which case he would look at a lot of faces after passing the second from the left. Any attempt by a suspect to avoid the witness's gaze only drew attention to him; but suspects standing second from the left had the best chance of being overlooked.

It might have been the intelligent thing for a guilty but clued-up individual to do. Or it might have been pure instinct: he'd done so many of these in the past that it came naturally.

Daniel did as Deacon asked, began at the left of the line-up and looked carefully at the man standing there—craning because every man there was a head taller than him—before proceeding to the next. Deacon held his breath—and then had to let it go unobtrusively when Daniel passed on from Ennis to the man beside him. And then the next, and so on down the line.

When he came to the last man he turned and did the whole thing again in reverse. Again he passed George Ennis with neither more nor less of an inspection than the others.

Deacon sighed. Of course, it had been dark but for the

meagre glow of a red torch. And they had been metres apart, and the fleeing man paused only an instant before hurrying on down the pier and out of sight. It was always a long shot. Deacon would have to make his case without identification evidence…

Daniel took a step back, looked over his shoulder to where the inspector was deliberately keeping his distance, hands behind his back lest mounting frustration turn a perfectly normal gesture into a pointing finger, and said quietly, "Yes. I can identify the man I saw on the pier. The man who killed Chris Berry and threw his body into the sea."

The funny thing about an identity parade is that, when it's successfully concluded, it isn't only the investigating officer who breathes a sigh of relief. The other people in the line-up do too. They glance at one another and trade relieved grins, as if a mistake by the witness would have projected them instantly into the dock of the Old Bailey.

Amid the general susurrus of escaping breath Deacon was resisting the temptation to cheer. He kept a tight grip on himself and went by the book. "Are you sure?"

"Absolutely," said Daniel.

"Very well. Will you please touch that man on the shoulder?"

But before he could do that there was a knock at the door and Sergeant Cobbitt came in. He looked surprised when he saw eight men lined up against the wall. "You've started."

Deacon nodded tersely, trying to bridle his impatience. "What do you want?"

The duty sergeant frowned. "I thought you were a man short. You sent out for another one."

Deacon frowned. "No, I didn't. We've got enough. Actually, we had a spare—I've just sent him home."

"Well, somebody told this gentleman you needed his services." Cobbitt opened the door wider. "That's right, isn't it, Mr—er—um—?"

Everything then happened very, very quickly. The door flew open much faster than it should have done, as if someone had kicked it wide. Another tall, rangy middle-aged man came through and slammed it behind him, at the same time extracting something long from the folds of his coat. A couple of voices were raised in alarm, until another that sent melt-water pouring down Daniel's spine stopped them.

"Against the wall, the lot of you. You too, Mr Deacon—no, don't look at me, look at the wall. You know who I am so you can guess what I'm doing here. And you know what this is. Anyone moves before I tell him, I'll blow his frigging head off."

IT'S OFTEN SAID that panic costs lives. But the failure to panic when appropriate costs them too. People die in survivable plane-crashes because they're too polite to make a dash for the emergency exit. People die in fires because they thought there was time to get their belongings.

In the same way, people confronted with an armed man let pass the moment in which an uncontrolled stampede for the door might have floored him and instead try to stay calm and co-operative. He's pointing a gun at them, he's made it clear that he's prepared to kill them, and they're trying to be helpful.

If Jack Deacon had been alone in this room when Neil Cochrane burst in, or if there had been only police officers here, he'd have wrested the gun away from him or died trying before the echo of the slamming door had faded. Before the intruder had time to arrange things to his satisfaction. He knew that if he moved Sergeant Cobbitt would throw his weight into the fray. Someone might get hurt. But *not* tackling a man armed with a sawn-off shotgun isn't a recipe for longevity either.

In fact Deacon never got a chance. He was at the far end of the room when Cochrane burst in, with seven innocent men, one guilty one and a vital witness between him and the gun. Even the duty sergeant was half-way down the room with his back to the weapon when the identity parade took its unexpected turn. Neither of them was in a position to jump Cochrane. And if the gun had gone off, neither of them would have taken the shot. Deacon's muscles actually jumped inside his skin, but he had the self-control to keep his feet planted where they were. All he could do from back here was get someone killed.

Among those close enough to tackle the gunman were some who would have done it if they had been sure what was going on. But this wasn't their show. The whole concept was so bizarre—they were standing with seven men they didn't know so that another whom they also didn't know could say if they'd committed a crime they knew they hadn't—that they had had to just go with the flow and do what they were told. Though the situation had now changed radically, psychologically they had yet to catch up. They were still compliant, waiting to be told what to do. Surreally, they found themselves wondering if this was part of the procedure. They looked blankly at Neil Cochrane, hostage to the very human fear of making a fool of themselves, and until they knew what was going on they were doing nothing.

Daniel knew what was going on as soon as Deacon did, and he was a lot closer to Neil Cochrane. But he was a fundamentally different sort of man. He didn't fight his way out of difficulties, he reasoned through them. Despite the difference in their build, he might have knocked Cochrane's gun aside, making time for the policemen to subdue him, if he'd acted immediately. But he didn't. He looked at the gun, and he looked at the man behind it, and he swallowed. "This is why I'm alive?"

Neil Cochrane gave a fractional nod. "You were the only one who could identify him. I needed you to tell me who wasted ten years of my life."

Daniel stepped back as if he'd been slapped. "No."

Cochrane said nothing. But his eyes were cold and admitted no doubt. He believed absolutely that Daniel would tell him who killed Chris Berry. He expected him to refuse at first, it was the decent thing to do: to resist, to decline to betray a man to his enemy. But Cochrane believed he could change Daniel's mind. If pointing out that the man was unworthy of his protection didn't do the trick, honest-to-God pain ought to. One thing was already acting in his favour. Daniel knew enough to be afraid of him.

At the far end of the line-up, now jumbled and peering anxiously from the policemen to the gunman, Jack Deacon too was wondering what Daniel would do. He came to the opposite conclusion. He was afraid that nothing Cochrane threatened him with would loosen his tongue if a man's life was at stake. Maybe he was wrong. Staring the wrong way down a gun-barrel changes people: perhaps it would change Daniel. Plant seeds of pragmatism among the lofty boughs of integrity. No one would blame him, whatever the consequences. He must know that. Deacon would remind him if the opportunity arose. Daniel exasperated the hell out of him, but he'd hate to see him lay down his life for a murderer. Already Deacon was thinking of Ennis in those terms. He could no longer afford to think of him as a friend.

Cochrane nodded calmly at the room in general. "Mr Deacon, everybody. I guess most of you know who I am. So who's going to shorten this by telling me what I want to know? One of you people is a killer. Who is it?"

There was some shuffling and mumbling, an exchange of troubled glances. Possibly from the best of motives the bouncer said, "We don't know. He didn't say."

For just a second the insane fury that had brought him here flared in Neil Cochrane's eyes. When it dimmed he was looking at Deacon again. "Is that right? I got here too soon?"

Deacon disdained either to confirm or deny it. "I don't know what you're doing here at all. You'd given us the slip: you should be half way to Tangiers by now."

The hatchet jaw came up. "Is that what you expected? That I'd run?"

"It was the only intelligent thing left to do." Deacon took a step towards him. "After you'd confessed your crimes to Hood and then let him go. The only sane thing."

"That lets me out then, don't it," said Cochrane with heavy

irony. "You know I'm not sane. You told the papers so ten years ago."

He had, too, before they had a suspect. Tom Sessions caught him in an unguarded moment, with the rage still burning from the discovery of the second boy's body, and he'd said what he was thinking. Ennis had torn strips off him for it. The killer would read that, he warned. He might agree with the assessment or resent it bitterly; either way his response could be another body. When Gavin Halliwell turned up on the town dump Jack Deacon had reason to remember that incautious quote.

He sniffed. Not even looking at Cochrane he took another step towards him. Just one, but if he kept taking just one step and the man kept not noticing, soon he would be within reach. "So this is you proving me wrong, is it? You walk into a police station, shut yourself in a room with one door and no windows, and produce a gun. And why? To find out what, if you'd waited twenty-four hours and then bought a newspaper, you'd have known anyway—that we'd charged a man with the murder of Chris Berry. You didn't have to come here. You could have been safe."

"I know what I'm doing," growled the farmer.

"Yeah?" Deacon barked a little laugh to cover his next step. "You think you're going to walk away from here? Cochrane, you're leaving this room in handcuffs."

Neil Cochrane's anger was mounting again. That may have been Deacon's intention but it was a risky ploy. If you take a dangerous, unpredictable man, arm him with a shotgun and shut him in a room full of panicking people, it isn't a good idea to annoy him as well.

"Don't worry about me, Mr Deacon. Worry about how the rest of you are going to leave. On stretchers, in boxes, that kind of thing. Because unless I get what I came for soon, people are going to start dying."

It was impossible not to believe that he meant it. "All right. So what do you want?"

Cochrane nodded slowly, a little of the tension going out

him now the strength of his position had been acknowledged. "First of all I want this door locked."

"All right," said Deacon again, expressionless, moving towards it. He got a couple more paces up the room before Cochrane stopped him.

"You stay where you are. Daniel, you're nearest."

"They're security locks," said Deacon. "You need to know what to do with them."

"So tell him."

Deacon did so. The man was too aware now of what he was doing. He'd have to wait for another chance, and hope there'd be one.

When the door was locked and he could put his back to it without fear of being surprised, Cochrane relaxed a little more. Enough to look properly at the people he'd come here to meet. He gestured them back against the wall and had them face him while he studied them.

When he came to George Ennis he blinked. "Good grief! You too?" Then he made a mistake. He looked at Deacon. "You must be pretty sure of yourself to want your old chief here. Of course, he was the boy's coach, wasn't he? Still, it was a nice thought, having him in at the kill. To coin a phrase."

His eyes travelled on down the line. But seeing no one else he recognised he turned back to Daniel. "Now, three—possibly four—of the men in this room know who killed Chris Berry, and I know who two of them are. You do: you saw him. And Mr Deacon does because he arrested him. Maybe he told Mr Ennis, maybe he didn't.

"And the other one who knows is the killer. So what we're going to do is this. If nobody's let me in on the secret in two minutes, I'm going to kill Sergeant Cobbitt here. If I still don't know in another two minutes I'll kill Mr Deacon. At that point, Daniel, it'll be down to you. If you don't tell me what I want to know, I'll kill every man in this room."

TWENTY-THREE

RIGHT THEN A PHONE rang. Half the people in the room patted their pockets but Deacon, heart sinking, recognised the tone. He'd chosen it because it was the least cheery one available. He said, "Do you want me to answer it?"

"Who is it?"

He looked at the display. "Chief Superintendent Fuller."

Cochrane barked a laugh. "Well, he's going to find out sometime. Maybe you should tell him what's going on."

Some of the men who looked vaguely like George Ennis, and indeed Neil Cochrane, still hadn't worked it out. They listened intently to the one-sided conversation in the hope of picking up clues.

Deacon said, "I'm still in the long room. We've hit a snag."

Then: "No, not exactly. Neil Cochrane's turned up. With a shotgun."

Then: "I haven't asked. Would you like to talk to him, sir?" He held out the mobile with an enquiring expression but Cochrane shook his head. "No," Deacon told the phone, "he's too busy pointing his gun at me. I'm guessing that *does* mean it's loaded.

"No, everyone's all right so far. Mr Cochrane's offering to blow my head off if I don't point our suspect out to him, but apart from that…

"Yes, sir, very witty. No, none of us is in a position to jump him. I think he's planning to keep it that way. No, I don't recommend forcing the door. In a confined space a shotgun can do a lot of damage.

"By all means, sir," he said then. "And while you're whistling up a negotiator we'll just talk among ourselves." He ended the call and observed judiciously to no one in particular: "Prat."

Cochrane was nodding approval. "Good. Keep avoiding the temptation to be a hero and you might all get home for breakfast. Well—nearly all." He looked at Daniel. "I believe I asked you a question."

Deacon knew what the response would be. He too had tried to get information out of Daniel Hood. He knew the man could not be bullied. Admittedly, Deacon hadn't had recourse to a double-barrelled shotgun, but he was afraid it wouldn't make any difference. Somehow he had to stop an armed and dangerous man, a man with a record of extreme brutality, from issuing an ultimatum that a quiet, gentle, stubborn man would die rather than obey.

There wasn't time for much subtlety. Daniel almost as much as Cochrane had to be steered away from the confrontation. Deacon cleared his throat noisily and said, "Mr Fuller wanted to know what you're doing here."

He'd succeeded in gaining Cochrane's attention. The man looked at him as if he was mad. "Isn't that *obvious?*"

"Yes. Sorry: not making myself clear. I mean, how you come to be here now. How you knew that this was the time and the place to get the answers you want. Have you been watching us?"

Even in the grip of his quest Cochrane couldn't resist the opportunity to brag a little. "Not exactly. I've been watching him." He pointed the strong jaw at Daniel. "Why do you think I let him go? Because you were going to need him to wind this business up. He couldn't tell me who he saw on the pier, but once you came up with a decent suspect he'd tell you. And what would you do then?—you'd put on an identity parade. If I stuck by him, sooner or later he was going to lead me to the man I was looking for."

Daniel couldn't believe what he was hearing. "You've been following me? Since I got out of the hospital?"

"Longer than that," chuckled Cochrane. "You haven't left

my ken since I set you free. I watched you come round and wander off down the lane. I kept an eye on you in case you fell in a ditch and drowned. I was never so pleased to see a bunch of police cars in my life—I thought I was going to have to baby-sit you all the way into Dimmock.

"I knew they'd take you to the hospital. I picked up the Land Rover and followed you down. I was no more than twenty yards from you all night—I sat in the waiting-room with a cup of coffee and nobody asked who I was waiting for. When that lanky foreign woman collected you I was a bit confused, but she didn't look like a police officer so I guessed you were going to stay with friends. I followed the taxi and saw where it dropped you. I put the Land Rover out of sight and found a spot I could watch from."

Daniel was cold under his clothes. After all he'd taken a killer to his friend's home. "You watched the house all day?"

"All day," nodded Cochrane, "and most of the night. You can get surprisingly comfortable in a shrubbery if you have to. A couple of times I slipped away for a bite to eat—it was a risk but a man's got to live—but you were still there when I got back. When you settled down for the night, so did I. Then in the early hours a police car turned up. I thought, This is it. They've got someone, I thought, they just need Danny boy to identify him.

"That was all there was to it, really," he finished modestly. "I presented myself at the desk here, gave a false name and said I was needed for the line-up. The sergeant believed me. Why wouldn't he?—I look pretty much like all the rest. And he's night-shift, and I was here in the day before."

Deacon regarded the man almost with admiration. It hadn't been difficult. It had required perseverance, and a little luck, but mostly it just required the will to do it. It needed someone prepared to devote twenty-four hours to the job for as long as it took. But then, what else had Neil Cochrane to do? Nothing that mattered to him more than being here right now.

And getting an answer to his question. Deacon's interruption dealt with, he tapped Daniel's shoulder with the muzzle of his gun. "If you've forgotten what it was I wanted to know," he rumbled, "I don't mind saying it just once more."

Daniel hadn't forgotten. And he hadn't changed his mind about how to answer. He realised Deacon had been trying to buy him some time, was sorry he couldn't put it to better use. He felt to be all out of options. "I can't tell you who I saw at the pier."

"You can't? Or you won't?"

Another man leaned cautiously forward. It was the bouncer again, and this time there was no question as to his motive. He wanted to help, all right: he wanted to help himself. "He recognised someone. He said so. Go on, tell him. Then we can get out of here."

Daniel felt the ground shake beneath him.

Cochrane looked at him; and getting no response there, looked back at the bouncer. "Who did he recognise?"

The man shrugged. "He never said. But what he said there, that's a lie."

Neil Cochrane looked at him with contempt. "That's not a lie, it's Daniel trying to do the right thing. Now, I may find that inconvenient, but you should know a brave man when you see one. So unless you've something more helpful to tell me…?"

He should have quit while he had the chance. But the bouncer was a big man with a sense of his own importance, and he thought he wasn't being appreciated. He said churlishly, "I'm telling you he *knows*—"

The cauldron of Cochrane's anger vented a bubble of hot fury. Abruptly the muzzle of the gun clipped the man under the jaw and he staggered back, whining and clutching his face. "I *know* he knows. Shut up while I find out *what* he knows."

Deacon had started forward again. But now Cochrane knew what he was doing. "Mr Deacon, you really don't want me to start pumping shots into these people. So keep still."

After that he kept his eyes on the policeman and spoke to

Daniel. "I'm not playing games, sonny. I know you have the information I want. *You* know I'll get it if I have to hurt you quite badly."

Daniel nodded jerkily. "I can't help that."

Cochrane scowled. He was the one with the gun: this shouldn't have been so difficult. Then he remembered. "Is this what you meant? In the barn, when I asked what you'd do to stay alive and you said almost anything. Is this the exception?"

Daniel nodded minutely. "I said I wouldn't let you hurt anyone."

Cochrane's hair-trigger temper fired again. "*Hurt* him? What do you think—I gave up my farm and my life there, and my only hope of making a new life somewhere else, for the chance to black his eye? It was all over. Nothing that happened in the last week was anything to do with me. But the man who killed the runner boy used me to hide behind. I spent ten years earning the right to a decent life again, and he trashed it. To take what I couldn't have any more and leave me to pay.

"I told you, Daniel, I can't do it again. I'm too old and too tired. I can't lie any more, and I can't do the time and look forward to being free when I'm eighty. But I can make him pay. I can make him regret using me. Hurt him? I'm going to kill the bastard."

Daniel felt the tremors start. It was one thing saying it, another seeing it through. But he had to try. "No."

"I can make you," warned Cochrane.

"I know you'll try."

"Sonny, you really don't want to make me angry!"

"I have no choice. I can't do as you ask."

For a moment they seemed to have reached deadlock. Twice his age, Cochrane could still have beaten Daniel to a pulp without a weapon to his hand. But he couldn't do it while holding the gun, and if he put it down ten big men, two of them policemen, would jump on him.

He turned the gun on Deacon. "I'll kill him. Right now."

Behind the thick lenses Daniel's eyes stretched. "Please…"

"You know what I want."

"I can't!" His voice cracked. "I can't give you some-one's life!"

Cochrane shrugged. "Then you're going to sacrifice a good man for the sake of a bad 'un. Either way you'll have a life on your conscience, only one of them deserves to die and the other don't."

Misery twisted Daniel's face. His eyes begged. Cochrane shook his head. "Mr Deacon can't help you. He won't talk. He hasn't the right to. He's paid to stand up to mad bastards like me. But you're not. He believes in what he does, he won't save himself, but you can save him. You can save Mr Deacon and every man in this room except the one you know to be a mur-derer. Any way you look at it, Daniel, that has to be a good deal."

Deep inside a tiny bit of Daniel's brain was riding the storm and still doing good work. He felt an answer starting to take shape. It was simple but hard—but not as hard as doing noth-ing. He reached for the door. "You won't hurt anyone if I'm not here to see it. There'd be no point. So I'm leaving now."

Deacon watched in astonishment, respect and deep trepi-dation. His voice was a warning growl. "Daniel—"

"Get away from that door," commanded Cochrane thick-ly. "Or I'll kill you where you stand."

Daniel had his back to the gun. "Then you'll never know what I saw."

Exasperation fermented in Cochrane's brain. "You know what you're saying, do you? That you'd give your life for a killer?"

"Not exactly." Daniel sounded troubled, as if he was still working it out. "It's not really about anyone else. I can face dying. I don't want to die, but it doesn't terrify me. Not as much as living with everything that matters to me gone. Hon-our. Integrity, self-respect. You can't take them by force, they have to be surrendered. If I do as you ask there'll be nothing left. If that sounds pretentious I'm sorry."

No one thought it was pretentious. They were all bigger

men than Daniel: now they found themselves wondering if they could have defended the things they held dear with the same courage. Perhaps they could, but they didn't think so.

"All right," snarled Cochrane, "then go. But the first sound you hear will be Jack Deacon's innards hitting the wall."

Daniel shuddered. "If I go, Mr Deacon's the only one who can help you. You won't kill him either."

He still had his back to the farmer. They couldn't see one another's faces. Daniel's was white: despite his brave words he was waiting every moment for the impact of close-grouped shot that would tear him apart. His eyes were shut tight.

Cochrane's expression was pensive as he considered the logic of the situation. Reluctant as he was to admit it, Daniel had a point. "Oh well, in that case…"

Everyone knows a gun is a deadly weapon because of the charge it carries. What people forget is that, even unloaded, it's a steel club longer than a man's arm. Cochrane swung with all his strength and the heavy barrels smashed into Daniel's shoulder and cannoned him into the wall.

"…Perhaps you'd better stay," finished Cochrane mildly.

Teeth clenched, fists balled, Deacon was ready to take his chance. But Cochrane already had him covered. "Stay where you are, Mr Deacon."

"He's hurt," gritted Deacon.

"I dare say he is. Teach him to do as he's told."

"I mean, he can't get up."

Cochrane spared him a glance. Daniel was an untidy knot where he'd hit the wall and fallen. He might have been dazed but he wasn't unconscious. His glasses had come off and his light eyes blinked owlishly.

"Get up," said Cochrane.

He tried again, sank back with a moan.

"Do as you're told," growled Cochrane. "I don't care if it hurts. Get up."

He'd hit the wall with enough force to shatter his collarbone. One arm hung uselessly. Whining in his teeth, he somehow got his feet under him and pushed himself up the wall. He stood swaying, whey-faced, cradling his right arm with his left.

"Now let's try that again," said Cochrane. "The man responsible for all of us being here is in this room right now. Point him out."

Daniel shook his head. The pain grated.

"For pity's sake, man," hissed Deacon, disgust twisting his lips. "He isn't going to do what you want. Are you going to kill him an inch at a time?"

Cochrane looked at him. Deacon thought that if the farmer could have been sure of reloading he'd have shot him right there and then. But he wasn't. And he wasn't going to risk what he'd gambled everything for just to stop Deacon's mouth.

Instead he grabbed Daniel's sleeve and swung him between himself and the room. "You keep prodding me, Mr Deacon, and you're going to regret it. What am I going to do? I'm going to get what I came here for. From him, or from you."

What stretched the thin lips wasn't a smile. It was cold, and cruel, and intelligent, but there was no humour in it. There's no satisfaction in hurting a man who's chosen martyrdom. He just wanted to finish this, and he thought he saw how. "And I'm getting pretty bloody tired of holding this gun." Calmly, deliberately, he dropped the heavy barrels onto Daniel's right shoulder.

Daniel gasped and his knees buckled. Cochrane shook him. "Stand up! Fall down now and by God you'll never get up. Now talk. Somebody, start talking."

It was nasty and brutal, and it was clever. It isn't easy to watch someone in pain when you have the means to end it. Every muscle in Deacon's body clenched. But if he jumped Cochrane he'd be risking the lives of innocent civilians. And a broken collar-bone was only a broken collar-bone. It was the sort of injury little girls get tumbling off ponies. You could fairly expect a grown man to set his jaw and deal with it.

Deacon had no idea what a shotgun weighed, but it would feel more resting on broken bone. A lot more; too much. Cochrane moved it around and Daniel tried not to whimper.

Deacon was trembling with impotent rage. Cochrane watched him over the gun, his eyes speculative. They both knew he'd have ripped Cochrane's throat out with his bare hands to stop this, and they both knew he dared not try. There was only one thing he could do to end Daniel's pain, and all his instincts and all his training forbade him to do it.

In spite of which he took a deep breath and said, "All right—"

"All right," said George Ennis, stepping out of the ragged line-up.

Daniel had known him the moment he came into the room. He had said nothing until he'd inspected every man standing with him because that was what Deacon told him to do. Even sick with pain he could say nothing again, because he wouldn't be any man's executioner. But if Ennis intended to confess... But why would he—now, when it was clear how Cochrane meant to repay what he'd done? Perhaps he had another lie prepared. Or was he just trying to get close enough to grab the gun? Daniel tried to stay with the action because if something happened to alter the balance of power, however briefly, he didn't want to be busy fainting and miss it.

Ennis reached out carefully and lifted the steel barrels off Daniel's shoulder. His eyes held Cochrane's over the younger man's head. "I'll tell you what happened. Leave him alone. I'll tell you everything."

"I don't need to know everything, Mr Ennis," growled Cochrane. "I just need to know one thing. Who killed Chris Berry?"

As the pain eased its grip Daniel sagged. Ennis caught him before Cochrane could jerk him upright again. "Hang on in there," he said softly, "this won't take much longer."

To Cochrane he said: "The man who killed Chris Berry isn't here. He isn't anywhere you can hurt him. Vengeance, however, is still an option. But you'll have to hear the story to understand how."

Cochrane acceded with a bad grace. "Go on. But don't take all night. If I lose interest I just might fire a few shots to relieve the boredom."

Ennis nodded. "I'll remember that. You remember this. You've thrown away everything you had for the information I'm about to give you. If you don't pay attention you may not get another chance."

"Tell your damned story."

TWENTY-FOUR

THEY WERE TWO YOUNG men, drawing wages in their first full-time jobs, at last with a bit of disposable income. It was inevitable that wheels would be high on their list of priorities.

Because they were friends, because they spent virtually all their spare time together, it made sense to combine forces. It was still an elderly car, but either buying alone would have had to wait another year.

They obeyed Chris's mum's injunction and were sensible about it, agreeing in advance how they'd share the use and the expenses. But because they were young men and thought they were great drivers, they never considered the possibility that one of them would make a silly, expensive mistake. It could have been either of them but it happened to be Nathan, driving home from his girlfriend's house late one evening, who saw a builder's skip too late and reduced the nearside wing to tinfoil.

The car was—Mrs Berry had insisted—comprehensively insured. If it had been a write-off, probably they would have stayed friends. But the damage came to £400: too little to justify a claim so early in their insurance history, too much to be easily found. So they quarrelled. Chris insisted that the kitty was to pay for unavoidable expenses like tax, insurance and maintenance, not for careless mistakes on the part of one of them. Nathan argued that the repair of damage too small to claim from the insurers *was* maintenance, and anyway he hadn't the means to pay it out of his own pocket.

Chris was adamant. The mistake was Nathan's, the damage his responsibility. He wasn't prepared to subsidise his friend's bad driving.

They had been friends most of their lives. They had done things for one another that money couldn't buy. But a £400 dent soured the relationship. Chris couldn't let the subject drop. If Nathan didn't have the money, could he borrow it somewhere? The car needed fixing, it would only deteriorate until it was done.

Nathan would have paid up, if grudgingly, had he had the means to do so. But his savings had gone into buying the car, he had nothing more. His family didn't have any money to spare, even as a loan. There was no one else.

There was one person. He asked George Ennis.

Ennis thought about it. He'd lent money to athletes before, mostly for kit or competition expenses. Repairing a bent car was a bit different; but the three of them had been important to one another for a lot of years now, Ennis didn't want this to come between two young men who needed one another's support to achieve all they were capable of. So he gave Nathan the money and they agreed to call it a loan until he'd worked it off—cleaning the gym, fetching and carrying, helping with classes. And he could start that very night. A busy weekend had left the place a tip.

Nathan was still working at twelve-thirty. Finished or not, he was about to knock off because he started work in the carpet warehouse at eight. Then Chris turned up looking for him, wanting to know what was happening about the car.

Chris had seen him, as Nathan had seen Chris, in all kinds of extremes—exhausted, in pain, in the humiliation of defeat. He'd seen him in tears. He had not, before now, seen him cleaning the ladies' lavatories.

They were young men, there were things they hadn't yet had time to learn. Things like discretion, kindness and the ability to laugh at oneself. If the same events had taken place in another year or two the ending would have been quite different. But Chris saw Nathan wielding the mop, and instead of feeling humbled by what his friend was prepared to do to keep his regard he laughed.

Nathan slapped him in the face with the wet mop.

The tragic thing was, they weren't angry. Even after the fight began, both of them knew it was more than half a joke. They were rolling on the wet floor, wrestling like they did when they were children, when a fight could last an hour and end with giggles and not a mark on either party.

But time had passed since they last did this. They were men now, physically at least, with the strength of men, and when they landed a blow it hurt. Instead of dissolving in tears and threatening to involve their bigger brothers, they responded with adrenalin-fuelled determination. They were two competitive individuals. At some point, as the fight moved out of the ladies' changing-room, across the hall and into the gym, it stopped being a joke and became a contest. They still weren't trying to injure one another. But they each wanted to win.

The blood ran high, the sweat poured, the muscles swelled and strung. The violent ballet took them the length of the gym and back again; and with every step the humour of the situation, the friendliness of the challenge, was buried under ever deeper layers of effort until the struggle was entirely serious.

Even so, they fought not as enemies but as gladiators, men with something to prove. The wet mop remained their only weapon, wrested by one from another and snatched back, until by chance Chris used it to send Nathan spinning against the rack of weights by the lifting bench.

No thought came into it. As he fell his hand closed on the metal bar, and he surged to his feet panting with exertion, swinging it.

Chris never saw it coming. His teeth were still bared in triumph when one end of the bar smashed him across the temple with all the force of Nathan's strong, angry young body.

While all this was going on George Ennis was in the flat upstairs. He was used to the sounds that percolated up when athletes were working out. The first warning he had that something was terribly amiss was a low, drawn-out howl that barely sounded human in its horror and distress.

He got downstairs to find Nathan Sparkes on his knees on the gym floor, bent over and keening, the broken head of Chris Berry dragged into his lap.

GEORGE ENNIS had been a policeman for thirty years. He knew when he was in the presence of death. He knew immediately that nothing they did now would alter the stunning reality that one of his golden boys had just killed the other.

"It was too late to do anything for Chris," he said softly. "My next priority was Nathan. He couldn't believe what had happened. It took him ten minutes to tell me: he kept going into some kind of spasm. Shock, of course. He couldn't get the words out. He couldn't let go of the body; I had to pry his fingers apart and drag him away. I didn't dare leave him to call for help. I thought his heart was going to burst. I thought I could lose him too."

If he'd been able to get to the phone and call Deacon right away he'd have done it. It wouldn't have occurred to him to do anything else. But for twenty minutes he sat on the floor nursing Nathan Sparkes through a storm of emotions so violent they threatened to rip him apart, and after that it was no longer quite so obvious what he should do next.

"I couldn't alter what had happened," Ennis said with a quiet urgency, as if it mattered to him that they understood that. "Chris was beyond help. But as I held Nathan to stop him dashing his brains out on the wall, slowly it dawned on me that there were two boys involved in this tragedy, two promising young men with families who loved them and futures waiting, and maybe the other one could still be saved.

"He'd go to prison for what he'd done. It was more than half an accident, but the court would see one boy with his head stove in and the other swinging a weight bar, and Nathan would go to prison. He was eighteen years old: I knew what would happen to him. He'd be brutalised. He wasn't going to the Olympics. He was going to get some corrective dentistry and a new walk, and when he came out he'd drift into crime.

Those boys were the best athletes I'd ever had the privilege of coaching, and now one was dead and the other was never going to run again. Unless I helped him."

There were better coaches in the country, Ennis freely admitted; there were better men. But possibly no one else could have done for Nathan Sparkes what Ennis did next. He wrapped the body of Chris Berry in a foil sheet, partly to contain the blood but mostly so that Nathan wouldn't have to look at what he'd done while they carried their burden out to the van. Ennis located his wheel-brace, then he drove to the pier and slowly, quietly, moving the barrier and avoiding the gaps, to the end of it.

His sole intention at that point was to hide the actual cause of death under damage he knew Jack Deacon would recognise. Chris's body, accompanied by a passable blood-spatter pattern, would be found by some angler or dog-walker, and ten minutes later Deacon would be on his way to Manor Farm.

Ennis laid Chris gently by the ruins of the concert-hall, wrapped himself in the foil blanket and—gritting his teeth and hating himself—delivered four or five massive blows with the wheel-brace, mumbling apologies to the dead boy as he did, explaining why the desecration was necessary.

"I knew what I was doing was wrong," he murmured. "I hoped maybe it wasn't *as* wrong as letting the law run its course. But one thing I was certain of was that Chris would have wanted me to try. He might have been pretty pissed off at what happened but he wouldn't have wanted his best friend to pay for an accident with the rest of his life."

It couldn't have taken half a minute; it felt like hours and left Ennis spattered with blood and filled with shame. He took off the blanket, bundling it carefully inside out, and returned to the van, meaning to leave the scene and never return. He thought he'd done enough. The part of him that was still a policeman knew he'd done far too much.

"Then I saw a light come on in one of the netting-sheds. My first thought was that someone had heard the van and I was about to be discovered. I thought Nathan and I were both going to jail. Then I remembered who lived there."

He glanced at Daniel. But Daniel was taking minimal interest: if Ennis had let him go he'd have slid to the floor. In a way that made it easier to continue.

"I didn't know him but I read the papers, I knew who he was. I knew what he did on starry nights when sensible people are in their beds. I guessed that if I waited a few minutes he'd come outside with his telescope."

All at once the time of which there had seemed so much was racing. Mere random chance had presented him with an opportunity he couldn't refuse: an eye-witness to tell Deacon what he had to believe. The discovery of a young man's body on the pier, bludgeoned about the head by a wheel-brace, certainly suggested a fourth murder in the ten-year-old series. But Jack Deacon was an experienced detective, he wouldn't necessarily jump to the obvious conclusion. He'd wait for the forensics, want to know if Chris had died at the pier or been brought there, want to know what the blood spatter pattern revealed. And it just might raise questions Ennis didn't want asking.

Now he glanced at Deacon. "But if a reliable witness told you he saw Chris die at the end of the pier, and he saw the killer silhouetted by starlight and described a tall rangy individual, I couldn't see you waiting for the forensics. I thought, even if they came back with some inconsistencies you wouldn't be too worried. You'd reckon you knew where Chris died, when he died and how he died; and you'd be pretty sure who killed him."

It was almost as if he'd forgotten that Cochrane was standing there, pointing a gun at them. He was explaining himself to Deacon, not the man he'd made his scapegoat. As long as he talked Cochrane did nothing to stop him, but Deacon was aware of fury building in the man as vulcanologists are aware of the magma chamber filling beneath their feet.

Ennis had no idea how long an amateur astronomer would stay outside on a cold night. Perhaps only a few minutes.

Quickly, before Daniel came outside, but also as quietly as he
could he drove off the pier and back to Fisher Hill and *The
Attic Gym*. He found Nathan where he'd left him, curled on
the floor, sobbing as if his heart was broken.

But there was no time for that. Ennis dragged him out to
the van and explained why as he drove back to the seafront.

He parked away from the pier this time, checked that Hood
was now outside, then shook some steel into Nathan's back-
bone and pushed him out onto the pavement. They both knew
what they had to do, it was too late to start discussing it now;
anyway, Nathan Sparkes couldn't have framed a sentence to
save his life. But he could run. He could always run. He ran
away up the pier, feet thundering on the suspect timbers, and
Ennis gave chase.

In case the sound of running wasn't enough, Ennis threw in
a few shouts, some angry, some afraid. When he looked across
at the netting-shed the astronomer had already left his telescope
and was approaching the pier. As if this was a playground dis-
pute that had got out of hand. Ennis raised the wheel-brace with
a roar of anger and Nathan cried out in terror.

Neither of them found the acting hard. Nathan *was* terrified, had every reason to be; and George Ennis was angry. God
alone knew how angry: with the boy cowering under his raised
arm and the other hidden close by. A golden future had
slumped to ashes in a second, in an argument over a dented
car. He wanted to knock their stupid heads together. He
wanted to scream at them to see what they'd done. Their lack
of discipline had quite possibly destroyed three lives. Unless
Ennis could make this credible, in which case two of them
might yet be redeemed.

When the murder scene had been played, with Nathan lying flat on the deck, Ennis pulled the body of Chris Berry towards him and heaved it into the sea. Then he ran back towards
the van, pausing just long enough to pose against the stars.

He managed a rueful grin. "I never thought he'd have a
torch. At least it was red and didn't carry too well. I knew he'd

seen me, I hoped he hadn't seen me well enough for an ID. Even so, I tried not to give him the chance. A couple of times Mrs Farrell wanted us to meet but I found excuses not to. Was that deliberate?" he asked Deacon. "Did she suspect me? Was she trying to bring us together, to see if Hood would recognise me?"

Tight-lipped, Deacon shook his head. "I don't think so. I think she thought you were trying to help. I wouldn't want to be in your shoes when she realises you were using her too." He stopped abruptly then, his eyes flicking to the gun. Brodie Farrell's wrath, impressive as it could be, was the least of Ennis's problems.

Deacon returned to Ennis's account. This might be his one chance to hear of these events first-hand. Two of the participants were already dead and he wasn't putting money on Ennis's chances. "So what happened to Nathan?"

Ennis nodded. "He stayed on the deck, out of sight, while I ran away. I expected Hood would hurry indoors to dial 999, at which point Nathan would sneak back up the pier. But Hood didn't go inside. He waded out to look for Chris." He sucked in a deep breath. "I felt badly about that. He was risking his life for a dead man. Thank God he got back safely. Nathan waited until Hood was fully occupied then he bent double and slipped away before anyone else turned up."

And from that moment onward Detective Inspector Deacon had concentrated all his efforts on pursuing the wrong man. Not an innocent man, as it turned out, but not Chris Berry's killer. He hadn't looked any further than he'd been meant to, and that was the real reason they were standing here at gunpoint today. If he'd wondered about the inconsistencies, which were there for a discriminating eye to see, he'd have widened the search. He'd have asked himself who knew enough about the earlier murders to lay a false trail that persuasive, and he'd have come up with the name of George Ennis a good deal sooner.

If he'd closed this case two days sooner, Daniel would not have gone looking for Cochrane and Cochrane would have gone on doing what he'd done for the last ten years—keeping his head down. Deacon blamed himself. None of this would have happened if he'd been a different sort of detective. Ennis had been able to take advantage of his weaknesses only because they were so predictable.

In other circumstances he'd have been standing here with his fists clenched at his sides to prevent them swinging of their own accord. The rage that was in him was like a force of nature, almost too massive to be contained within a human frame. He felt betrayed, used and defiled.

But he also knew that all of them were in danger, Ennis most of all, and it was literally a matter of life and death that he keep a clear head and a tight rein on his tongue. If they left this room safely Ennis would learn what Deacon thought of him. If they didn't, it was beside the point.

He looked at Cochrane, and refused to look at the gun. His voice was steely. "You have your answer. Now, there are seven men in this room whose only connection to all this is that they look a bit like Mr Ennis. They're just in the way. Let them leave."

Cochrane gave it some consideration. He seemed to be absorbing what he'd just heard, unsure what it meant, as if he hadn't thought what he'd do if he got the information he came here for. Finally he nodded. "All right. Phone your boss, tell him they're coming out. And tell him, if there's anyone in the corridor when the door opens I'm going to start shooting and I'm not going to much care who."

Deacon did as he was told, relayed Chief Superintendent Fuller's message back. "There'll be no one in the corridor. No one'll try to come in."

"Good. Unlock the door, then stand back. I'll tell you when to open it."

Again Deacon followed his instructions. Then he said, "Let Daniel go. There's nothing more he can do for you."

There was another long pause while Cochrane thought. "Yes. You take him— I don't need you here either, or Sergeant

Cobbitt. You can all get out, right now. The only business left is between me and Mr Ennis."

Deacon felt his whole body clench. "You know I can't do that. Sergeant, will you take Daniel?—I'm staying here."

Cochrane shook his head, just once, crisply. "Mr Deacon, you can do anything I tell you to do. You want to save lives, you'll do *exactly* what I tell you to do. Help the lad, he won't make it on his own. Take the rest of them and go, and don't look back. It's your job to protect the innocent, yes?—well, do it. Neither me nor Mr Ennis is your concern."

Deacon went to protest again but Ennis stopped him. He was quite calm, calmer than he'd been all week. "It's all right, Jack. I've handled hostage situations before. Mr Cochrane and I will sort something out. Take Hood and get these people safe." He put Daniel into Deacon's hands as if bestowing a gift.

Daniel was in pain and his senses were swimming. But he understood enough of what was going on. He lifted his head until the bones in his shoulder grated, and held Ennis's eye for a moment. His voice was thick. "I wouldn't have told him."

Ennis smiled. "No, I don't believe you would. But Jack would. He had no choice. As Cochrane said, it's his job to protect the innocent, not the guilty."

Deacon steered Daniel towards the door. When his knees went to string Deacon stooped briefly and straightened up with the younger man draped over his shoulder. He looked hard at Cochrane. "I will be back." Then he walked out of the door, and Sergeant Cobbitt ushered the rest of the hostages out in his wake.

As soon as they cleared the corridor, Deacon bent and eased Daniel to the floor. "Call an ambulance," he told Cobbitt, "I'm going back for George."

But before he could turn a shot rang out, filling the building like the blast of a cannon. And although he immediately started to run, the second shot crashed before he reached the door.

TWENTY-FIVE

IT WAS MID-MORNING when Brodie walked up the hospital steps, a bunch of flowers in her hand. The first nurse she saw, pushing a wheel-chair across Reception, nodded her a friendly greeting and said "M3, second floor, right-hand corridor, second bay."

It was ridiculous, Brodie thought irritably. In the ten years she'd lived in Dimmock she'd been in this hospital perhaps three times. In the three months she'd known Daniel she'd become so familiar a sight here that the staff treated her as one of themselves and the lady on the flower-stall started conversations with, "What's happened to him now?"

She'd got a brief account of what had happened from Detective Sergeant Voss in the early hours, when he found time to call her and say Daniel wouldn't be coming straight home, and why. She'd got an update from the hospital when she phoned at eight. The fracture had been set, they said, but he'd be groggy for a few hours. She meant to wait until noon before visiting, but curiosity got the better of her shortly after ten.

She'd have been better waiting. Daniel tried to stay awake for the sake of politeness but it was uphill work. Brodie shook her head. "Tell me the whole story tonight." He nodded and within minutes was asleep.

She sat with him a little longer, then she left, dropping a kiss onto his forehead. She smiled to herself. It was a good job he was asleep. That wasn't the sort of kiss a woman gives a man: it was the sort a mother gives a child. It wasn't because he was five years younger than her, it wasn't because he was shorter. It was something to do with the way he approached life, as if it was new and fresh and irresistibly interesting. When he wasn't taking on the world he could give the impression of being not quite old enough to be out on his own.

As she was going down the hospital steps Jack Deacon was coming up. He halted, shoving his hands deep in his pockets. "How is he?"

"I think he's fine," said Brodie. "He's asleep at the moment. I couldn't get much sense out of him, but he's on the mend. If you need to talk to him, you'd better leave it a few hours. I thought I'd try again this evening."

Deacon nodded, turned and fell into step beside her. "I don't need to talk to him, not yet. I just wanted to see if he was all right."

Brodie looked along her shoulder at him, quizzically. "Have you changed your mind about Daniel, Inspector?"

Immediately defensive, he sniffed. "No. What do you mean? Changed how?"

She smiled. "Oh, I don't know. You seemed to think he was the result of all the inmates of Pentonville holding hands and asking for something to be sent to annoy you. Or did I imagine that?"

The detective looked a little shame-faced. "Not entirely. It's just, I never know quite how to deal with him. It's like, my office if full of files, yes?—there's a lot of them, and everyone who comes through the door slips into one or another. Except Daniel doesn't. Daniel refuses to. I know he's not a villain, but he doesn't behave like an innocent bystander. When I ask him a question he thinks too long, and half the time I can't get a straight answer.

"He doesn't behave like a victim either. Typical victim behaviour is to pull up the draw-bridge, put up the shutters and refuse to look over the parapet until I can swear on a stack of Bibles that nobody's going to bother them any more. It is *not* typical victim behaviour to pay the suspect a visit in order to discuss the crime with him!"

"I don't think that's quite what he had in mind," demurred Brodie.

"But then, whoever *knows* what Daniel has in his mind?" demanded Deacon. "He never says. He does exactly what he thinks and leaves you to wonder why. Is this your car?" They'd stopped beside it.

"Yes."

"Leave it here. Let's go for lunch."

She laughed. "It's only eleven o'clock!"

"It's twenty-two hours since I last ate a hot meal," said Deacon firmly. "In my book, that makes it lunchtime. You were up half the night too. Did you have a proper breakfast?"

"Well…"

"Coffee and toast, right? About eight o'clock?"

"Half-past seven."

"Come on." He waited expectantly until she shrugged and joined him.

THE SMALL FRENCH restaurant at the back of Hastings Street came as a pleasant surprise. She'd been expecting curry.

Because it was early the kitchen was only starting. They sipped wine and ordered, and sipped some more wine.

"I'd have thought you'd be up to your eyeballs this morning," said Brodie.

Deacon shook his head. "Too late and too early. Too late to prevent a disaster, too early to have to explain it. By two o'clock I'll have the Chief Constable, the Assistant Chief Constable, the Press Office, the Home Office and Tom Sessions of *The Sentinel* to answer to. But right now there's nobody needs me as much as I need this." He looked at her. "Thanks for coming."

She smiled. "Thank you for asking. I'm glad of a bit of company just now as well."

"I expect there are things you want to know."

"I can wait till Daniel wakes up."

Deacon shrugged. "There's no need for secrets any more. It'll be headline news by one o'clock." He told her everything that had happened.

Or almost everything. As the first man into the long room after the gunfire, he was the only one who knew that he'd found the weapon in George Ennis's hands. The two men had wrestled for it and Ennis had won. It didn't make much difference: there was only one way out for either of them. But Deacon was obscurely glad that his friend had made the final decision. That Ennis had got his man, even if it took ten years, and not the other way round.

On the other hand, it was the sort of thing that didn't need to go down on the record, which is why Deacon had taken the gun from Ennis's dead hand and dropped it on the floor between the two men in the few seconds before Charlie Voss ran in behind him.

Brodie listened in silence. Only when Deacon ran out of words did she venture some of her own. "This must have been dreadfully difficult for you."

He darted her a little look, half grateful, half haunted. "George Ennis was more than just my boss. He was my teacher, my friend—the policeman I admired above all others for his intelligence, compassion and dedication. He was the one I consulted about problems, even after he wasn't there any more. 'What would George do about this?' I used to ask myself. OK, I didn't always do it, but that was because I was a different kind of policeman. Less patient, less perceptive. George Ennis was the detective I wanted to measure up to and never did.

"And now I don't know how I feel about him. He's dead, and half of me's grieving and the other half reckons he had it coming."

"You're in shock," Brodie said gently.

Deacon shook his head impatiently. "I'm angry, I know that. And—I feel so *stupid*. George Ennis knew me better than I knew him. He knew what I'd do if he laid the bait right. I danced for him like a damned puppet. Now three men are dead who'd be alive if I'd done my job better; and all right, one of them killed for pleasure and another perverted a legal system he'd sworn to uphold, but one of them was an eighteen-year-old boy who shouldn't have had to pay with his life for a momentary loss of control. I should have seen what was happening to him and asked why. I should have held onto him."

His hand was gripping the stem of his glass so tightly that in another moment he would break it. Brodie laid her own lightly on top. "You were fooled by someone you trusted. It's happened to all of us. You don't question what they tell you: that's what trust *is*. When you realise you've been duped, the world turns upside down. If *that* could happen, and you didn't even see it coming, how can you count on anyone ever again?

"But you have to. You can't go through life believing in nothing and no one. That would be too lonely. It's better to be let down occasionally than never get close enough for another person to hurt you. I know what I'm talking about: I thought I had a good marriage until my husband told me he wanted to marry someone else." For perhaps the first time she was able to smile about it. "I thought I'd been stupid too. But I hadn't—I know that now. He'd gone to a lot of trouble to keep me from knowing, partly to protect himself but partly to protect me.

"Yes, George used you. He was in a position where he had to hurt someone who mattered to him, and he thought you could handle it better than Nathan."

"He should have come to me!"

"Of course he should. But I understand why he didn't. He already had a tragedy on his hands: he saw one chance to limit the extent of the disaster. He didn't succeed. But if he had done, maybe it wouldn't have been so terrible. Neil Cochrane would have gone to prison for a murder he didn't commit; but prison was where he should have been, for the three that he did. Nathan would have gone free, and maybe he'd have gone on to be a great athlete. I don't think Chris would have minded."

"But it's not that simple, is it?" said Deacon doggedly. "What about Daniel? He's in hospital now because of the choices George made. All right, he'll be out soon, you can say it's a small price. But what if he'd drowned trying to save a man who'd been dead for half a hour? What if Cochrane had killed him—raped him and killed him?

"And Nathan's dead and shouldn't be. I'd have had him seeing a psychiatrist, and on suicide watch while he was on remand. Four or five years from now he'd be making a fresh start. He'd have come through this if George had called me instead of staging a pantomime."

"Yes," Brodie agreed. "Which means that what followed is his responsibility, not yours. And he paid for it. Whatever your Chief Constable decides, I don't think you have much to reproach yourself for."

Deacon said nothing, poured more wine. He'd need to get a taxi back to the office, and he'd have to avoid Chief Superintendent Fuller for a couple of hours, but he didn't care. Brodie was right: a kind of justice had been done, and if it wasn't his kind it also wasn't his fault. That was worth a bottle of Beaujolais at the end of a week like this.

He cleared his throat. "Er—this is maybe a bit of a nerve, and anyway you've probably got other plans, but— Well, we've got an office bash coming up next Friday night. Nothing very formal, just Dimmock's finest. I can't remember what it's in aid of—someone's birthday or engagement or divorce or something. Thing is, I'm always the spectre at the feast. They feel they have to ask me, I feel I have to go, but because I'm on my own they think they have to talk to me. I'd count it a real favour if you'd come—just for an hour, if you like, we could make our excuses before the cabaret begins. Would you? Or am I way out of line?"

Brodie was trying to keep a straight face. "Cabaret?"

He gave a gloomy shrug. "It might be a stripper. That I can cope with. But it might be Sergeant Cobbitt singing Songs from the Shows while accompanying himself on the piano accordion."

Brodie laughed aloud. "It sounds an unmissable evening. I'd love to come."

* * *

AFTER LUNCH Deacon had the taxi drop her home before taking him back to work. Half-way up the stairs he was already shouting for Charlie Voss.

Voss had been asleep with his head on his desk. He'd been on duty as long as Deacon had. He tried to unscramble his brain as he headed for the door. "Now what?"

"You've got to do something for me, Charlie," said Deacon thickly, and his face was the colour of old concrete. "You've got to arrange some sort of an office bash for next Friday night…"

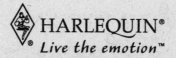

HARLEQUIN®
Presents

The world's bestselling romance series...
The series that brings you your favorite authors,
month after month:

Helen Bianchin...Emma Darcy
Lynne Graham...Penny Jordan
Miranda Lee...Sandra Marton
Anne Mather...Carole Mortimer
Susan Napier...Michelle Reid

and many more uniquely talented authors!

Wealthy, powerful, gorgeous men...
Women who have feelings just like your own...
The stories you love, set in exotic, glamorous locations...

HARLEQUIN®
Presents

Seduction and Passion Guaranteed!

HPDIR104

Harlequin Historicals®
Historical Romantic Adventure!

From rugged lawmen and valiant knights to defiant heiresses and spirited frontierswomen, Harlequin Historicals will capture your imagination with their dramatic scope, passion and adventure.

Harlequin Historicals . . . they're too good to miss!

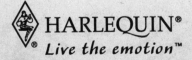